A DA

Dr. Wetmore gave Winston a poke in the stomach. "Come on, city dweller." Winston watched her disappear inside the first rows of corn. Hesitating, he took a gulp of air and jumped in.

Dr. Wetmore had already vanished in the forest of stalks. Ten more feet and the world outside the cornfield ceased to exist. The closeness and the eerie silence made Winston uneasy. Then he spotted Dr. Wetmore again, a crouching figure moving quickly through the stalks. Old women aren't supposed to move like that, he thought . . .

"Winston!" She grabbed him by the collar, her eyes round with fright. "There's someone lying down over there!"

She pulled aside some stalks and pointed into the adjoining furrow. Winston glanced hesitantly into the next row. A man lay face down in the dirt, hands at his sides. Winston's eyes shot to the large knife handle sticking from between the man's shoulder blades. A broadening red stain on the Kelly green sport coat had spread to the back of his white pants. He reminded Winston of a broken Christmas tree ornament.

ED MCBAIN'S MYSTERIES

JACK AND THE BEANSTALK   (17-083, $3.95)
Jack's dead, stabbed fourteen times. And thirty-six thousand's missing in cash. Matthew's questions are turning up some long-buried pasts, a second dead body, and some beautiful suspects. Like Sunny, Jack's sister, a surfer boy's fantasy, a delicious girl with some unsavory secrets.

BEAUTY AND THE BEAST   (17-134, $3.95)
She was spectacular—an unforgettable beauty with exquisite features. On Monday, the same woman appeared in Hope's law office to file a complaint. She had been badly beaten—a mass of purple bruises with one eye swollen completely shut. And she wanted her husband put away before something worse happened. Her body was discovered on Tuesday, bound with wire coat hangers and burned to a crisp. But her husband—big, and monstrously ugly—denies the charge.

Available wherever paperbacks are sold, or order direct from the Publisher. Send cover price plus 50¢ per copy for mailing and handling to Pinnacle Books, Dept. 17-479, 475 Park Avenue South, New York, N.Y. 10016. Residents of New York, New Jersey and Pennsylvania must include sales tax. DO NOT SEND CASH.

THE GOOD LUCK MURDERS

BRIAN JOHNSTON

PINNACLE BOOKS
WINDSOR PUBLISHING CORP.

to Akiko

Special thanks to Ann La Farge,
Jan DeVries, Peter Devers and
Marta Greene.

PINNACLE BOOKS

are published by

Windsor Publishing Corp.
475 Park Avenue South
New York, NY 10016

First printing: February, 1991

Printed in the United States of America

Chapter 1

A short, rotund man of quick step, Vicar Tart nego-
tiated the hill behind the vicarage with difficulty,
using his walking stick to pole himself up the
steeper parts. Not a man of athletic fancy, he nonetheless labored through these modest acts of contri-
tion every Sunday after the ten o'clock sermon.
Vicar Tart most enjoyed the ascent when there was
a "blow," as he put it—the more forceful the better.
The dark cape he affected pounded and snapped
against his body, keeping him off balance and making the climb all the more difficult. At these moments Tart felt a warming kinship with the *peregrini*
he so admired, the Irish monks who, far from their
beloved Ireland, suffered great hardships bringing
enlightenment to the pagans of the Continent. Not
that Tart's hometown of Port Washington, Long Island was that much closer than the village of Wistfield to the center of civilization, which for him was
New York City, but in Simon Tart's dense fantasy
world any place with more trees than people was
considered a cultural frontier, a land where the civi-
lizing traditions of religion, art, and the sciences
were marginal at best, thin veneers covering a deep
morass of pagan dualism and animistic idolatry.

Was it not true that in Wistfield people not only deified dogs and horses but slept with them, that rumor was more satisfying than truth, that the feudal system had yet to be routed by any renaissance? Armored in a mantle of righteousness, Tart, ever vigilant, kept a holy eye on the movements of his parish. Evil was afoot in Wistfield and Simon Tart welcomed the challenge.

At the crest of the rise Tart rested, looking down on the hamlet of Wistfield much in the same way he envisioned his God looking down on him: with considerable charity and an acceptable quotient of pride. Below him on his right stood his church, St. Peter's, a charming little pastry of Carpenter Gothic that had flourished under his tutelage. There was now talk among the vestry of expanding the size of the church to accommodate the ever-growing number of newcomers. There *was* a smattering of opposition by those who considered the church a historical landmark and therefore off-limits to the architect's whim, but the new financial report would win them over, reasoned Tart. After all, they *were* Episcopalians. The vicar took a halfhearted swat at some wild bergamot.

Moving twenty more feet down the crest, Tart sat himself on his "rock of ages," as he called it, a jutting of granite that afforded a splendid view of the valley. Settling his large stomach between his thighs and letting out a long, calming breath of air, he considered today's climb. Almost too pleasant. The October weather was warm and balmy, a slight breeze rolling the tall grass in a soothing rhythm. Tart felt protected at this height, closer to his God. Together they considered the view.

To his left was Meadowbrook Farm, certainly the

largest and most stately of the mansions that graced the hills around Wistfield. He could just make out the help putting up long tables on the lawn to board the hunt feast that would be laid while the Phillipses and their fellow beaglers were out tramping about the countryside. This afternoon was the first day of beagling season, so an unusually large crowd would be on hand. Vicar Tart knew that most of the people came just to enjoy what would be placed on those very tables now being set up below him: pots of venison stew, piles of steaming sweet corn, homemade breads, fruit pies, the much-needed warmth of the Johnny Walker Black. He himself had once eagerly blessed that feast, but the ensuing run after the hounds had eventually dampened his enthusiasm and now he restricted his physical exercise to this weekly climb. What's more, the hunters always thinned considerably as the season turned to winter, and *he* didn't want to be known as a fair-weather beagler. Vicar Tart forced the panorama of food from his thoughts.

Beyond the Phillips place was Jack Glenn's weekend retreat, the chimney pots just visible above the trees, and a few miles beyond that the Bantram house. Now *there* was a man who could spend more time sitting in a pew, thought Simon. Charity for James Bantram certainly began and ended in his front foyer. On the hill across from him, partly hidden by a stand of tall hemlocks, stood the old Worthwell estate, now owned by that silly man, Mr. Joyce. Tart snorted. He certainly had his thoughts concerning *that* man. Tootling around Wistfield in a chauffeur-driven limousine. The impertinence. Oddly enough, Mr. Joyce's chauffeur had started showing up on Sundays. A quiet but pleasant man,

7

he had a habit of sitting alone in the church long after the sermon had ended and everyone else was chattering away in the vicarage enjoying coffee and cakes. Said he believed in a quiet sit with his God in an empty church. Tart wondered if the man was privy to all aspects of his master's life, if he sat alone with his thoughts for a reason. He must have a long talk with the man one of these Sundays. All the . . . trouble had started just after Bill Joyce had moved into the area. And wasn't Joyce always endearing himself to the older ladies: an armful of perennials here, a flattering word there, escorting them from function to function. Tart smiled into the middle distance, going over in his mind what he thought he knew. The police were no closer to solving the murders than they were before. Tart's smile faded as he remembered the look on that Captain Andrews' face—the pained grin, the casual rebuff. The police didn't need any outside assistance, he had said, adding that the clergy should stick to consoling the bereaved and that he and his experts in forensic matters were more than capable of investigating and solving the crimes by themselves. Of course, if the vicar had any information he wished to share . . .

What did the police know about evil? Real evil? Or good for that matter. Nowadays they spent their time feeding data and statistics into computers, peering at lab tests, and trying to outmaneuver lawyers. Not like the old days, when the police investigator's instincts were as important as his evidence. Police chiefs went to church in those days; understood the real battle. What Captain Andrews failed to realize was that he, Simon Tart, did more than quiet the guilty minds of the privileged, that he saw more than just large homes from his exalted position. He saw the self-conscious look and embarrassed smile, the cleverness behind a boyish grin, the hate when no one was supposed to be looking. The vicar had studied people, his flock, all his life and felt he could discern evil when it lurked behind the masks they wore. If his evidence was slim it didn't bother the vicar; his instincts were honed indeed.

Tart huffed himself to a kneeling position. Arranging his cape out behind him, he raised his eyes to the cloudless heavens.

"Dear Lord . . ." Tart's voice rose to a stentorian whisper. "With Your blessing and strength I shall be Your lightning to pierce the dark shadow and expose the evil for all to see. As you did use Saint Columba before me to turn back the beast, this terror shall be routed and sweet grace once again restored to our . . . to this small kingdom. I remain, as always, Your humble servant. As it was in the beginning, is now and ever shall be, world without end, Amen. Until next week."

Looking out across the valley, Vicar Tart noticed the people beginning to arrive at Meadowbrook Farm. Rising, he gave one more glance up to the sky and then, quickly checking his watch, braced himself for the tortuous descent back to earth.

Chapter 2

The corner of 14th Street and Eighth Avenue in New York City is not the most obliging spot to nurse a hangover. Winston Wyc was made painfully aware of this as he balanced his forehead against the cool metal of a lamppost, gently cursing the noisy ebb and flow of taxis, the jostling crowds, and the fragrance of the bag lady next to him. Mrs. Swartz, the neighborhood ladies called her. A Jewish bag lady? But then, the neighbors were elderly Irish women, forever wondering out loud to each other what in the hell their lazy policemen sons were doing living out in Bensonhurst when the neighborhood was taking a nose dive. It would have taken two of the burly fellows to remove Mrs. Swartz; she was a formidable mass of old clothes and deep resolve. The van from the homeless shelter had tried many times to introduce Mrs. Swartz to a better world. She wasn't buying it. Usually Winston liked Mrs. Swartz, donating often to her marginal upkeep, but this morning her spirited concern to banish the evils of liquor from the face of Jupiter was not meshing well with Winston's personal concern, namely, trying to line up the arrows on a bottle of Tylenol with his eyes closed.

A vigorous whack of her cane on the post sent Winston careening backward and straight into a man standing behind him. Fighting nausea, Winston stared up into the face of a tall, muscular ramrod dressed like a 1920s chauffeur, complete with military cap and square, charcoal gray tunic buttoned to the throat. The knee-high black boots sparkled. Winston wasn't sure if the man was sneering at him or reacting to the smell of Mrs. Swartz. A large hand reached out to steady Winston.

"Excuse me, sir, I noticed your suitcase. Perhaps you're waiting for someone?"

Winston slowly bobbed his head in affirmation.

"Mr. Winston Wyc, then, I presume?" The chauffeur deftly fended off Mrs. Swartz's attempt to pierce him through the chest with her cane.

"Presumably." Winston spoke through his fingers.

"Daddy Grace was a Gentoo!" shouted Mrs. Swartz with another lunge. The thrust going wide, she stumbled over one of her many Macy's bags, and rolling down the sidewalk, scattered pedestrians like ninepins.

"My name is James, sir. I'm Mr. Joyce's driver. His car awaits."

Winston winced as the tumbling bag lady came to a disorderly stop against a Korean vegetable stand.

James picked up Winston's suitcase, and with a nod indicated a limousine idling at the corner. Trying to affect some semblance of personal order, Winston straightened and presented a trembling hand for an introductory handshake. James stared down at the extended hand as if it were a dead cat.

12

With a weak smile, Winston watched his fingers flutter back to his side.

"I must be coming down with the flu. I don't feel very well."

"Certainly, sir."

James pivoted his head slightly toward Mrs. Swartz, who was preparing for a rush up the sidewalk.

"Perhaps we should go, sir. Mr. Joyce will be expecting you for beagling."

"Beagling?"

"Yes, sir."

The limousine door closed out the noise of the city with a solid whoosh.

"No one goes anywhere good in one of those fancy cars," shouted Mrs. Swartz just before a small Korean woman brained her with a casaba melon.

But Winston was unaware of Mrs. Swartz's caution. Gingerly resting his head on the tucked leather, he wondered about beagling and chauffeurs and vernacular architecture. He smiled. Friends at last night's going-away party had warned him about the dangers of farmers' daughters, unleashed dogs, fresh vegetables, and possible Indian raids. Feral cows. They hadn't mentioned limousines and chauffeurs. If working in the country was going to be this comfortable, he could handle all the rest. From his privileged window, Winston watched the squalor of the New York City streets pass by, a poverty he'd been nominally aware of but able to shut out as he walked among its ruin. Suddenly the filth and misery seemed unconnected to him, like viewing a black-and-white documentary film of depression in some Third World country. Reaching up, Winston pulled down the window shade. Con-

13

cern for his fellow man would have to wait until the pounding in his head subsided. Closing his eyes, Winston could feel the limousine move smoothly away from the morning after, and as it moved, the night before became only a vague memory.

Chapter 3

Dr. Janice Wetmore ran the comb over Skippy one more time with a flourish. Leaning away, she admired the small bundle of gray fur with its flat face and drooping mustache who, barking his approval, awaited the final caress he knew to be coming. He was not disappointed.

"Now off the table, you scoundrel. I've work to do. Preparations. Today is opening day of beagling, and you know what that means."

A spritely seventy, Dr. Wetmore moved her thin, athletic body quickly and surely around her kitchen. Having never married, she had spent a life expending her excess energies working late or staying physically fit. Swimming, mountain climbing, and gardening had filled her few leisure hours. Strangers were always incredulous when she told them her age. Health was her only conceit.

On the counter she had arranged a neat row of small bottles, each containing an essence that reputedly matched that of various woodland creatures. If applied properly on the ground, the discerning dog nose might believe itself hot on the trail of a deer or woodchuck or the elusive hare. Janice Wetmore had become a master of false trails.

15

The fact that a hare had not been killed at the Wistfield hunt for over four years attested to her proficiency in the art of nasal illusion. Dr. Wetmore gave Skippy a loving look. It was his tiny paws that laid down many of these misleading aromas.

Holding a bottle to the light, Dr. Wetmore uncapped it and took a cautious sniff.

"Seems weak, Skippy, although the instructions promised a three-year shelf life." She poured a small amount into a more convenient and safer plastic vial. Dr. Wetmore smiled to herself, remembering how she used to bring the scents in glass bottles until the day she dropped one on a rock, splattering the back of Elaine Brooks's raccoon coat with essence of catamount. Poor Elaine had barely made it out of that coat alive. When the hounds had eventually ended their feeding frenzy, nothing had been found of the coat. Miss Brooks had given up beagling after that. Some of the more demented wags in the crowd still referred to a false trail as a "Brooksy's Raccoon."

"We'll go with Idaho jack rabbit today, Skippy, my dear. The hounds have always responded well to it."

Crossing to the window over the sink, Janice took a small charm off the sill. Flo Perkins had given her this silver bugle as a joke two years before she died . . . was murdered, that is. Janice shuddered at the memory. Flo had been the backbone of the hunt for decades, carrying it through the war years and building up the local interest it enjoyed now. Unbeknownst to everyone was the fact that Flo and a few others who dearly loved animals had finally realized that one could have one's cake and eat it too. That you could have beagling without the unnecessary death of another creature. Flo Perkins had been such an extraordinary hunt master that up until she had retired ten years ago no one had ever suspected her of directing the hounds away from their quarry. They had all taken it for granted that she was not very good, and many were happy to see her retire.

Janice rubbed the charm for good luck and placed it in her pocket. Why Flo Perkins had been killed was the mystery of Janice Wetmore's life. And then there was Cynthia Hall, found murdered in her bed. Two old friends brutally killed for no apparent reason. Their deaths had made all the elderly ladies of Wistfield recluses, hiding behind multiple locks and fearful expressions. Although the last killing had been over a year ago, it was still darned hard to get a hearts game together after the sun went down. And the police didn't seem to have a clue. In fact, that Captain Andrews had stopped returning her phone calls. Dr. Wetmore considered herself something of a mystery buff, her library full of hundreds of mystery novels collected over a lifetime of avid reading. Following Flo's murder, she had spent many weeks searching each book, looking for any similarities that might direct a little light on the dreadful event. Captain Andrews had been quick to point out that real life and the world of the novel and were not the same thing. Dr. Wetmore wasn't convinced. She placed a can of mace in her bag next to the vial marked "cat."

"Well, Skippy, that should do it."

Standing by the hall mirror, Dr. Wetmore wrestled her thick gray hair into a loose bun. Touching the silver horn one more time, she gave Skippy a

whistle. "Shall we go? It's a beautiful day for beagling."

Stretching at the door, Skippy bounded into the
clear October afternoon, ready and eager for the
task ahead.

Chapter 4

Winston Wyc awoke to James's not-so-gentle coaxing.

"Mr. Wyc? Welcome to Wistfield." The chauffeur stood back, allowing Winston a moment to collect his senses. "Mr. Joyce has promised to be only a second. He regrets not waking you personally and hopes you don't mind waiting for him by the cottage."

"Thank you . . . eh, James."

Winston accepted James's assistance.

"Feeling better, sir?"

"Yes, thanks."

James's look implied he could care less about how Winston felt. Nonetheless, the ride up the Taconic Parkway had proved restful and therapeutic; a silent motion picture of late summer turning into autumn as the car glided northward. Winston wondered if James was new at his job.

"James, you mentioned beagling earlier. Could you give me a hint as to what that might be?"

"An afternoon of chasing dogs, I believe. You'll have to ask Mr. Joyce." James obviously thought the pursuit ridiculous. Winston watched the man polish his way back into the driver's seat. James seemed more the bodyguard than driver. He had the demeanor of a pro football player who had been fired for meanness. The man didn't seem comfortable in his role as chauffeur, or perhaps he resented ferrying Winston around. Raising one finger, Winston wiggled a good-bye to the quickly departing limousine.

Now where was he? Winston turned to face the guest house. The once crude dwelling had been done over to resemble a Cotswold cottage; even the surrounding plantings had the authentic look of an English perennial garden, with its painstakingly casual rat's nest of flowers. The cottage, built into the side of a low rise, was buried in roses, hollyhocks, and wisteria. Beyond the cottage lay open fields, then dense woods. Not a taxi, bag lady, or for that matter another human being could be seen or heard. The quiet landscape was slightly unnerving to Winston, so unfamiliar was he with the countryside and its expanse. Experiencing a fleeting sensation of being the last person on earth, he began moving and humming aloud.

Wandering among the flowers, Winston sniffed at the remaining bee's balm and wondered if he was appropriately attired for the sport of beagling. Running amok over hill and dale with a raging hangover was not his idea of the perfect afternoon, preferring as he did the cozy interiors of research libraries and the darkened, quieting humor of the barroom.

Winston swatted the head of a tall black-eyed Susan into the air and across the drive just as a Volvo station wagon roared up from behind the hedge. The car stopped abruptly, and Winston had to jump and tiptoe his way quickly through the flower beds to avoid being struck by flying gravel.

Unraveling his long frame from the car, Mr. Joyce regarded his vehicle with suspicion.

"Sorry! Can't seem to get the hang of the darn car thing. Of course, it might have been the shock of watching you manhandle that poor rudbeckia." Mr. Joyce offered Winston a cross look and a handshake.

"Rudbeckia?"

"What Linnaeus called a black-eyed Susan. Welcome to Wistfield. Home of the Wistfield Warriors. That's a polo team. Can you imagine? Look, didn't mean to keep you waiting so long, but I've been reprimanded soundly by the local gentry for ploughing around the countryside in the stretch Lincoln, so I'm trying my damnest to learn how to *pilot* one of *these* things." Mr. Joyce finished paragraphs like a man who'd held his breath for too long under water. "As our friend Macbeth said, 'The attempt and not the deed confounds us.' Actually, maybe you'd like to drive. I *had* promised you the use of an auto while you were working up here."

"I'm afraid I'm a bit rusty on driving. Native New Yorker and all." Actually, Winston had become quite proficient at driving while piloting a cab around New York to make ends meet at college. Hacking had seemed the perfect way to make money until one night his ride had placed a very large gun next to Winston's brain and demanded all his hard-earned pay.

"Practice begins immediately. I'll navigate."

"Eh . . . where are we going? James mentioned . . . beagling?" Winston wondered if there was any possibility of begging off—bad leg, allergy to dogs, sudden migraine, anything. Pounding hangover probably wouldn't do it.

21

"The sport of minor kings, Winston." Mr. Joyce said this as if he were a major monarch. "I've told everyone about your coming. You'll love it."

"Oh."

Winston cautiously made his way up the drive and past the main house, which was crisscrossed by skeletal towers of scaffolding.

"What do you think, Winston? Just drape the damn ironwork there in something chintz. Keep the flowers small and we'd blend right into the countryside."

"Camouflage?"

"It's all camouflage, Winston." The long hands fluttered in the direction of the house.

"But then you wouldn't need me, Mr. Joyce."

"True. Could save myself a bundle, heh? And please call me Bill."

Beneath the metalwork, Winston could make out the large, Classic Revival house that he was being hired to assist in renovating. Balustrades seemed to outline everything, including the roof. The exterior was extensively ornamented.

"Before we get too far into the afternoon, I'd like to thank you for taking a chance on me," Winston said. He had met William Joyce only twice in New York, a long interview at the university and a shorter interrogation at the Carnegie Deli. On the strength of those meetings, a recommendation from Professor Hamilton, and Winston's suggestion to try the hot turkey gumbo, Mr. Joyce had offered Winston the job of architectural and historical consultant for a project involving restoration of an old, recently purchased mansion. Winston's portfolio was slim on historical renovations, but Mr. Joyce

22

had liked Winston's enthusiasm, his school record, and most certainly the turkey soup.

"Don't be silly. Your specialty at N.Y.U. was nineteenth-century architecture. That's what we have here. The way your face lit up just *talking* about it, well . . . how could I deny you the chance? But more importantly, I think we will get along, and for me that *has* to be the deciding factor." His gaze into Winston's face lingered a beat too long. Winston was annoyed to feel himself redden and turned his eyes quickly back to the road. "If I may speak freely, Winston." Bill Joyce paused, taking from his sport coat a silver cigarette case. "This is certainly a proper little community, everyone so Edwardian, but people will talk, and since I'd like for us to be friends, I'd like to clear up something from the very start. I am a harmless gentleman of epicene tastes, Winston, in the classical mode. Because of a few flamboyant . . . shall we say . . . gestures on my part, certain people tend to misread me."

"Yes?"

"Since you're from New York, I'm sure the term *intersexual* doesn't bother you. This is not the case everywhere. Go straight through the rotary and then take a left at St. Peter's church. The gentlemen of this privileged community think of me as a 'walker,' that is, a man they can trust to escort their wives here and there while they pursue . . . other matters."

"The knaves."

"Yes, well it works out just fine for all of us."

"Your secret is safe with me."

"Under that boyish charm, Mr. Wyc, do I also detect a hint of the knave?" Mr. Joyce blew smoke rings at the windshield.

"My good mother and the parish priest eliminated knavery from my soul at a very early age."

"Uhmm. Well I wouldn't mention *that* to anyone else in this wasp's nest."

Winston laughed. "I'm looking forward to starting work, Bill."

"Then we understand one another. I'm glad. Meadowbrook Farm is up here on the left. And I would leave Mr. Phillips's flowers intact, if I were you. He's our host today and he adores his gardens."

"I'll keep my hands to myself."

Mr. Joyce started to iron out his perfectly pressed corduroys with his hands. "How do I look?"

The man looked as if he'd just stepped off the cover of *GQ*, thought Winston. "Next to me, you look like a million bucks."

Bill Joyce was wearing a hand-spun Scottish tweed sport coat over a fawn-colored cashmere sweater. A lime green paisley ascot bristled at his throat. The green Wellingtons had never touched rough ground. Winston felt uncommonly drab in his tan cotton pants, wrinkled blue pinstripe shirt, and corduroy sport coat. His tennis shoes had seen plenty of action.

"You'll be just fine. All the younger folk come dressed like thrift shop specials. Not at all interested in hunt couture." Joyce chuckled at his little pun. "Actually, you don't *look* all that well, Winston. Are you okay?"

"An uncharacteristic bout with demon rum. A leaving-the-city celebration."

"I see." Mr. Joyce looked doubtful.

"A good run with the dogs, Bill, and I'll be back

24

in shape for Monday. Is that what we do? Run?" The thought horrified Winston.

"They're called hounds, Winston. And you don't have to run. A quick walk is acceptable."

"What actually *is* involved?"

"Just look intelligent and follow the crowd. There's no expertise involved unless you're a whip or a huntsman."

Winston interrupted his contemplation of the word *whip* to marvel at the white fencing that stretched along and beyond the driveway for as far as he could see, dividing the land into neat, separate pastures. The Catskill Mountains in the distance highlighted the horse barns that dotted the horizon. At the top of the drive sat an imposing Palladian villa with the side wings stretching out in an elegant curve: a welcoming gesture. Winston was open-mouthed at the size and beauty of the structure.

"People live here?"

"Certainly people. Now don't embarrass yourself by walking around with a four-inch gap between your lips."

"Sorry. All the houses I've studied that were this big either belonged to Third World rulers or were national landmarks."

Several horse-drawn carriages stood poised at the entrance, the drivers leaning casually against the high wooden wheels, blowing smoke into the air, talking.

"I'm impressed. The carriages are a nice touch."

"Those are not props, Winston, they're the real thing. It's horse country. The one on the left is a cabriolet, and that one's Mr. Leyton-White's surrey. Isn't it wonderful?" Mr. Joyce stared at the carriages like a fox at the chicken coop. "Once the house is finished, I plan on a coach or two of my own."

Winston had a vision of William Joyce at the reins of his limousine.

"Horse-drawn barouche parked next to the pavilion, a warm night, the orchestra playing Liszt, swirling dancers . . ."

"Sounds like another century."

"Oh, that it was." Bill collected himself. "Shall we?"

Winston let Mr. Joyce hurry on without him, saying he wanted to study the magnificent house for a moment when in truth he was feeling decidedly rumpled, inside and out. The thought of meeting strangers seemed a harrowing proposition. A little exercise of the self-confidence muscles might prove beneficial.

The facade followed correct Palladian lines, not at all like the birthday cake house so admired by Bill. The small portico at the main entrance had probably been added some years after the original house was completed. The entablature above the four tall, ionic columns supporting the pediment was quite simple, as were the gently curved lintels gracing the lower windows. The side wings mirrored each other: curving, one-story additions that terminated in two-story structures that Winston thought would make decent homes in and of themselves. Clouds appeared to swirl about the four chimneys that towered above the main roof, forcing the eye to gaze high into the heavens. For all its size, the house was undemanding and hospitable to the surrounding landscape, possessing a harmony Lord Burlington would have applauded.

The weather was mild for October, and the clear

skies and warm breeze, along with the house and coaches, lent the setting a fair-tale quality that dazzled Winston as much as the sunlight playing off the white facade. Curious, Winston went up the steps of the front portico, past the columns, and in through the arched doorway, which had been opened to the warm day. Finding himself alone in the large entrance hall, Winston ran his hands over the Hepplewhite gaming table and two Early American, hand-painted ladder-back chairs that stood just inside the door. A carved mahogany staircase led up to a wide entresol overlooking the entrance, continuing up to a second- floor balustrade.

Winston's inspection of a seventeenth-century refectory table was halted by an inquiring cough. A tall young woman stood in the rear of the hall giving him a quizzical look. She was dressed casually in cowboy boots, jeans, and a faded blue flannel shirt under a navy sport coat. Her dark shoulder-length hair was loosely pulled back over her ears. Light blue eyes shone angrily above the high cheekbones. She was startlingly pretty.

"Yes?" she said, raising an eyebrow and shoving her hands into the pockets of her jeans. A gesture from a Western: going for her guns.

"Sorry if I'm trespassing. I was looking for a washroom."

Winston held up his hands for inspection. The woman only frowned at him, cocking her head to one side.

"You're right, I'm lying. I was being a snoop. I find this house simply amazing, and since no one was selling tickets at the door I took advantage of the situation and dared to trespass. I'm a guest of

Mr. William Joyce. He seems to think I'd enjoy . . . beagling."

Pursing her lips, the woman gave Winston the once over. Winston gave himself the once over.

"A little shabby, perhaps, but then, never having run with the doggies, I was confused as to appropriate attire. Hope I won't offend them."

"Our . . . eh, dogs, are bred to ignore what they see. It's the nose that counts."

Winston realized the woman was really angry. She had crossed her arms and was flicking her head back and forth in an exasperated manner.

"I *am* trespassing and I apologize. I'll take my shabby body outside right now and throw it in front of a carriage."

Winston turned to go but stopped at the woman's laughter.

"Although that might be fun to see, I don't think it's a good idea. I'm sorry, I'm not mad at you but at someone else." The woman hissed out a long stream of air. "In fact, I should calm down right now." She forced a smile. "A guest of Bill Joyce is always welcome. You didn't arrive on a large white horse, did you?"

"A horse?"

"Never mind. I'm Erika Phillips." Erika strode across the foyer offering her hand. "You don't appear . . ." she wiggled her fingers, ". . . so shabby up close."

"Thanks. Bit of a rough night, I'm afraid. I'm suffering the consequences of my acts. I'm Winston Wyc."

"Happy to meet you, Winston. Now that we're all properly introduced and apologetic, you may even use the john."

"I take it you live here."

"Yes. Me and my father."

"Just the two of you?"

"Am I supposed to apologize?" Tense lines returned to the corners of Erika's mouth.

"Of course not . . . I mean . . . well, actually I'm a bit out of my environment here. I'm sure it shows. It's a beautiful house. Remarkable, really."

"Well, thank you. We're rather fond of it."

Winston realized he'd better do some fast talking if he wanted to keep this beautiful woman on his side.

"Yes, of course. My business, if you can call it that, is studying houses. I'm an architectural historian. I always seem to get really stupid around buildings I find this wonderful. If I could have a tour someday, I'd be in seventh heaven."

"We don't usually give tours, but maybe . . ."

"As a gift? For a poor student of the builder's art."

"Well . . . for art . . . maybe."

"I will praise your dogs to the world."

"Please call them hounds, Mr. Wyc, or people will think you a visitor from Mars."

"Wouldn't have that, and please call me Winston."

"If you're still interested, the john is behind this door. I'll wait for you on the back porch. Go through that room and out the double doors."

"Thanks." Winston was happy to see the smile return.

Closing the door behind him, Winston pressed his forehead against the mirror. He felt remarkably light, as if the air were falling away from him, taking

29

clothes, hair, skin, everything with it, leaving him completely exposed.

Love rears its ugly head. I've been weakened by the drink, he thought. Oh, God, make me whole. Winston did a little jig and splashed water on his face.

The room across from the bath was a high-ceilinged salon with a wall of tall mullioned windows looking out on the rear lawn. Giving himself another few minutes before he had to be bright again, Winston examined the family portraits arranged on a Steinway piano next to the door. Erika with her arm around the family labrador; in jodhpurs and hard hat sitting on her horse; by the pool in a ruffled two-piece bathing suit; her round little eight-year-old belly protruding over the suit. Winston smiled to himself. She had the same impatient look in all the photos, as if posing for pictures was an intrusion into her busy world. In the photographs of Erika with what must have been her mother, Winston was startled by their close resemblance. It was as if someone had magically taken a snapshot of Erika in the future and then spliced it with one of her as a child. He wondered what had happened to Mother.

Standing in the door, Winston saw Erika talking to a tall blond man wearing a green sport coat and white pants. He was dressed like an usher but seemed a shade too earnest for Winston's liking. Beyond the back portico was a planted terrace and then a wide, flat lawn on which a large gathering milled about some long bare tables.

No refreshments as yet, observed Winston. A little hair of the hound, as it were, might hit the spot. Of course, can't have the masses tearing through the heather half crocked. Might turn an ankle or fall off a log.

People stood in small animated groups, eager and noisy. The atmosphere was light and convivial. The older men and women were appropriately booted and tweedy, faces red and blustery, in charge of their smiles, all slightly wind tossed. Those in their thirties supported Mr. L.L. Bean, looking for the most part like clothes-conscious campers. The younger crowd seemed to confirm Bill's assessment of them, wearing the outsized crumpled attire that was popular with kids at the moment. Winston wasn't sure where he fit in, feeling a little old and unsuccessful for wrinkled chic.

"Oh, Winston. I'd like you to meet Jack Glenn." Tall and physically aggressive, Mr. Glenn was one of those hearty fellows who like to rearrange hand bones, measuring another's manliness by how hard you squeezed back.

"Jack, this is Winston Wyc. Winston, Jack."

Jack rolled the name around in his head. "Wyc. That's a strange one. British?"

"Carnassian," said Winston. "It's hard to recognize, I know. My grandfather dropped the 'o' when he immigrated to this country." He shot Glenn his warmest smile. "Please call me Winston."

"Of course." Mr. Glenn was not amused. "You're here to fix something?"

"Winston's a guest of Bill," Erika said quickly.

"Of Bill Joyce?"

"He studies houses or something. Have I got that right?"

"Close. I'm a house historian. Mr. Joyce hired me to assist him with . . ."

"Ohhh. Oh, damn, of course, you must be the architect, or whatever. He did mention something about you. I don't know why, but from what Bill has said, I expected someone older. He thinks you're a true find." Jack's expression showed he would reserve judgment.

"Jack, could you introduce Winston around. I have things to get ready. I'll catch up." Without waiting for a reply, she left them both standing there, staring after her.

"I'm a lucky man, Winston. She's a helluva creature."

"You and Erika are . . . betrothed?"

"Betrothed? Oh, engaged. No, but soon. I'm playing hard to get." Glenn's indecent laugh was interrupted by Winston slapping him hard on the shoulder.

"Why, you devil! Is Erika aware of your intentions?"

Glenn steadied himself, unsure whether or not to poke Winston in the nose.

"Sorry, didn't mean to hit you so hard," said Winston.

"No problem."

Jack Glenn dropped the affable mask for only a split second, but Winston was startled by the hardness of the eyes.

"I'd say she had a pretty good idea of what was going on and was content with the program, Winston."

A man who knows what he wants and goes after it. Surely an admirable quality in men *and* dogs. Wonder how Erika feels about it, thought Winston.

Bill Joyce touched Winston's arm.

"There you are. Hello, Jack. I see you've met Winston."

"Yes. I thought he was a delivery man."

Mr. Glenn didn't give up.

"It's the chic New York rumple, Jack. Hasn't reached the fortieth floor of Wall Street yet."

"Can't wait."

"Winston's a well-known architectural historian. He's graciously consented to assist Paul with the renovation. I feel pleased to have him working with me."

Winston wished Bill wouldn't beam at him.

"Winston, I want you to meet our host. You'll excuse us, Jack."

Jack Glenn wished Winston a pleasant hunt.

"A friend of yours? Seems a little tightly wound."

"Jack's okay. Takes upward mobility too seriously, but once he gets to know you he'll turn on the charm."

"Can't wait."

"Don't be hostile."

Bill led Winston toward three men who were standing apart from the crowd.

"Fletcher, I want you to meet Winston Wyc. He's the young historian I was telling you about."

"Certainly. Mr. Wyc, it's a pleasure. Fletcher Phillips here. May I introduce James Bantram and his son, Hugh."

Hellos all around. Mr. Phillips was of medium height, but broad and powerfully built. His head was covered in snow white hair, and under his nose was a neatly clipped white mustache that stood out like neon against his crimson face. He too wore the Kelly green sport coat and white pants Winston had noticed on Jack Glenn and others in the crowd. Obviously the habit of the beagling fraternity. Mr. Bantram, a slight man with large hands, nodded and spoke.

"Mr. Wyc. What would you think of a son who ridiculed his father in public?"

"Now, Dad, that's not true. And Mr. Wyc is certainly not interested in our family disputes."

Hugh Bantram was a younger James Bantram. The slight build, the high forehead, and the same sincere brown eyes.

"I don't give a damn what Mr. Wyc hears, I'm asking his opinion."

"Jim, please. My guest is unfamiliar with the situation."

Mr. Joyce's was an unappreciated voice of reason.

"James, Bill is right." Mr. Phillips spoke. "Let's not ruin a good hunt."

"I didn't come here to ruin anything." Mr. Bantram's voice rose in volume as he addressed his son. "You think I don't see the greedy hand here, young man. You'd sell your birthright to the highest bidder!"

"Better to do that than keep up stupid appearances. You couldn't even provide Mr. Potter with a decent pension when you let him go. A man who worked twenty-two years for you. The whole conservancy thing is nothing but . . ."

"Stupid!" Mr. Bantram gave Winston and the others an embarrassed, angered look. "This coming from a . . . a dreamer who sponges off his father. A son who can't finish school or hold a job." He stumbled in his son's direction. "A good throttle is all you . . ."

"Gentlemen, gentlemen. Please! No one's going to throttle anyone. Unless the hounds should catch a hare." Mr. Phillips tossed a laugh around as a buffer. Bill Joyce took Hugh by the arm.

"Hugh, let's take a walk. Warm up the legs." Bill started away from the group.

Frustrated, Hugh threw up his hands. "Okay. Mr. Wyc, I'm sorry that you were needlessly dragged into this. Dad, I . . ." But James Bantram was already stomping off across the lawn. Hugh shrugged and hurried after Joyce.

Fletcher Phillips eyed Winston curiously.

"Not a close family, Mr. Wyc. A boring situation all around. You don't look like a beagler."

"Afraid it's my first time, sir. Not much beagling in New York City."

"I suppose not. Too much traffic." Mr. Phillips chuckled. "Well . . . this your first time out, heh?"

Winston nodded.

"It's a credible endeavor, Mr. Wyc, although there are those among the uninitiated who scoff at the idea of grown men and women spending their Sundays chasing after a bunch of hounds, but I'm telling you it's a game of life and death—and all the brambles in between."

"Sounds exciting."

"Oh, but it is, Mr. Wyc." With a low intensity, Mr. Phillips bent into Winston as if to impart a great secret. "You start with the beagle, shorter and slower then the foxhound, but smarter and with wonderful patience. You have your whips and spotters to keep the hounds under wraps—the technicians. And you have the master of the hounds, that's me, the director, as it were, cajoling, demanding . . . guiding the whole show, drawing the field for a scent and inspiring his hounds, his beloved hounds, to rally and run the hare to ground."

Mr. Phillips's voice rose as he began, in slow motion, to chase invisible hares across his lawn. "Ahhh . . . then there is the hare." Mr. Phillips pointed to a spot twenty feet away. "A difficult quarry, sir. She doesn't leave as strong a scent as the fox, so the hounds must be patient, the ground covered thoroughly. They can't race. She can use a creek bed or a stone wall to her advantage. No Einstein, certainly, but full of cunning and a well-developed instinct for survival."

A crowd had begun to gather around Winston and Mr. Phillips, and it grew as the man's voice rose in passion and his gestures took on a life of their own.

"Mr. Wyc, the huntsman knows his hounds like he knows his own mind. He has raised them, taught them what he knows, developed a bond between himself and them, and it is through this common knowing that he will be able to interpret their cries. And they, in turn, will listen for the horn and the whip to guide them to victory over the crafty hare."

Fletcher Phillips threw his arms up in a gesture of triumph, bowing his head in a humble acceptance of the gathering's applause. Winston half expected someone to shout "cut!" and they would all go home. Instead, everyone was more eager than ever to take to the field, inspired by their master and their own enthusiasm.

"Bravo, Father. Let the hunt begin." Erika emerged from the crowd with an older woman in tow.

"Yes. To the kennels!"

With a great clamor the believers shot off toward the barns.

"Winston, I'd like you to meet Dr. Wetmore. Dr. Wetmore, this is Winston."

"Call me Janice, for goodness sakes. I see Fletcher found a novice to receive the party line and inspire the multitudes."

Winston liked Dr. Wetmore immediately. She seemed of the crowd but distinct from it. Exuding more health and glowing good purpose than an entire championship rowing crew, she constantly re-shaped a tumble of quietly rebellious gray hair that kept falling out from under a large brimmed hat.

"I'm an easy mark, Dr. Wetmore. I feel like Alice in Wonderland."

"And so you may be."

"Oh, Janice. Wistfield is really no different than anywhere else."

"Erika, dear, Meadowbrook Farm is *very* different from anywhere else. And so is Wistfield nowadays, full of antique malls and gourmet food shops. People sit on their overpriced, hand-doodled farm chairs and stuff themselves with Mrs. Somebody's original country jelly while normal people can't find a sensible pair of shoes or an inexpensive ice cream cone. You mark my words, Winston, the . . ."

Suddenly the lawn was full of hounds. They came bouncing and barking up to where Erika was standing. Winston found himself knee-deep in them. Calling each by name, Erika lavished endearments on some, pats and hoots on others. To Winston they all looked the same in height, markings, and enthusiasm. Each tail was pointed upward and thrashed wildly—a sea of overwound brown and white metronomes.

"How can you possibly know which is which?" shouted Winston. "Where are the name tags?"

"When you raise them from puppies, it's not too difficult. They're all individuals when you love them."

Winston watched as the dogs clamored around her and she accepted their licks and nuzzles, her hair coming loose and falling about her face, her obvious joy. He wanted to join them.

And then a bugle sounded and the hounds turned and headed across the lawn toward Mr. Phillips, who was roaring encouragement to hounds and by-standers alike. Following Dr. Wetmore, Winston and Erika strolled casually over to the excited crowd.

"Beagling happen all the time?" asked Winston.

"Every Sunday from October to March. You will come again, won't you? It's excellent exercise and you get to see people you might not see during the week," said Erika.

"Social hour with pets."

"Hardly pets, Mr. Wyc." Erika moved them through the crowd toward her father, who was ex-plaining to the whippers-in and the crowd exactly where he wanted to go. The first draw would be the field just over the hill.

"What happens if they actually catch a hare?" whispered Winston.

"The mask and pads are awarded to the worthy or lucky hounds. The young hounds, if this is their first hunt, will get their noses rubbed in the blood to acquaint them with the smell. They have to know what it is they are looking for."

"Seems a little atavistic."

"We're not Druids, Mr. Wyc, it's just part of the training. You're not a hunter, I take it."

38

"I'm a historian. I stalk the elusive building. In New York, I usually find myself being the prey."

"You're not like the other city dwellers who come up to Wistfield, are you, Mr. Wyc, enjoying the countryside with kid gloves on?"

"Call me Winston, please, and this is all too new for me to have any idea, but I promise you that if any blood comes my way, I won't put my gloves in it."

"There's never any blood, anyway," smiled Dr. Wetmore. "A few character assassinations, maybe, but no dead hares."

The whole mob suddenly began moving rapidly for the hills, the beagles, like a riot of schoolchildren on a field trip, pushing against the boundaries of discipline, their green and white ushers demanding order with whips and shouts, reprimanding the younger ones who wouldn't stay with the pack.

"It's like a moving carnival," shouted Winston. "The noise must alert every hare for six counties."

"The hare will hear and wait them out. Like us, they can't believe that death is heading in their direction."

"Janice, so glum. You enjoy the run as much as anyone." Erika turned to Winston. "Janice comes every week to exercise and gossip. She'd be lost on Sundays without it."

"I might finally finish my mystery club selections. But I'm addicted, Winston. It's like a bad habit. We know it's wrong but we can't stop."

"I'll have to reserve judgment until after it's over. But shouldn't we try to catch up?"

"Winston, why don't you escort Janice. She can offer you another viewpoint concerning beagling."

"And you . . . ?"

39

"I really must stay here and get ready for the returning crowd."

"Don't look so sad, young man. I'm not such bad company." Dr. Wetmore had Winston by the arm.

"I'll see you afterward," said Erika. "I'm sure Janice is hiding Skippy somewhere and is dying to rescue him."

"Skippy?"

"Skippy's my dog," said Dr. Wetmore. "Fletcher thinks dogs shouldn't be allowed on the hunt. Says their scent distracts the hounds in some way, which is bunk, of course. Skippy hasn't smelled like an animal in years."

"Shall we collect him then? I'm beginning to feel a surge of primal instincts."

After good-byes, Winston found himself once again watching Erika walk away.

"Did I really look sad?"

"Like a hound on a tether. Come on. Skippy's waiting."

Chapter 5

With a toy poodle the size of a short sigh tucked into her coat front, Dr. Wetmore led Winston toward the hills behind the farm. Winston had to jog to keep up. Noticing the hill rose steep and long to the crest, he hesitated.

"Cardiac Rise, it's called. Good for whipping city dwellers into shape." Chuckling, Dr. Wetmore held onto Skippy with one hand and her hat with the other as they started up the hill.

"Is there anything I should know?" asked Winston.

"Well, to hear the faithful you'd think there were all kinds of interesting things to know, but unless you're caught up in the sport, I'd say knowing how to watch and stay out of the way is good enough. They go on about winds and scents, this line and that, the dryness of the summer months and its effect on the hare population. There's always this theory or that, but if you want my two cents worth, I'd say it all boils down to man and his dog chasing nature through the woods. To tell you the truth, I don't think half of them have the mother wit of a hare. They never catch one."

41

Winston nodded and tried to keep up, appreciating the breeze off the tall, browning grass.

"What brings you to Wistfield, Winston? A visit?"

"I'm doing some work for Mr. Joyce. Helping with the renovation of his new house."

"You're a carpenter, then?"

"No . . ." Winston paused, not sure he was willing to explain himself every time he met someone, but he liked Dr. Wetmore. "I'm an architectural historian, or will be with a few more jobs under my belt. I'm just out of school, actually."

"What brings you to the country? They've got some old homes in New York, or so I hear."

"I thought I had a job at the Landmarks Commission but it fell through. Seems I didn't have the proper connections in the mayoral theocracy. Bill Joyce came to the school looking for someone young and willing to go outside New York. Professor Hamilton recommended me."

"Students come fairly cheap, I imagine."

"There was that, I'm sure, but I feel qualified."

"I don't doubt that, and I for one am glad he chose you. I don't know Bill Joyce very well, although we certainly see enough of one another. The occasional social event, that sort of thing. I've often wondered just what it is Bill does."

"Actually, I don't know. I've never asked. There are some people who look like they've always had money, born to it, I guess. Bill acts much that way."

"Hmmmm. Wouldn't know." Dr. Wetmore smiled graciously and continued to the top of the hill. "And another thing. The hare is always referred to as a 'she.' "

"Why's that?" puffed Winston.

"Some nonsense about being born to suffer. I

42

think it has to do with men liking the idea of chasing women."

They were both laughing when they crested the hill. A panorama of rolling countryside fell away from them, with Meadowbrook Farm below. Beyond lay miles of woods and meadowed farmland, and in the distance, the village of Wistfield. Winston was reminded of a picture he once liked in his fifth grade civics text, a photograph of rural New England taken from the air. To a young boy living in Brooklyn, it had looked like heaven. It still did.

The other side flattened out quicker, and Winston could see a large cornfield a half mile down the hill—a wash of pale yellow on a field of reddish brown and gold. And beyond the corn, coats of green pursuing invisible hounds, the beagles hidden by the tall grass. The high chorus of the beagles carried clearly on the breeze that ruffled the hilltop, the dogs like ghost hounds to Winston, chasing a spectral hare that they would never catch. Mr. Joyce and a few others had also stopped on the crest and were watching the action below.

"Isn't it wonderful, Winston? You can see everything from up here," said Bill.

"I thought you'd be chasing behind them, Bill. Enjoying the exercise." Winston motioned with his hand toward the moving figures below them.

"Are you kidding? My legs turn to aspic at the thought. I may make it to the other hill, but *that's* it. Everything in moderation. Don't you agree, Christopher? Oh, forgive me."

Winston and Dr. Wetmore were introduced to a couple posing next to Bill. To Christopher Leyton-White a handshake meant grabbing the other person's fingers at the tips and giving them two uncere-

43

monious pumps. The less physical contact the better. Sylvia Leyton-White held Winston's hand in both of hers, looking earnestly into his eyes and welcoming him with heartfelt emotion and no sincerity whatsoever. Mr. Leyton-White stood, his best foot forward, like some fop from the court of Louis XIV.

"Up for the weekend, Mr. Wyc?" Christopher pulled his lined, full-length, black leather coat tighter around his shoulders.

"Winston's working for me on the house, Christopher. He's an architectural historian."

"Is he?" Christopher's response was a curious blend of surprise and pity.

"And he's quite good," said Bill with a curt nod. "You two have something in common, Winston. Christopher's an architect. Many of his designs are photographed for national publications." Christopher had turned back to watching the hounds. He spoke without looking at them.

"Renovation. I've always thought one should just dig a hole in the ground and throw money in it. Personally, Georgian fronts or gingerbread or what-have-you bore me to tears."

"I've always thought the future, particularly in architecture, was shaped by the past," said Winston, beginning to be irritated.

"I have studied the past, Mr. Wyc, but I do not wallow in it."

"I just read Van Loon's *Lives*," said Mrs. Leyton-White to Winston. "It's full of history."

Christopher rolled his head back in his wife's direction. "Don't be an ass." He gave Winston a look of endured suffering. Sylvia Leyton-White's smile never cracked.

44

"I think I'm ready for the next hill," broke in Bill Joyce. "Coming?"

Everyone said their good-byes. Winston watched the three descend the hill, delicately picking their way around the dirty parts.

"That fellow's the north end of a horse headed south, if you ask me," said Dr. Wetmore, who had remained outside the little group. "Excuse my French."

Winston laughed. "I've never heard of him. How's the beagling going?"

"They drew a hare in the far field and pursued it through that stone wall down there. I think they lost her."

Cries of "killo" came from the human pursuers.

"What in the world are they shouting?" asked Winston.

"Whoops, they've raised her again. You can tell by the hounds' cry. If there's a viewing, the person who spots the hare yells "killo." In fox hunting they'd be yelling "tally ho." Same thing. It makes the blood race, does it not?"

Still breathing hard from the climb, Winston didn't need the scene below to get his blood racing.

"Run, you little fool. Cheat the devils. Come on, Winston, the hare's gone into the cornfield. She'll get away for sure now."

A horn sounded.

"Why the bugle?"

"Horn, Winston. They're regrouping the hounds, and the spotters will take positions around the field to try and spot the hare if she should exit."

"She won't stay in the corn?"

"She should, but she probably won't. She'll look for an opening and try to get back to her neck of the woods. Very parochial in that way. She's going to need some help."

"And that's why we're here, I take it." Winston had to smile. Dr. Wetmore's face shone with mischief.

"We provide the red herring." She gave Skippy's nose a tweak. "You know, that's where the term comes from. Years ago the more sporting types would drag a smoked herring across the path of the hare to bewilder the hounds. Throw them off the scent."

Dr. Wetmore was off and running. She pulled up short of crashing into the corn. Winston followed as best he could, but his sides had begun to ache. He rested his palms on his knees. "Maybe I'll stay here and tell the spotters the hare went thataway."

"We can't stop now. There's a life to be saved."

"What about my life?"

Dr. Wetmore gave Winston a poke in the stomach. "Come on, city dweller." Winston watched her disappear inside the first rows of corn. Hesitating, he took a gulp of air and jumped in.

Dr. Wetmore had already vanished in the forest of stalks. Ten more feet and the world outside the cornfield ceased to exist. Noises were filtered to a murmur. Winston's height put him at a disadvantage, for his face was just level with the heavy foliage at the top of the stalks. Even bending down, his visibility was limited. The feeling was of standing up against a wall with another wall fifteen inches behind. The closeness and the eerie silence made Winston uneasy. He had a vision of himself stumbling around in this maze for years, lost and forgotten. Dr. Wetmore could rescue the devil for all he cared, this was worse than subway rush hour. Turning to retrace his footsteps, Winston heard a muffled cry behind him, and suddenly Skippy went racing between his legs and deeper into the darkening rows.

"Which way did he go?" shouted Dr. Wetmore.

"Christ, you scared the hell out of me."

Dr. Wetmore pushed past him. "If he raises that hare and old Phillips finds him, he'll have Skippy *and* me for the hunt stew next Sunday. He's never taken off like that before."

Winston watched her disappear again, a crouching figure moving quickly through the stalks. Old women aren't supposed to move like that, he thought. Somewhere up ahead, Skippy began yelping. Reluctantly moving in that direction, Winston swatted at corn silk and swore never to eat popcorn again.

"Winston!"

"Yoooo. Would you stop appearing out of nowhere. Let's get out of here. This place is giving me the willies."

Dr. Wetmore grasped Winston by the collar, her eyes round with fright.

"There's someone lying down over there."

"What do you mean, 'lying down over there?' "

Inching Winston over, Dr. Wetmore pulled aside some stalks and pointed into the adjoining furrow. Winston glanced hesitantly into the next row. A man lay face down in the dirt, hands at his sides. Winston's eyes shot to the large knife handle sticking from between the man's shoulder blades. A broadening red stain on the Kelly green sport coat had spread to the back of his white pants. He reminded Winston of a broken Christmas tree ornament. Dr. Wetmore and Skippy moved beside him.

"Is he dead?"

"He doesn't look at all well. I think this is taking character assassination a little far," said Winston, moving two steps away. "I don't feel so well either," he muttered.

"This will ruin refreshments," noted Dr. Wetmore.

Chapter 6

"For goodness sakes, it's Jim Bantram. And he does look dead, the poor man."

Dr. Wetmore went down on one knee, her eyes inspecting Bantram's body, the stiffened legs, the arms tight to the sides. With her forty years as a physician, she didn't need to go looking for a pulse. The murder weapon was a large knife, its handle having the corded look of a bayonet. It had pinned the diminutive Bantram to the ground like a butterfly on a cardboard display. Jim either must have been kneeling or have been knocked to the ground, she reasoned. His body had been forced into the dirt by the knife thrust, and that wouldn't have been the case had he been standing. Dr. Wetmore ran her hand lightly over the man's skull. Hesitating, she lifted the hair and found a raised contusion on the back of his head. Sounds of the hunt came to her. Quickly she surveyed the ground around the dead man for clues: a footprint or items dropped in a struggle. Leaning over, she brushed aside the dirt from around Bantram's face. She thought she could see a hint of fur.

"Here, give me a hand. I want to pick his head up."

"You're kidding. It's a little late for mouth-to-mouth."

"Just lift his head a little. He can't hurt you. There's something *in* his mouth and I think I know what it is."

Winston reluctantly assisted in turning Bantram's head slightly.

"What the . . . his tongue's gone all furry or something." Winston dropped the head in disgust. "What in the hell is wrong with his tongue?"

"That's not his tongue. It's a rabbit's foot," murmured Dr. Wetmore.

"A what?"

But Dr. Wetmore didn't have time to answer, for all of a sudden the hounds came bounding up from nowhere, hounds from hell come to claim their man. The older dogs recognized Bantram for what he was, a dead man lying in a cornrow. Picking up the hare's scent on the other side, they continued the pursuit. Yelping and sniffing, five of the younger dogs stayed to investigate this stranger fetor of death. She watched Winston shoo away one brave pup trying to remove Bantram's boot.

"I should go for help," said Winston.

"By the sound of things, I believe help is almost upon us."

Mr. Phillips came smashing through the corn and tumbled over the canine melee. Unable to stop, he crashed into the next furrow, taking cornstalks and hounds with him. He sat up, his angry red face sputtering corn silk. He tossed a hound into the air.

"What in the hell is this? Damn you, Doctor, what are you up to now? Ahhhh." One of the pups had grabbed the horn around Phillips's neck, and taking off, pulled the enraged man over backward.

The scene exploded with a mass of green jackets and concerned prattle. Jack Glenn tried raising Mr. Phillips off the ground. "What happened, sir? What's going on?"

"Why are we stopped?" Hugh Bantram spoke.

"There's been an . . . accident," said Dr. Wetmore, looking over to the next row where Hugh's father lay partially hidden. Joyce stumbled over, curious to see what could be wrong. Turning back to the gathering, Joyce sputtered a few incoherent sounds, let out a shriek of disgust, and fainted.

Watching the faces of the people as they reacted to the body of James—each one turning to look at Hugh Bantram, and then away—Dr. Wetmore wondered if any of them there had wielded the knife. If so, they were damn good actors. Winston caught her eye. The poor boy, she thought, looks ready to faint himself. He's white as snow.

Walking a short distance from the gathering, she could hear Hugh Bantram call out his father's name and then break into sobs. Peering vacantly down the cornrows, she fingered Flo Perkins's good luck charm in her pocket, absently wondering if the hare had escaped the hounds.

Chapter 7

Simon Tart looked up from his desk, wondering if there might be a fire nearby. For the last half hour every emergency vehicle in the county seemed to be going by the vicarage. Stepping out on the porch, he gazed down the road. To his surprise, they seemed to be going into the Phillipses' cornfield next door. Back in the house, he put away the photographs he'd been going over, and slipping on his cape, went outside to investigate. Bill Joyce's limousine was parked in the far drive next to the church: that strange man James having a quiet moment with his God. Tart could see the man's dark profile against a back window. Hurrying along, Vicar Tart wondered if they prayed to the same deity.

Having already climbed the hill once today, Tart decided the road would be more accommodating. Besides, he liked the road and the fact that it had never been paved. It lent the church a more rural character. Walking Coonden Road in the evenings, Tart could imagine himself at the edge of civilization. There were no streetlights, and as the sun set the surrounding tall grass and scrubs grew dark and mysterious, full of the high chatter of crickets and peepers. Often the sudden rustle of a groundhog became in Tart's imagination a small, winged women, dancing naked just on his periphery. Unable to turn his head for fear he might succumb to her entreaties, and fingering the silver cross that hung from his neck, he would quicken to the distant safety of his porch light, a Christian beacon in the pagan dark. The tension that gripped him on the road would suddenly dissipate as he hurried onto his lawn. His heart in his throat, Tart felt titillated, aroused by the experience. He would not admit to himself that the excitement was in any way sexual, but the idea had occurred to him.

Noting that Mr. Phillips's cornfield was a mess, Tart worked his way past the many parked vehicles until he reached a yellow ribbon that had been strung between cornstalks. Printed on the ribbon were the words "Police Line. Do Not Cross." On the other side of this boundary a number of policemen and three men dressed in suits stood around peering at the ground. He could see Janice Wetmore and a young man he'd never seen before standing beside a parked patrol car. Tart felt a sudden tinge of jealousy that Janice Wetmore was behind the line and he wasn't. He and the doctor were always competing in one way or another, whether it was the Sunday *Times* crossword puzzle or figuring out a whodunit on television. Tart suspected he might take the competition more seriously than Janice did, but that didn't bother him. He thoroughly enjoyed the contest. Spotting Erika Phillips and Jack Glenn among the crowd on the hill, he decided to brave the incline after all. Information was needed here, and Erika would be a pleasant conduit.

"Erika, my dear." Tart's breath came in quick gasps. "What in the world is going on?"

"Mr. Tart, how kind of you to join us. A body has been found."

"Found?" Leaning over, Tart tried supporting himself by placing his hands on his knees. A difficult task given his extreme girth.

"Are you okay?" asked Glenn.

"It must be that extra shrimp at lunch. I'll be fine in a moment."

While Tart caught his breath, the three stared down at the gathering crowd of pickup trucks. A television van had arrived.

"How in the devil do these people find out about things like this so quickly? Really! The television," said Glenn.

"They use their CBs. Many local people keep a police scanner going in their homes," answered Erika. "I know Carl, our gardener, does."

"How clever," said Tart with a touch of irony. "You say a body was found."

"That of Jim Bantram."

"Jim!" Tart's eyes grew round. He turned away. "How interesting."

"Interesting? How do you mean?"

"I mean . . . well, I don't know, really. It's just that . . . that I was talking to him in church this morning and . . ."

Erika waited, an inquisitive look on her face.

". . . and he said he didn't feel he was going to be around much longer." Tart finished the thought quickly.

"He'd been threatened?" Erika and Glenn were all ears.

"Well, not exactly. I think he meant since he was getting along in years."

"Oh." Erika looked doubtful.

"What's Janice doing down there?" Tart changed the subject.

"She found Jim's body."

"She did?"

"She and Winston."

"Who's he?"

"Winston Wyc's here to help Bill Joyce renovate his house. He's a historian or something," said Glenn.

"Hmmmm."

Tart pursed his lips and smiled a secret little smile. If his theory was correct, then Bantram had to die next, but why had it taken so long? And a new man arrives on the scene to assist Joyce. *How convenient*, he thought. Janice might have found the body, but *I* know the answer, he chuckled.

"What's so funny, Simon?" asked Jack Glenn.

"Oh . . . nothing."

"You find humor in murder?"

"Heavens, no, I was merely trying to catch my breath."

"Do murdered people go to Heaven? I've always wondered," asked Glenn.

"It's not the dead man that concerns the church, Mr. Glenn, it's his killer. The murdered is already on his way. We can only say a prayer for him at this point."

"That little smile of yours hinted at some secret knowledge, Simon. You holding out on us?" Glenn grinned at Erika.

"I only wondered if Jim Bantram had a rabbit's foot in his mouth?"

"You don't think . . ." Erika was appalled.

"What would make you think that, Simon? It's been over a year since the other murders. And they were elderly women." Glenn picked a piece of lint off Tart's cape. "This doesn't fit the pattern."

"Maybe it does, Jack. Maybe it does."

"Do you have some information we don't know about?" asked Erika.

"Only a guess . . ." Tart hesitated. Glenn and Erika leaned in. "Between me and my God." Tart looked at them both, a wry look on his face.

"That's a bit unfair," said Glenn.

"You should tell the police," said Erika.

"I've tried that. They don't listen to the clergy in matters such as this. Anyway, I'm probably all wrong. Best not to spread careless rumors." He peered up at the darkening clouds. "Think I'll try and get a closer look. Ta."

"Come by the house later if you like. I know some of us appreciate company at times like this," offered Erika.

"Thank you," called Tart over his shoulder. "I'll do that."

Tart approached the yellow ribbons again. Raising an arm, he tried to attract Dr. Wetmore's attention, but she was getting into one of the patrol cars and didn't see him. Wait until she saw what he had found only this afternoon. The timing was uncanny. Or maybe he would hold out for a few days. It was always good to keep something back from the competition.

His mind turned to Erika's invitation and thoughts of the beagling feast that must certainly still be intact after all this chaos. God moves in mysterious ways, he thought. In very mysterious ways.

57

Chapter 8

The afternoon had turned dark with the gathering of storm clouds from the west. Winston sat in the police car watching the flashing colored lights strobe their eerie patterns against the cornstalks. Each emergency vehicle cast its own distinct mood: the hot red of the fire engines, the jaundiced yellow of the ambulances, the icy, inquiring blue of the patrol cars. Why the fire trucks were needed, Winston hadn't a clue, and there seemed to be an unnecessary collection of pickup trucks with their own variety of twitching colors, an army of volunteers, their citizen's band radios crackling, keeping the people at home up to date on any new happenings.

The forensic crew appeared almost finished and was preparing to leave, giving the boys with the black bag their chance at the body. The local media, cordoned off behind a yellow ribbon that designated the crime area, played with their own lights and revolving communication disks, broadcasting news without having access to the actual event.

Up on the hill, Winston could make out the few remaining members of the beagling party staring down on the proceedings. Erika Phillips stood between Jack Glenn and a man wearing a black cape that played out behind him. From this distance the man looked like a short fat highwayman.

Winston and Dr. Wetmore had stood around for two hours waiting for the police and the obligatory interrogation. A Captain Andrews had been questioning Dr. Wetmore for the last twenty minutes while a Sergeant Miller took notes.

"Mr. Wyc, you have anything to add to that?"

Winston shook his head.

"You saw nothing or heard nothing out of the ordinary?"

"I think Janice covered everything." Winston wondered what "out of the ordinary" really meant. The cornfield had scared the hell out of him.

"You're from New York?"

"Yes."

"Thought so. Brooklyn, right? Could tell by the accent, although you cover it pretty well. I'm from Brooklyn myself. Was a cop there for twenty-five years."

"Oh yeah? What brought you up here?" Winston could feel himself slipping into Brooklynese.

"Sorta semiretirement. Been here about a year and a half now. What brought *you* up here?"

"I'm doing some work for Bill Joyce. Restoration."

"For Joyce. No shit." The idea seem to amuse the captain. "You people are free to go. Just give Sergeant Miller here your full names and addresses. Phone numbers, etcetera. Now these TV and newspaper creeps, they're gonna try and get hold of you and ask all kinds of dumb questions. Don't talk to them. Let's keep our little conversation off the airways and outta the *Wistfield Roundabout*, can we? This isn't gossip, it's murder." The captain combed back his hair with his hands and patted himself down. "The press burns my ass," he said to no one in particular.

Winston and Dr. Wetmore avoided walking where the captain was meeting with the television cameras. Skirting the small group of remaining emergency vehicles, they started back up the same hill they had come down. Winston noticed that Erika and party had gone. Below, most of the pickup trucks had left and the few remaining were gunning their engines, passing along one more observation, putting off going home for a few more minutes. Winston was so exhausted the hill seemed to go straight up. Cradling Skippy in one arm, he assisted Dr. Wetmore with his other. She had taken off her hat, and hair tumbled about her shoulders.

"You feeling better?" asked Dr. Wetmore.

"I'm okay. What did the captain mean by calling it another 'good luck' murder?" asked Winston.

"Because of the rabbit's foot stuck in Bantram's mouth. About a year ago two elderly woman were brutally murdered in Wistfield about a month apart. A rabbit's foot was found on both bodies. You know the kind. Comes with a little chain to hang keys on. Since a rabbit's foot is considered a charm, the papers took to calling them the Good Luck murders. I found it appalling. Those women were good friends of mine."

"I take it they never found the killer."

"That's right. It had been long enough, I thought maybe the maniac had left the area. I was wrong."

"Unless he came back."

They were both silent for a few feet.

"Just like the city, heh? Murder and mayhem." Dr. Wetmore nudged him in the side.

61

"I wouldn't know. Dead guys always seem to be only on television. But you know, it was odd. After the initial shock, the body didn't seem to affect me at all. It could have been a pile of old clothes or something. Part of a 3-D movie. Maybe that's what comes of living in the city for so long. Your soul hardens over like dried mud."

"Dried mud can be washed off. You didn't look all that well out there," suggested Dr. Wetmore.

"It wasn't the body," said Winston. "It was the look on Hugh Bantram's face when he realized it was his father. That look really shook me."

At the top of the hill, Winston turned to look back at the cornfield. The sky had really darkened by now, and Miller and Andrews were standing in the patrol car headlights, going back over the spot where Bantram's body had lain. They looked like two Beckettian actors rehearsing a scene. Everyone else was gone.

"I feel sorry for Hugh Bantram, although I guess I shouldn't. I mean, it would appear he's finally got his wish."

"What do you mean?" asked Dr. Wetmore.

"Hugh and his father were having an argument just before the hunt began about the mismanagement of the estate or something. It won't be a problem anymore."

"We'll see. Hugh Bantram has a hard time getting dressed by himself, much less running a farm."

Winston could see Meadowbrook Farm below him. The carriages were gone and the hounds back in the kennels. The house with its warm lights, the distant hamlet of Wistfield snuggled beneath the hills, the absolute silence of the valley—all seemed so secure and fanciful to Winston that the murder today could have been merely some aberrant parlor game played by these people from another century. He would go into the house and there would be Mr. Bantram, drink in hand, being congratulated on a fine performance.

A drink. What a wonderful idea! Was I really in New York last night cheering the inner man? I feel like I fell down that rabbit hole. Or is it hare hole?

The lawn was brightly lit, a large ring of safety in the darkening hills. Shadows could be seen moving behind the lace curtains of the drawing room. Dr. Wetmore had shot ahead and was bounding up the patio steps. Winston wondered momentarily if the woman lifted weights. Muted voices could be heard, and the clinking of ice in glasses, a most calming sound.

"Winston!" Erika called to him as he entered the room behind Dr. Wetmore.

"Winston, you're back!" yelled Bill Joyce.

"It's true, we're back, for goodness sakes," said Dr. Wetmore.

The small group of people in the room suddenly came alive as though given permission to make noise again. Gathering around the two of them, they interrupted each other asking questions and offering condolences.

"You poor things," sighed Bill, "having to go through such an ordeal."

"Jim Bantram's the one to feel sorry for," shot back Dr. Wetmore.

"Of course!" shouted Fletcher Phillips. "We all feel terrible about this. What a hell of a thing to happen. What a day. What a day." Mr. Phillips glowed from the excitement.

"Are you okay?" Erika came over to Winston.

"I'm okay. I think we could both use a long night's rest. And a scotch."

"But of course," stated Mr. Phillips, who still looked rosy from the afternoon and more than a little drunk. "A most sensible request." He trotted off.

Erika forced Dr. Wetmore into a large wingback chair. "Janice, I want you and Skippy to stay upstairs tonight. And no argument." Mr. Phillips returned with a drink for Winston.

"Thanks," said Winston.

"I'm sure you need it," said Joyce.

"That, forty hours sleep, and the first train back to reality."

"Don't talk like that, Winston. Tomorrow is a new day and we have lots of work to do. You'll feel differently in the sunlight. Christ, I sound like the Prince of Platitudes."

"It's true, your first day in Wistfield hasn't been much fun," said Erika. "But you must stay and let us introduce you to the nicer side of the village. You *will* let me show you around."

"I'd like that." Winston noticed Jack Glenn off to the side, his face beginning to redden and stretch.

"Good. Maybe tomorrow?"

"I'm at your command."

Glenn spoke harsh and loud from the corner. "Why don't we just trot him up the stairs, too? Have a damned slumber party."

"Oh, Jack," Erika murmured under her breath.

Winston noticed Mr. Phillips giving him a curious leer.

"It's Mr. Wyc, is it not?"

"Call me Winston, please."

"My daughter seems to have taken a shine to you. What is it you do again?"

"I'm a historian."

"That's right." Mr. Phillips's face showed he wasn't quite clear what that meant. "What'd the police say?"

"Father, Winston's been interrogated once today already."

"So he has. My apologies, Mr. Wyc, but I'm a nosy old hound. Later, maybe?" Mr. Phillips stole a look at his daughter. The three were joined by Simon Tart, who had stayed around waiting for Janice Wetmore.

"What if the killer was in this room?" said Tart.

"What does that mean, Simon?" asked Erika. "You've been acting very mysterious this afternoon. May I introduce Winston Wyc. Winston, this is our illustrious vicar, Mr. Tart. Watch him, he's full of strange thoughts this evening."

"We always find what is unknown to us strange. Isn't this true, Mr. Wyc?"

"So I hear." said Winston, unsure as how to react to this man staring at him. The Reverend Mr. Simon Tart was a short, round man in his sixties, dressed all in black, who carried a supercilious air about him that contrasted sharply with his pudgy, farm boy looks. Winston thought he looked like Elmer Fudd playing the role of Richard II.

"It's a pleasure to meet you." The vicar went to proffer his hand but thought better of it. "Erika says you're a historian."

"I research old houses, old buildings, and assist the architect with advice on how they might have originally looked."

"Ah, a detective of sorts. I like that. We are possible kindred spirits then, Mr. Wyc. We both study

65

the past and bring its . . . enlightenment to the present."

Joyce stepped between them. "Winston, I'm afraid I've got to get home. I'm dying to hear what the police officers said, but I'm about to fall down."

"I feel the same way. It's been nice talking to you, Mr. Tart."

"We'll talk history sometime soon, shall we?"

"That'd be fine." Winston looked around for Erika, who was whispering with Jack Glenn. He crossed to Mr. Phillips. "Mr. Phillips, thank you for the lesson on beagling this afternoon. Maybe next week the hunt can return to normal."

"Damned exciting, I tell you. Of course, we can't have someone littering the countryside with corpses, but nevertheless . . ." Mr. Phillips shook his head as if to dislodge his next thought, which never came.

"Oh, Winston, you're leaving." Erika came over and took his arm. "Once again I'd like to apologize for this afternoon. I wasn't very friendly at our first meeting."

"Forget it."

"I think tomorrow the real tragedy of the day will begin to affect us." Dr. Wetmore took his other arm. "It would be a good idea if we all got a good night's sleep."

Another round of good-byes and Winston was outside with Joyce, heading for the Volvo. Winston turned back to see Simon Tart staring at them from a window.

"That religious fellow sure's an odd duck," mentioned Winston.

"Poses a bit, but he's hell in the pulpit."

"What's the story between Erika and your friend Jack Glenn?"

"There's talk of an engagement, but who knows?" said Bill sleepily. "Nothing's been officially announced. You'll have to stay with me in the guest cottage tonight, Winston. Tomorrow we'll get you settled into your own place."

Winston watched Bill fumble under the dash trying to release the emergency brake. Settling his head against the window, he had almost drifted asleep when he felt the Volvo suddenly shoot backward down the driveway, forcing him awake. The car came to rest in a hedge. "Bill, maybe I should drive." Winston received no answer. It seemed Joyce had gone to sleep.

Chapter 9

Winston was unsuccessful in willing himself back to sleep. The growls from his stomach became more determined, and soon he was lying face up, both eyes wide open, listening to his peptic juices play a hunger concerto and remembering the events of yesterday: a vague recollection of Bill Joyce showing him to bed and . . . a murder.

Winston lay on his back, drawing an outline of James Bantram on the ceiling with his eyes. Don't think of that, he pleaded with himself. Thoughts of murder would have to wait until after coffee.

Forty minutes later, showered and dressed, he stood in the tiny living room of the cottage, sipping a cup of coffee from Bill's Mr. Coffee machine, staring out the mullioned windows into the garden. The day before still made no sense to him. His cynical saloonmates in New York might have warned him about the dangers of the country, but they had failed to mention falling in love or finding a man with a knife in his back.

Turning back to the room, Winston automatically began going over its contents. It was a game he had developed while in college: trying to identify furniture in a room as to period and style and then arranging the room in chronological order. What had started as an educational diversion had become a habit. He was seldom wrong about a piece.

The ceiling was crisscrossed with styrofoam beams. Between the beams and covering the walls was an off-white sand paint, to give the walls a textured, stucco appearance. The drapes and upholstery matched: large, red-flowered chintz. The Oscar-Wilde-meets-Zorro look, thought Winston, looking for rubber cobwebs in the corners. If this was Bill's idea of period renovation, then Winston had his work cut out for him.

The furniture was real, though, and expensive, much of it being light and airy Federalist, although so much had been crammed into the small room that the effect was destroyed. Running his hand over the fine craftsmanship, Winston could easily imagine this furniture up in the big house, especially since the cottage was so damp. This humidity would ruin the furniture in no time.

The only jolting piece was a huge Gothic armoire that loomed against the back wall. Winston half expected Quasimodo to open the cabinet door and clang forward. Finding it locked, Winston was trying to peer behind it when he heard a car door slam. Joyce, wearing a Mandarin red sport coat over tartan plaid trousers, came through the front door. James positioned himself in the doorway.

"Snappy outfit." said Winston.

"I've always imagined Pandora's box to look something like that wardrobe," said Joyce, ignoring Winston's comment. "It's so evil looking I just had to buy it. I see you found the coffee. Everyone's running a little late this morning, due, I suppose, to the horrors of yesterday. *I* feel like I'm moving through water. Every time I think of that poor man . . . but then, I'm the sensitive type, aren't I, James?"

"That's always been the case, sir." James had the look of man who wouldn't blink if a bomb went off in his mouth.

"James is going to take your things over to the Cogs's boarding house, that's where you'll be bedding down, and *we* can go over at lunch for your personal perusal, but I know you'll just love it. Now, is there anything else? No? Then shall we begin work."

It had rained hard during the night. Winston could remember waking at some point to the heavy pounding on the roof, but the morning was balmy and the day would once again be bright and blue. October had been unseasonably sunny, delaying the turning of many leaves. Winston closed his eyes to the warm sunlight. Maybe winter never comes to Wistfield, he thought. While the rest of the Northeast is buried under snow and ice, this small community remains an Eden, untouched by the cold.

Winston lagged behind, watching Bill walk ahead of him. He noticed James watching him from behind a curtain in the cottage's kitchen window. An impulse to quit came over him. He had a sudden overwhelming feeling that something was wrong, that a piece of the picture was missing or that something was askew. Too many people were staring at him from behind windows.

"You'll be meeting a Mr. Worth and a Mr. Grimes." Joyce stopped and waited impatiently for Winston. "Ed Worth is the carpenter and Paul Grimes is the architect/contractor. Both are from New York. Both quite good." Turning, Joyce started back up to the house, stopping in the drive

71

when he realized Winston hadn't moved. "Are you coming?"

Shaking off his uneasiness, Winston started up the drive.

The Joyce house had an intricate exoskeleton of thin metal scaffolding that enveloped almost the entire front of the building. Wooden planking ran vertically at different levels so the workers could have access to every part of the exterior. Winston noted that the roof had been reslated and water-damaged areas restored. Broken cornice and window crests had been removed.

Joyce had done extensive work on the grounds and cottage, leaving only the house to bring the entire estate back to the original. Winston would spend the fall sketching and copying design elements, measuring and figuring out exactly what needed replacing, determining what belonged and what didn't. The winter would be spent finding the workshops and craftsmen who could reproduce the design elements needed: doors, windows, moldings and ornamentation, and by spring all would be ready for the completion process. By the end of summer, Joyce would be able to move into his new house, just in time to entertain for next year's beagling.

Winston passed under the scaffolding and in through the front door. The entrance, which would have had narrow sidelights originally, had been replaced with two large solid-core doors that would have discouraged a charging elephant. Restoring the door would be next on the agenda. Winston couldn't bear to look at this travesty of remuddling. The interior looked like all houses under renovation: empty and echoing, filled with the black dust of demolition. Voices could be heard in the back of the house.

The back parlor had been made into an office of sorts. Sawhorses topped with plywood served as desktops, and various prints and plans had been laid out for inspection. Joyce stood talking to two men, whom he introduced to Winston as Mr. Worth and Mr. Grimes. The two could have been brothers. Both were short and wiry, with cigarettes hanging from the same sides of their mouths. Both men had elongated faces, the skin pulled tightly over the cheekbones, giving them a shiny, hollowed look. Each had dull, slicked back yellow hair. Anorexic Tweedledee and Tweedledum. Mr. Worth had large, callused hands—the palms of a man who worked wood. Mr. Grimes's hands were small and soft. Worth wore the overalls of a carpenter, Grimes wore a plaid sport coat.

"Mr. Wyc, it's a pleasure. Mr. Joyce says we share a reverence for the old buildings. Not that there isn't a place for the new, but please, not at the expense of the fine designs of the past. Don't you agree, Ed?" His partner grunted. "Country renovation is not really my forte, Mr. Wyc, but I've always been eager to participate, and I'm looking forward to learning from an expert." Mr. Grimes actually gave a short bow. "I believe we can drop the formality here. Please call me Paul, and this is Ed." Hands were again shaken all around.

"And I'll be Winston. Are we the only ones here?"

"Until the reproductions come back. What's left to do can be handled by Ed and myself, if he needs a hand." Winston couldn't see Paul lifting a finger.

"Bill says you're from New York."

"That's right. Queens. You ever do any work in Queens?"

"Can't say that I have," said Winston.

"Paul, you and Ed can go over with Winston what we discussed last week. I see no need for me to stick around, so I'll just scoot along. See you at twelve, Winston, and we'll go visit the Cogs." Joyce left the men alone.

"Let me show you what we have, Winston, and I'll try to answer your questions."

Winston and Paul went over the blueprints. Ed hovered on the periphery, looking sullen and offering an occasional grunt of approval. Paul Grimes certainly knew what he was doing, but Winston kept having the feeling that he was being sold a used house. They had anticipated most of his questions and the plans seemed thorough and professional.

"So now it's up to you, Winston, to put the icing on the cake and make the old lady tasty once again. We've managed to salvage some of the decorations, like the outside balustrade urns, and store it all in the basement. You can wander around down there if you like and maybe shorten your shopping list somewhat."

"Thanks. I think I'll just nose about the house for a while and acquaint myself with things. Is there an extra set of blueprints?" Paul produced another set and Winston left to explore the ruins.

The walls were pockmarked with holes where new pipes and electrical wiring had been installed. Some of the cornice moldings had been damaged in the process, and he would have to make imprints of these so reproductions could be made. Ornamentation had been excessive. Festoons of fruit and flowers covered the walls, garlands of ribbons served as

74

window aprons, while each doorway was guarded by matching pilasters topped in acanthus leaves. Egg and dart and dentil bands supported cornices decorated with plaster roses and smiling Cupid's faces. Much of the embellishments were repetitious, which would make Winston's job easier, and the first floor had not sustained as much damage as Winston had feared. Some walls didn't seem correct. He'd see if Joyce had any original floor plans.

Roaming the other floors, making notes, Winston tried to visualize what the rooms might have looked and sounded like when inhabited: the whispers of young lovers, political arguments among friends, a Christmas party. Winston couldn't separate the present physical interior from the past life that had walked its rooms. Once he envisioned the human elements, reconstructing the material environment was simpler. Winston listened now for the voices that would give him the clues he needed. Closing his eyes, he focused his mind on the sounds of the house. An eerie silence suffused his thoughts, as if the ghosts of the past were there but were unwilling or unable to confide in him. Quickly opening his eyes, Winston glanced around the room. The strange quiet had frightened him. Instead of voices he had felt movement, close and silent and sinister. An image of James Bantram lying in the cornfield had come back to him. I'm still spooked about yesterday, reasoned Winston, shaking off the sudden chill and continuing his investigation of the house.

The basement was actually two large rooms, one of which had a door to the outside where the hillside fell away from the house. The workers had saved everything, and much would have to be thrown away. The urns were there, as were sections of balustrade, an Ionic column, piles of plaster molding and chunks of cement with hints of designs on them. He could use some pieces as models, though, which would speed up the process. Winston usually felt at ease in old cellars, but this one was giving him the shivers. He had the feeling that things moved when he wasn't looking. Going over to the outside door, he let the sun shining through the glass warm his face and relax him. I've got to forget about Bantram, he thought. It cheered him to realize that he could handle the job, and it looked as if he might have the time after all to pursue some personal writing. After an unusual start maybe it would all settle into a quiet winter in the country.

The basement door looked out on the back drive to the cottage, and Winston could see Erika Phillips coming toward the house. He took pleasure in watching her walk, the light sway of her hips, the long legs, her hair brushing her face as she moved.

"Hello!" Winston stepped out and shut the basement door behind him.

"Good morning. What a beautiful day."

"It keeps getting prettier."

"If that's a compliment, then thank you. I've come to take you to lunch."

"That would be nice. I think I might have to go with Bill over to my new quarters, though."

"All taken care of. I just had Bill release you into my custody."

Erika took Winston by the arm and led him back toward the cottage. "Now you're not one of those serious people, are you? Devoted to their work and nothing else."

"Work is very important in my life. I try to get in at least two, three hours a day."

"That's what we like to hear. And what about people? Are we devoted to anyone in particular nowadays?"

"And aren't *we* being a little nosy?"

"That's a possibility. But how else am I going to learn about your private life?"

"Through observation. You stay very close and after a number of years all the questions will have been answered and I won't feel I've been unduly probed." Winston smiled to let her know he didn't mind her interest.

"Close, heh?" They had reached her car, a cream-colored BMW. "Anyway, I've already locked your bag in my trunk, so you have to come with me. You don't mind, do you?"

"You could lock *me* in your trunk."

Erika squeezed his arm and laughed. "Mr. Wyc, I like my gentlemen in the front seat where I can get at them."

"I don't let anyone 'get at' me unless they call me Winston."

"I like the name Wyc. Do you mind?"

Bill Joyce came out of the cottage.

"Well, well. You waste no time, Winston. Immediately after the prettiest girl in town."

"I'm an innocent bystander."

"That hasn't seen a thing, right? Listen, I hate to break up this little group, but since you are going to be using the Volvo, would you mind taking it into town with you now? That way I don't have to drop it off to you later and you aren't stuck at the Cogs's. I may have to take off this afternoon. Antique hunting in Connecticut."

"I see no problem with that. How about my guardian?" Winston bowed in Erika's direction.

"We're to meet Dr. Wetmore at the Wistfield Inn in town."

Winston noted that Erika said this more to Bill than to him. How close were Bill and Jack? he wondered.

"Then it's settled. Stay away from the fish and chips, Winston. Ghastly stuff. You'll find the keys in the car. Ta." Bill stopped to sniff a hollyhock before entering the cottage.

"Follow me, Mr. Wyc. The village of Wistfield awaits."

Chapter 10

Dr. Wetmore sat on a bench in the village green watching Skippy chase ground sparrows. She had managed a long walk that morning and was feeling better for it. The finding of Jim Bantram had unsettled her more than she had been willing to admit to anyone yesterday, and exercise always helped her to relax. Last night had been a difficult one. Every time she closed her eyes, Flo Perkins would appear, offering in her outstretched hand a dangling rabbit's foot. Dr. Wetmore shuddered even now at the recollection.

Across the wide lawn she could see Simon Tart making his way toward her, his cape shadowing behind him. She wished he'd get rid of that darn thing; it made him look like a pretentious fool. She liked him, though. He was a good competitor. They'd had many an amusing tête à tête.

"Good morning, dear doctor. I hope this day finds you content and reconciled with the events of yesterday."

"I'll live. And yourself?"

"I fear I might have lost a few pounds climbing that damn hill twice," he chuckled. "I feel like a stick."

"You must really watch your weight, Simon. You're going to end up a skeleton."

"As we all will. I've spent a life waiting to see the Boss, Doctor. Death doesn't bother me."

Tart settled himself on the bench, which Dr. Wetmore noticed rose perceptibly on her end as he did. The two took a moment to enjoy the sunshine. The village of Wistfield was still blessed with its original green, its wide lawn and small pond untouched by the disfigurements of progress. Large Victorian houses and a number of shops ringed the green, and although some of the homes had been converted to multiple dwellings or stores, the remodeling had been tasteful and in most cases inconspicuous. A stoplight at the far end had caused quite a stir ten years before but was now taken for granted.

"Skippy's looking well," said Tart. "Not often he finds a murdered man."

"Once in a life time is plenty for him *and* me. You have that glint in your eye, Simon. You didn't call me this morning to talk about Skippy. You know something or think you do and you can't wait to tell me, so why put it off any longer?"

"You know me too well, Janice. It's true I have a hunch as to these murders, but I thought I'd run it past you first before making a fool of myself with the police." Tart stared off into the middle distance, his fleshy mouth formed into a perfect "O." Dr. Wetmore busied herself with her hair.

"There will be another murder before you pass on this jewel of a hunch, Simon."

"Yes, well . . ." Tart looked all around him at the green.

"Oh, for goodness sakes!" said Dr. Wetmore.

"I'm arranging my thoughts, so just be patient. Up until now no one could figure out why these particular people were killed. They seemed like random murders with no connection. But I've found a link."

"You have?" Dr. Wetmore was doubtful but couldn't suppress her look of curiosity. Skippy came up and barked at the vicar's pants leg.

"I have." Tart leaned down to retrieve a stick that lay at his feet. Skippy danced back in anticipation. The size of Tart's stomach prevented him from quite reaching it; his short fingers flailed at the stick. Straightening back up, he took a quick look at Dr. Wetmore and faked a few coughs.

"Some time today would be nice, Simon. Skippy can find his own stick."

"Hmmm. As you know, I'm working on this history of Wistfield for the bicentennial, and Sunday after my climb I was going through some old newspaper clippings from the *Wistfield Roundabout* and I came across a picture showing some hunt club officers giving money to the town library to buy books on beagling. Can you imagine? As if everyone in town would be interested."

"Go on."

"Well, there they were all lined up. Cynthia Hall, Florence Perkins, and James Bantram."

Dr. Wetmore only stared.

"At the time I didn't know about Jim Bantram, but I thought it odd that two of those in the photo had been killed. Later, up on that hill, it all suddenly fell into place. The thing is, the article mentions five members of the committee but only names the three shown in the photo. Just like the *Roundabout*."

"Who were the other two?"

"Just hold on. I've looked through all the papers for that year but I couldn't find anything else pertaining to the committee. Unless the hunt became directly involved with the village in some way the committee didn't make the news."

"What was the date on this newspaper?"

"March 1955. It would have been the end of the beagling season." Tart took a deep breath. "Now what I did was call around this morning to see if I could find anyone who might remember the committee and ask if they'd had any trouble with anyone."

"Trouble?"

"Well, yes. It would seem somebody has it out for that group of people, wouldn't you say?"

"Curious." Dr. Wetmore wasn't won over. Yet.

"Tracy Bump said she thought John Hardwell had been on the committee during the fifties, although she wasn't exactly sure when. John was her neighbor at that time."

"But John Hardwell died of natural causes."

"How do you know?"

"I know. I was his doctor."

"Oh. That's too bad."

"What is it, Simon? You look crushed."

"I had thought that maybe we could go to the police and have Hardwell's body disinterred. Look for foul play."

"We? I hate to disappoint, but John Hardwell died of lung cancer. I was at his side. Besides, I think the police would need more to go on before they started digging up thirty-year-old bodies."

Tart managed a small rally. "Doesn't mean a

82

thing. I think it's too much of a coincidence that the other three were on that committee."

"It does seem odd. So who's killing people?"

"That's the sticky part. Since I didn't find anything in the paper for 1955, I went back to the previous year when the hunt season began. In November of *that* year I found an editorial written by one Samuel Berry lashing out at the hunt committee for being elitist and so on and so on."

"That's not true. Anyone can go beagling. You just have to show up."

"I know that, but Mr. Berry seemed to be of a different opinion and was rather miffed. The letter turned out to be a defence of his policy not to let the club beagle on his land."

"His land?"

"That's right. Now I had no idea who this fellow was because I wasn't around in those days, but Bump remembered some Berrys who lived on the Joyce estate when it still belonged to Alice Worthwell. She later left it to the Berrys in her will. I vaguely remember hearing about it. You think it's the same Berrys?"

"That's right. The Berrys. It caused a minor stir at the time. I don't remember their first names. But what are you saying? That the Berrys are in some way responsible for the murders? I think they're both dead. I seem to recall that the husband took off or something, deserted the wife. I don't remember. Mrs. Berry moved away soon after that. At least I think she did. That would have been in the late fifties. I would imagine they are both dead at this point. Either that or well past a hundred. From what you're suggesting the committee should have been killing the Berrys."

83

"Hear me out. Bump told me the Berrys had a young son and that he'd be in his late forties now and . . . well, I don't know, maybe he's here in Wistfield . . . somewhere . . ." Tart arched his eyebrows.

Dr. Wetmore arched her eyebrows back at him. "You think the Berry son is running around killing people? You're a crazy man, Simon Tart."

Tart had lost on his first hunch and he wasn't going to let this one go so easily.

"It's only a theory, you understand, but what if there was more to it? I think that's what we have to find out. Maybe this boy has returned to seek revenge."

"He's hardly a boy and revenge for what?"

"I don't know, but obviously . . ." Tart shrugged. "Whatever it was has demented the man. He . . ."

Tart screwed his face up into a painful expression, his hands beating the air. Dr. Wetmore waited as long as she could.

"Simon Tart, you're holding something back. You look like the boy who stole the cookie. He . . . what? Do you know who this person is?"

"I'm not sure yet, but I'm working on it."

"You're working on it. Bah!" Dr. Wetmore gave the middle distance some scrutiny herself. "It doesn't make any sense, Simon. What could have happened to cause the deaths of three people? Surely the town would remember such an injustice. Besides, there's no one new in the village. Certainly no Berrys."

"Oh, Janice, he's not going to come back as a Berry if he's a murderer. And there *is* someone who moved to the area recently. Within the last two years."

"Who?" Dr. Wetmore racked her brain to think of someone Simon might mention. No one came to mind immediately, but it would come.

"That's for me to know and you to find out."

"Simon Tart! That's not fair."

"I have a meeting with a certain person tomorrow. After that I will be more positive."

"Simon, that's crazy. You can't go by yourself to meet with a killer."

"Who said anything about meeting with a killer?"

"If what you say is true, and I doubt it at this point—sorry, but that's the way I feel—but *if* it's true then you're putting yourself in great danger. You should notify the police, take them with you."

Tart pursed his lips and said nothing.

"This is the silliest thing I've ever heard coming from you, Vicar Tart."

"Do I detect a note of jealousy?" Tart brushed off a layer of invisible dust. "Tomorrow the forces of good do battle with the forces of evil."

"Save it for the pulpit, Simon. This is not some intellectual melee. This is murder."

"I'll be careful. I'm a little disappointed in you, though." Tart sucked at his front teeth.

"About what?"

"You haven't asked the million-dollar question, Janice."

"What question's that?"

"Who was the fifth person on that committee? And is he still around? He or she, that is."

"Lordy, you're right. Who was it?"

Tart ignored her entreaty. Looking across the lawn at Skippy he rocked himself to a standing position.

"How's Skippy's nose?"

"You're making no sense, Simon Tart."

"You don't think Skippy saw the killer, do you?" Tart chortled.

Dr. Wetmore glanced quickly around the lawn, finding the small dog frolicking over by the pond. The thought actually hadn't occurred to her. But what if Skippy *had* seen . . . She looked up and watched Simon Tart rumble away across the grass, cape billowing, short determined steps carrying him into unknown dangers.

"Simon Tart!"

Darn him, she thought. He knows more than he's telling and he's heading for trouble. What he needs is a little help.

At that moment Erika Phillips and Winston Wyc drove up in separate cars and parked in front of the Wistfield Inn.

Dr. Wetmore knew just who could help . . . and how.

Chapter 11

The Dutch had built their villages in the New World in straight lines, on a grid pattern, logical and sane. The early English settlers, on the other hand, had fashioned their villages like the ones they had left behind, around a common, with the streets working outward as they were needed, unmindful of practicality or future zoning problems. Winston was happy to see that Wistfield was a village in the English manner, its homes and shops circling a broad expanse of lawn. But Winston noted that like many old towns in New England, Wistfield was in danger of becoming a victim of an idealized past. The local planning board obviously had a Disneyland idea of what a quaint New England town must look like. Already some shops had remodeled their facades to resemble something from Charles Dickens. The Wistfield Medieval Festival, with jousting and jesters ruining the green, wouldn't be far in the future. The original settlers would have looked on in bewilderment.

Winston parked beside Erika in front of the Wistfield Inn. The building was bounded on one side by an antique store and on the other by the Gourmet Shoppe, each with its own hand-carved sign swaying above the door. Glancing down the sidewalk, Winston saw other wooden signs announcing a variety of wares. No civilized neon here.

Dr. Wetmore caught him and Erika at the door.

"Winston, what a pleasure. I've thought of no one but you since yesterday's . . . eh, unhappiness. Who knows what might have happened if I'd been alone. I like to think that you saved my life." She stood beaming up at Winston.

"I wouldn't say that was true, Doctor. I'm not the hero type. I'd say we owe our lives to Skippy and his fierce bark.'"

"Skippy couldn't scare an old shoe and you know it."

"Maybe. I wonder if Skippy saw the killer."

"Simon Tart wondered that same thing. What if the murderer thinks *we* saw him?" She grabbed his arm. "We might be next." Janice Wetmore seemed to relish the idea.

"That's not possible, Doctor. The murderer knows we would have told the police by now." Or would he? "It won't help to become paranoid."

"Paranoid implies imagined dangers, Winston. This danger is real enough. Maybe we should figure out who did it. Get the drop on them."

"Well . . . I don't know. I think this might be a job for Captain Andrews." Winston smiled over at Erika, who was frowning at Janice.

"Oh, where's your sense of adventure? Come on in, we can discuss strategy. And how are you, my dear? I haven't seen you since breakfast." Janice took Erika by the arm, escorting her into the restaurant.

The interior of the Wistfield Inn wasn't fake country colonial, as Winston was expecting, but looked quite authentic. The floor was composed of enormous, smooth slabstones, closely joined, with a large fieldstone fireplace in the center of the room. An oak bar, with raised panel front, stood along the left wall. The other walls were lined with blackened oak banquettes, the benchfronts worn round and smooth from many sittings. The heavy beamed ceiling had the darkened dun-color patina applied by generations of cigar and fire smoke. They chose a table near the fire.

Dr. Wetmore removed her hat, and her hair immediately fell over her face and onto her shoulders. She began wrestling it into a bun.

"Janice, what in the world were you talking about outside? You didn't tell me you had seen someone."

"Well, we didn't actually. But what if the killer *thinks* we have?"

Erika gave Winston a skeptical look. She placed her hand over Dr. Wetmore's.

"Janice, I think you're being an alarmist. Don't you agree, Winston?"

Winston cleared his throat and brought his hands together. "Well . . . I'm not sure. I'd say somebody pretty ruthless murdered Mr. Bantram in that cornfield. If they thought for one minute . . ." Pulling his mouth down, Winston widened his eyes at Erika.

"I don't think it's amusing. Janice, just because you found the body doesn't mean you saw anyone." She looked from Winston to Dr. Wetmore.

"Yes, but do they know that?" asked Dr. Wetmore.

"Perhaps I'll invest in one of those red-tipped canes. Blind architectural historian stumbles over body in cornfield," said Winston.

"Very clever," chided Erika. "You and Janice might be in serious danger."

"I don't think so," said Winston. "If we had seen the killer we would have said so right then and there. He has to know that."

"I think Winston's right," said Dr. Wetmore, who relaxed, nodded to herself, and began rummaging in her handbag. "Of course, if they should miss the obvious, then it would be best if we got to them first." She extracted a notebook and a pen. "Now, to begin with, you two have to promise that anything said at this table will remain confidential."

"Wait a minute, Janice. You're not suggesting that the three of us get involved in this in some way?" Erika was dismayed.

"Why not?"

"Mr. Wyc here has already mentioned the brutality of this horrible person, and *I* think the police should handle it. Don't you agree?"

Winston nodded. "I didn't know Mr. Bantram, so it's hard for me to want to stick my neck out for the guy. I'm concerned about what happened, but . . ."

"Well, I didn't know him all that well myself, but two dear friends of mine were killed by this same maniac." Dr. Wetmore opened her notebook. "I feel most involved already."

"I think it's a job for the police," repeated Erika. "Besides, I wouldn't have the slightest idea where to start. If Captain Andrews can't solve this mess what makes you think we can?"

"If you both promise not to say anything, I've had some interesting information passed on to me."

Winston and Erika exchanged puzzled looks. Dr. Wetmore received reluctant nods.

90

"I know an important link between all those killed."

"You do?" Erika and Winston spoke in unison.

"They all served on the hunt committee together back in 1955." Dr. Wetmore sat back. Erika and Winston looked at each other with blank expressions.

"You think that has any significance?" asked Erika.

"It's too much of a coincidence, if you ask me."

"You're saying somebody had it in for the hunt committee?" said Winston. "If that's true, then who is it?"

"Well . . . that I don't know yet. That's what I thought the three of us might figure out."

"You're talking to someone who's straight off the boat around here," said Winston. "How could I be of any help? That's if I was willing to help."

"My mother used to talk about the good old hunt days all the time," said Erika. "She never mentioned any trouble with anyone. Not the kind that would precipitate this kind of reaction. And so long afterward. I don't know, Janice."

"Simon thinks it might have something to do with the Berry family."

"Who were they?" asked Erika.

"They lived at the Worthwell estate. Old Alice Worthwell left it to them when she died. I remember everyone was amazed when she did. The Berrys were her cook and gardener. I thought at the time it was a nice thing to do."

"Did that upset anyone?" said Winston.

"I don't think anyone really cared all that much. I had just moved to Wistfield and I don't think I ever met the Berrys. They were very reclusive."

"Where does all this lead, Janice? What makes Simon think the Berrys are involved?"

Dr. Wetmore took in a deep breath, expelling it slowly. She gave Erika and Winston an animated recap of the conversation she'd had with Tart that morning, ending with the fact that the Berrys had a son.

"Simon and I think he's come back for some kind of revenge."

"Revenge?" said Erika.

"That might explain the rabbit's foot, if it had something to do with the hunt," said Winston.

"I hadn't thought of that," said Dr. Wetmore.

"How grisly," shuddered Erika.

"Would you like menus?"

The sudden inquiry caused all three to jump. A skinny young man with long blond hair and an earring stood holding menus.

"Sorry to startle you folks. An afternoon libation? Bloody Mary? Mimosa?"

Winston and Erika settled on Bloody Marys. Dr. Wetmore wanted tea. Quiche and salad was ordered all around.

"That fellow gave me a fright. I didn't see him come over." Dr. Wetmore shook her head.

"So those are your sources. Mrs. Bump and Simon Tart." Erika clucked. "Those two are the biggest busybodies in town. What other tidbits did the vicar have to offer?"

Dr. Wetmore looked sheepish. "I wasn't supposed to tell anyone. You won't mention it to him, will you?"

"Your secret is safe with me, but really, Janice, I wouldn't get all excited about this. Simon's in the ozone half the time."

"I don't know," said Winston. "I think Janice is right. It's too much of a coincidence not to look into, but I feel the police should do the looking."

Dr. Wetmore was horrified. "Not yet, Winston. Give me and Simon a little more time."

"It's too dangerous," said Winston.

"What do you want us to do?" asked Erika.

Drinks were placed on the table.

"You find the body yesterday?" The waiter's question was directed at Winston.

"That's right," said a surprised Winston. "Me and Dr. Wetmore here."

"I've never found anything like that."

"Bodies are a rarity. I hope you never find one," said Dr. Wetmore.

"I don't know. It might be neat. Did you see who did it?" The young man lowered his voice.

"No!" Winston and Dr. Wetmore spoke together. They grinned at each other.

"Tell me. How did you know it was us?" asked Winston.

"Overheard your conversation. Some of it. Sorry." He shrugged a smile. "Anyway, it's all over town. Look, need anything else, just wave. I'm at the bar." The waiter grabbed his tray and left, his long hair following a moment later.

"Think I should get an earring?" Winston pulled at his ear lobe. "It's all the rage."

"If you're fourteen," said Dr. Wetmore.

"Oh, I don't know. Might give Mr. Wyc that swashbuckling, pirate look. Maybe a tattoo."

"That's a thought. Here on my forehead. 'Erika,' it'd say, with an arrow through it."

"Why, Mr. Wyc, I'd be truly honored." Erika laughed.

"Honestly!" Dr. Wetmore shook her head. "I'd like to get back to matters at hand. Erika, I want you to find the hunt committee minutes for the years 1954 and '55. Maybe there's something in them that would shed a little light on things."

"Jack Glenn's the secretary. I think all the old records are stored at his house."

"Well, he'd certainly let you in to see them. Also we need to know who else was on the committee."

"You mean there were more than the three killed?" asked Winston.

"Actually there were two more. We know that much. We think one was John Hardwell, who died of lung cancer, but the other one's a mystery. We must find out, and if he or she is still alive we should warn them."

"I'll ask Father if he remembers anything," said Erika. "And I guess I can look for those records."

"Winston, I'd like you to nose around the Worthwell estate and see what you can find."

"Where's the Worthwell estate?"

"That's the Joyce house now. I know all the old furniture was still in the house when Bill bought it. Maybe there's something there. What, I have no idea." Dr. Wetmore shrugged. "I wonder if Bill bought that house from the Berrys' son. Bill might know who he is. You could ask him." Dr. Wetmore had become inspired. Her hand flew over her notepad.

Winston grinned over at Erika. "I'll see what I can unearth. You think this fellow was lurking in the cornfield waiting for Mr. Bantram?"

"I hadn't thought about that," said Dr. Wetmore.

"Well, *someone* was waiting out there," said Winston. "Of course, I can't imagine how anyone could find someone in that maze. Or maize."

"Are you always so silly?" asked Erika.

"Don't listen to me. I'm still in shock."

Erika shook her head. "Maybe they followed him in."

"I didn't see anyone at the hunt I didn't know," said Dr. Wetmore.

"I didn't know anyone there, but I thought I spotted one unsavory character," said Winston. "A big blond guy in a green sport coat."

"That's unfair," admonished Erika, enjoying the suggestion of jealousy, nonetheless. Catching Winston's eye she grinned and made a face.

"You think it might have been someone at the hunt?" Dr. Wetmore's face glowed with promise.

"Unless Bantram had an appointment to meet the killer at some definite spot there's no way he'd have found him in that field," said Winston.

"Somebody followed him," whispered Erika.

"I was introduced to Bantram's son at the hunt," said Winston. "He was in a heated quarrel with his father. What's his name?"

"Hugh."

"That's him. Bantram threatened to throttle the boy."

"We should have found Hugh, then, and not Jim," said Dr. Wetmore.

"And Hugh mentioned a Mr. Potter, who'd just been fired by his father."

"Barney Potter? He's been with the Bantrams forever," said Erika.

"He might have been angered by the firing?" said Winston.

"Barney had a hard time poisoning gophers," said Dr. Wetmore. "Wonder why he got fired?"

"Hugh said something about keeping up appearances. I got the feeling that finances were tight and that the Bantrams had different approaches to the problem. A conservancy was mentioned."

"That's the Wistfield Conservancy. It was set up by a few of the larger landowners to help protect the land against future development. My father's a member," said Erika.

"It was set up to keep Wistfield in the nineteenth century and land values high," snorted Dr. Wetmore.

"It's a way of keeping Wistfield's rural character intact," retorted Erika. "Janice is for development. She thinks it would help the merchants in town."

"Who are dropping like flies. Used to be we had services in this village."

The quiche and salads arrived just in time to postpone any further disagreement. Winston felt he'd better change the subject.

"Suddenly it would seem we have a spate of suspects: the shadowy Berry lad, the greedy son, and the irate gardener."

"I'll have to ask people if they saw Bantram with any of these people," said Dr. Wetmore.

Pushing an orange slice around his plate, Winston said to no one in particular. "If the killer *was* beagling, then he was standing right next to us in that field."

They all sat staring at each other in silence.

"That's too weird to think about," said Erika to her salad.

"And if he wasn't beagling, then he escaped out

96

the other side of the field. Anyone be able to see him if he came out by the road?"

"That'd be right by St. Peter's. Simon didn't mention seeing anyone. I wonder . . ." Dr. Wetmore sat up straight, a bemused look crossed her face.

"Think the old boy held out on you? Or *did* he mention someone?" Winston gave the doctor a reprimanding look.

"Simon was only speculating." Dr. Wetmore rose. "I've found most clergymen do. If you'll excuse me a minute I must powder my nose."

Winston and Erika sat uncomfortably silent for thirty seconds. Winston noticed Erika's skin was stretched taut on the high cheekbones, her full lips drawn tight. "Tired?" he asked.

"I guess I am. I didn't get much sleep last night. Truth be known, this whole situation bothers the hell out of me. Murders don't happen in Wistfield. It's a nice, quiet community where you can leave the keys in your car and the door to your house unlocked." Erika stared into the fire. "I guess I'm a little frightened, too. Mr. Bantram wasn't really a friend of ours, he stayed very much to himself, but still . . . he's dead. Murdered."

Winston and Erika both stared into the flames.

"How long have you known Dr. Wetmore?"

"Janice Wetmore has been the local GP for as long as I can remember. She delivered me, so that means I've known her since I was born."

"Janice is a doctor?"

"Janice is a wonderful doctor. She's retired now."

"I don't know why I'm so surprised. I guess I thought she might have been a professor at some local college, teaching something obscure, like the mating calls of wildflowers, or some such."

97

Erika laughed. "Now you're trying to cheer me up." She reached over and laid her hand on Winston's arm. "Thank you."

Dr. Wetmore sat back down. "I'll be on my way. Now, Winston, I want you to give this affair some serious thought."

"It's at the front of my frontal lobe."

"That doesn't sound very serious. Where will you be staying?"

"Bill's booked me into the local boarding house. Mrs. Cog's?"

"Amy and Herb Cog run a very tidy, very comfortable place. You'll like it there. Hmmmm. The Cogs are a wealth of local lore. You could ask her about the Berrys and the possibility of a son. I think I'll pay Hugh Bantram a visit. As a doctor, of course. And Erika, if you could get those records from Jack it would help immensely."

Dr. Wetmore collected her notebook and placed some money on the table.

"No, no. Let this be on me." Winston pushed her money across to her.

"Winston, if you want to ask me out for dinner some night, I'll let you pay, but as for lunch, you're just another one of the girls. Both of you take care. And thank you, Erika, for last night."

"Don't be silly," said Erika. "How about coming over for dinner tomorrow night, you and Winston? Father's going out of town for a couple of days. I'd like the company. I'll call Simon. We can have a powwow. Winston?"

"I'd love to," said Winston.

"Count me in too," added Dr. Wetmore. "Maybe I'll have some news to report. Isn't it exciting?"

Stuffing her unruly hair back under her hat, Dr. Wetmore smiled at each of them and exited.

"I hope she doesn't get herself into any trouble," sighed Erika.

"You can almost hear her buzzing. Hopefully she'll run around in circles until the whole thing blows over."

"Still, I wish she'd go to the police."

They waited for the check in silence.

Once outside, Winston was reluctant to part. "Can I walk you anywhere?"

"That's okay, I'm only going to the corner. I own the gallery there." She smiled at him.

"You do?"

"I do. Girl has to do something besides take care of her father's estate. I have an opening this Thursday, so everything's a mess at the moment or I'd invite you in. You should certainly come to the opening."

"I'd like to." Winston went to leave. "How do I get to the Cogs's?"

"Just at the end of the village. There's a tall hedge just before the house; you can't miss it. If you go over the bridge, you've gone past it."

Winston watched her walk away, his heartbeat in time with her quick steps.

Chapter 12

Winston looked up at the impressive four-story Victorian and marveled at the gingerbread decorating the eaves, eighteen-inch knobbed shafts that hung down between large, bifurcated ovals. Oh, those repressed Victorians! mused Winston. The original covered carriageway was still intact on the east side of the house, and along the front ran a wide porch, its roof supported with Tuscan columns joined by latticed arches. Framed in one of the arches, sitting in a ladder-back rocker, was Captain Andrews.

"Mind if we talk a minute, Mr. Wyc?"

"Not at all." Winston's guard went up immediately. A left-over response from his teen years in Brooklyn.

Andrews laughed, motioning for Winston to sit. "Don't worry, I'm just looking for some help."

Winston settled against the porch railing. "What can I do?"

"I need a little assistance with this 'good luck' case. I can tell ya I'm getting nowhere." Winston nodded. "I need some ears and eyes and I was wondering if you'd be of a mind."

"What do you mean?"

"You seem pretty buddy-buddy with the doctor

there, and some time back two of her close friends were murdered. I know she was pretty upset by the whole thing, and for a while she was calling me every week: Possible motives, that sort of thing. Never made much sense. I think I pissed her off. She stopped calling. Anyway, now with this Bantram mess I'm sure the whole thing's gonna come up again and she'll be discussing it with her friends. Like you, maybe. Sure not with me."

"Uh huh."

Standing, the captain stood looking out at the lawn. "You can listen to what they think about the crime. Their own suspicions. They'll confide in you. You're part of the society now, but from the outside. You know what I mean? People tend to talk to strangers. Say things in front of them."

"You think one of these people is involved?"

"I don't think so, but they might know things, have heard things that they don't think are important. Gossip among themselves. Whataya say? For old Brooklyn, huh?"

Winston thought back on the morning's conversations. How loyal should he be to Dr. Wetmore's entreaty of silence? For now he'd let it go, but if the situation changed he'd go straight to the captain.

"I'll do what I can."

"Great. Probably nothing to report, but you never know. Here's my card just in case. Take care."

Captain Andrews ambled slowly down the stairs and across the yard, disappearing behind the hedge. Winston could hear a car start up on the other side. The smell of pastries baking drifted out the front door.

Amy Cog had a no-nonsense air about her that came from years of knowing what was right and living her life accordingly. She now stood in her hallway, arms folded across her massive chest, giving Winston the Cog eye. Winston's stomach growled under the intense scrutiny.

"That Mr. Joyce says you're an architect or something. That right?"

"Architectural historian, actually."

"Means the same to me, Mr. Wyc. You another one of those fancy pants from New York?"

"Fancy pants?" Winston had to stop himself from glancing down at his jeans.

"Come up here with your money and your pinky sticking out."

"Mrs. Cog, I'm not a fancy pants. I came up here to do a job for Mr. Joyce. I might even get my hands dirty."

"That so? Come into the kitchen, Mr. Wyc. I just made a fresh pot of coffee." Mrs. Cog bullied her way down the hall.

Sitting across from Winston, Amy Cog pushed over a plate piled with butter cookies.

"Try a few. Won a ribbon at the fair this year."

"Thanks."

"Coffee?"

"Not for me, thanks. If I drink coffee in the afternoon I'm out walking under the stars till morning."

"Caffeine does that," Mrs. Cog declared as if she'd just discovered the Salk vaccine for polio. She poured herself a cup of what looked like strap molasses.

"You found that Mr. Bantram yesterday."

Winston nodded, grinning to himself, wondering if there was anyone in Wistfield who didn't know who he was.

103

"Barney Potter's boy was there the afternoon it happened."

"Beagling?"

"Heavens no! Nobody I know would chase a rabbit through the woods, Mr. Wyc, without a gun. Except a hilltopper."

"Hilltopper?"

"That's how we refer to the gentry in these parts, Mr. Wyc. Barney's boy was in his pickup. One of the first to get there after the dreadful news went out. Any guess who did it?"

"No idea."

"Shame. Been up to the Worthwell place yet?"

"Wuffwall?" Winston mumbled through a cookie. "Oh ya, da Joose plaz."

"The Joyce place now. Was built by Mrs. Worthwell's father, back before the Civil War. Lady was a real loony, I heard. Of course, a person lives that long by themselves, everyone gets to thinking they're weird when maybe they're not. She passed on five years before I was born. That's some time ago."

Amy Cog stared into her past and bit off a chaw of her coffee.

"My mother knew Mrs. Worthwell, did some cleaning for her on occasion, and she told me the lady never did anything but sit in the front parlor with that Mrs. Berry and stare out the window."

"Mrs. Berry?" There's that name, thought Winston.

"Good cookies, aren't they? Mrs. Berry was the cook, married to the gardener. When Mrs. Worthwell died she left the whole shebang to them. Had no relatives, I imagine."

104

Winston figured Mrs. Cog could imagine almost anything.

"You want to know about that house, you talk to my husband. He knows about everything around here. If he don't know, no one does."

"I'd like to do that. These cookies are wonderful."

Mrs. Cog smiled, showing she already knew that.

"I'd like to see my room then, if I could."

"I'm a good judge of people, Mr. Wyc, and I think you'll be okay. Go all the way up the stairs, door on the right. You've got the top floor. Good view of the village from up there. Annie Boyle rents right below you. There's a girl I consider like my own daughter." The warning was not wasted on Winston.

The stairs were wide and oak paneled. A thick Persian runner swallowed all sound and lent the house the solemn quiet of an empty church.

At the top floor Winston entered a large sunny space comfortably furnished with an overstuffed Chesterfield and two threadbare wingback chairs. In the corner, next to a window, was a work table, and in the opposite corner, a sleigh bed. The wall across from the windows was covered with tall mirrors above and raised panel drawers below. The mirrors made the room appear larger and longer. Would have been the butler's room, reasoned Winston. Walking over to one of the windows, he looked down on the village. The fact that he was here still amazed him. The countryside had always been a foreign land to him, filled with farm animals and farm people who wore their hats sideways and spoke in tongues on Sunday. Winston suddenly realized they might be the normal ones after all.

Winston was staring out the window when, with a sudden knock, Mrs. Cog came barging through the door with an armload of linens.

"Brought you some sheets. Make the bed now if you like."

"Come in, Mrs. Cog." Winston imagined trouble ahead with his privacy.

"Call me Amy." She began a stroll around the room, picking up his things, examining them, and putting them back down. "Don't mind me. I'm as nosy as a body can get. You might as well know that right now."

Winston found her familiarity with his things unnerving. "How long have you lived in Wistfield?"

"How long? Thanks for the compliment but I was born and raised in this lovely hamlet, except for the two years my husband was in the service. Got to spend some time in Minot, North Dakota. Glad to get back here, I can tell you." Mrs. Cog finally started making the bed. "Exactly what will you be doing up at Joyce's?"

"I'm helping to renovate it."

"It was part of the Underground Railroad, you know. There's suppose to be a cave up there where they hid the slaves. My father said he saw it. You're from New York."

"That's right. Ever been there?"

Mrs. Cog shook her head. "Afraid not. Never crossed my mind. That Joyce says you'll be here for a few months."

"I guess so." Winston was wishing Amy Cog would go back to her kitchen.

"When I was a kid, we always thought the Worthwell place was haunted. The people who lived there were so weird."

"The . . . the Berrys?"

"That's right."

"What can you tell me about them? I mean, it might help in my work up there." Might as well make Dr. Wetmore happy while I'm at it, thought Winston.

"A little loose around the edges, if you ask me. Of course, you didn't."

"What do you mean by loose around the edges?"

"They did things different. They had a kid but they never let him go to school. Taught him up at the house, from what I heard. Tried to be self-sufficient. Didn't like the people of Wistfield."

"Why was that?"

"Don't know."

"You wouldn't remember what this kid looked like, would you? If he came back to Wistfield?"

"Can't say I would."

"Anyone around who might?"

"Might be." Mrs. Cog leaned into Winston. "Why?"

"No reason. You're a wealth of information." Winston leaned against the doorjamb.

"I'm a concerned citizen, Mr. Wyc."

"Please call me Winston. What time's dinner?"

"Seven thirty sharp. Don't miss it. Tonight's special."

"I can't wait."

Mrs. Cog searched Winston's face for any signs of irony. Satisfied that none existed, she thundered from the room.

Standing by his newly made bed, Winston stared at his possessions. His books, his shirts, his belt, his toiletries, they seemed different. Her touch had al-

107

tered them in some way; they seemed shared, less his. From below Winston could hear the faint sounds of dishes being mauled and Amy Cog singing hymns . . .

Chapter 13

The Joyce house still felt the same: lifeless, with no past, as if the people who had lived here, along with their lives, their dreams, their souls, had completely vanished, been swallowed up into some black hole of history that could not or would not release the spirit that these people had surely imparted to the house. Winston had always been able to get some response from an old house. He considered it a gift, without getting too mystical about it. Closing his eyes, he could often imagine the room and its inhabitants as they might have been in the past. The Worthwell house was devoid of a spiritual past, or at least any that Winston could discern. The thought depressed him.

It was the next morning and Winston had driven up to the Joyce estate early. Wandering the rooms, running his fingers gently over moldings and ornamentation, Winston savored the laying on of hands. The center hall stairs were particularly wonderful, the exposed tread ends being carved with woodland scenes. Winston had never seen or heard of that being done. Some master craftsman had spent many hours forming these delicate and woodsy works of art. Winston also liked the downstairs windows. They were twelve-over-twelve, the mullions and muntins finely crafted and very narrow. The hand-blown panes were thick and uneven, with many bubbles and swirls delightfully distorting the physical reality of the outside world. From the window Winston was inspecting, he could see a wiggly Bill sunning himself by the cottage, an elongated Ed Worth standing before him, nodding to Bill's instructions.

On the far side of the cottage, just inside the tree line, Winston noticed a man watching the house. The man was too tall be a woodland elf, thought Winston, although there was something of the fanciful about him. His dress? His long, grinning face? Winston wasn't sure. Looking up, the man noticed Winston at the window, gave him a brief salute, took three steps to his right, and disappeared back into the woods. Waiting to see if the man would reappear at some other spot, Winston watched the tree line for another two minutes. Who had the man been spying on? Bill Joyce?

Shrugging off the incident, Winston took the back stairs to the basement to sort through the materials he needed for making molds. His small carton with tools and beeswax blocks had been mailed up the week before. A little work would focus his mind for a few hours and might cheer him.

Winston made his own molding material for impressions out of beeswax, olive oil, and cornstarch. Hard when cold, the blocks softened with a little warming, and after dusting a design to be copied with talcum powder, Winston would press the wax mixture against the design, let it cool, and then remove it carefully, making sure not to leave any portion stuck to the object. The resulting mold would be filled by the artisan with plaster and burlap. This final product could be sawed, drilled, and nailed as if it were wood. Olive oil was used for fluidity and ease of removal. There were other methods of imprinting, but Winston liked this one because it handled well and removed fine detail easily. Best of all, the beeswax felt alive in the hand—warm, sensual, and tractable. Winston began opening the crate, eager to begin.

Chapter 14

Simon Tart moved cautiously into the Devil's den. Standing just within the door, he studied the arrangement, the contents of the room, making sure it was only Bill Joyce and himself. If there was evil it was well concealed. Tart left the door ajar and, inching over to his right, inspected some photographs on the wall.

"Yes?" asked Joyce.

Tart hadn't so much as given Joyce a nod.

"Sorry. I collect old photographs. These aren't of around here, are they?"

"Uh . . . no."

"They appear to be all of the same place, though. An old family estate?"

"Yes . . . my family."

"I thought you were from New York?"

"I am. My family is not originally. They lived in . . . Long Island. Have a seat, Simon. I may call you Simon? Or is it the Reverend Mr. Simon or Mr. Vicar or . . ."

"Simon is fine. Episcopalians aren't wrapped up in titular labels. Unless you're a bishop, of course."

"You're not a bishop then, I take it."

"I feel that the right place for me is with my flock.

Bishops, I feel, can lose touch with the people. At that level there's too much politics, fund raising, that sort of thing."

"I quite understand. Ambition has no place in the real church."

Tart's expression showed he couldn't agree more.

"But what a coincidence, Mr. Joyce. I'm from Long Island."

"Please call me Bill, Simon."

"Well, okay. You know, Bill, maybe our families are from the same town?"

"You're from Long Island? Really? Amazing. I don't know your background, of course, but when you come to mind I've always thought of places far more exotic then Long Island. The British Isles, maybe. Possibly Ireland?"

"No kidding. I've always thought of myself as connected in some way, some . . . other-life way, if you will, to the Hibernian shores. There's an interesting . . ." Tart caught himself. What in the world was he saying?

The two men stared awkwardly across the desk at one another. Tart thought Joyce could at least sit up straight or adjust his chair; the man was almost hidden from view behind the desk. From where Tart sat, Joyce possessed only a head.

"Yessss?" said Joyce.

Tart had to sit up if he wanted to see Joyce's mouth. Clearing his throat for what he realized was too long, Tart tried to remember his plan of attack and not fall prey to this man's . . . devilry.

"I've been asked by the town to write a history of the Wistfield area for the bicentennial. One of the

114

important points of interest, I feel, is the Worthwell estate."

"Ohhh."

Joyce seemed curiously relieved, thought Tart.

"It's been brought to my attention that much of the old estate was still in the house when you bought it."

"This is true. Much of it in a sorry state, I might add."

"That's too bad." Tart allowed a few moments of silence to show he could care about such things. "I was wondering if any old photographs . . ." Tart nodded in the direction of the wall, ". . . or written memorabilia had been found that we could use in the history. Pictures of the Worthwells or . . . the Berrys, even. They were the last to live here, weren't they?"

Tart thought Joyce took a beat too long to answer.

"Well, actually, there was a caretaker hired by the Berry estate who lived here for a while, but the house had been empty for almost twenty years when I purchased it. And it looked it. Thank God the roof had remained intact. You'd simply *die* if I told you how much this renovation has cost."

"It looks worth it, though, from what I can see. Passing by, that is. You don't happen to know or remember the name of this caretaker, do you?"

"That was twenty years ago. I've no idea. Probably dead by now, wouldn't you think?"

"Probably. As for the pictures?"

"There was a box of photos somewhere, but I'd have to look for it. I'll have my chauffeur drop off whatever I find that I feel could be used." Long fin-

115

gers suddenly appeared, waving next to Joyce's head.

"Thank you . . . Bill." Tart puffed himself up. "This is purely my own curiosity, but you didn't happen to meet any Berrys when you bought this place, did you?"

"Why?"

"Well, I was hoping you'd have met the son . . . if that's who sold it to you. I'd be interested in getting in touch with him. For historical reasons."

"Son? Hmmmm. I can't help you much there, I'm afraid. I bought the estate through a broker representing the Berry interests. I really couldn't tell you if a Berry existed. Checks were made out to 'the estate of,' that sort of thing. For some reason I always imagined the seller as being a woman." Joyce hesitated. "I could maybe get you in contact with the broker?"

"You could? Umm. Who might the broker have been?"

Tart fought to keep from smiling. Joyce was obviously annoyed at this question. He'd have to remember the broker or seem foolish.

Joyce lifted himself from behind the desk in a sudden explosion of animation, his arms and hands molding the air before him. Tart fell back in his chair, his hands out in front of him.

"You're going to think I'm a complete idiot, Simon, but I can't for the life of me recall exactly who the broker was." Reaching the window, Joyce attempted to open it but stopped as soon as he started. He turned quickly to stare at Tart. "Silly, I know, but that's the way I am. I could look . . ." Joyce shrugged.

"Mr. Joyce." Tart stood. The moment had come. "There wasn't any broker, was there . . . ?"

"I beg your pardon?"

Tart prepared himself for the worst. Joyce could deny the accusation or he could . . . Tart curled his cape around himself and calculated his distance from the door.

"I said there *wasn't* any broker. I don't believe this place was ever sold."

"I don't understand."

Much to Tart's dismay Joyce seemed genuinely confused.

"Are you saying that I've bought this house illegally?"

"I'm saying that I've done a little detective work on my own and I can't find a record anywhere that this house ever changed hands."

"You've been spying on me?"

"I've had my eye on you for two years now . . . Bill. Ever since . . ." Tart couldn't bring himself to say "the murders."

"Ever since what?"

Joyce was now completely still, his hands splayed at his sides. Suddenly, like a released bow string, he relaxed.

"Are you feeling all right, Vicar? You're white as a sheet. And all these odd questions."

Tart found Joyce's smile unnerving. It could have read "aren't you the clever one" or it might have said "what is this madman up to?" Confused, Tart took an even more dramatic pose. He knew how ridiculous he must look, but he couldn't back down now.

"Further, I have reason to believe that you are not who you say you are."

117

"How delightful. Who am I?"

Tart realized that the distance between him and Joyce was shrinking although he detected no movement from the man. Fumbling in his cloak pocket for his cross, Tart tried desperately to squelch a sudden, incapacitating sense of fear.

"Would you mind telling me who I am? No, wait. Let me tell you." Joyce, narrowing his eyes in deep thought, raised his chin toward the ceiling, his index finger almost to his lips. Bending his wrist, Joyce pointed his finger directly at Tart.

"You think that *I'm* the killer, don't you?"

"Please don't come any closer."

"And why would I kill these people?" Joyce laughed through his teeth at the thought. "Last Sunday I was surrounded by others the whole time. Have you checked with the people at the hunt? They would tell you the idea is absurd. I don't remember seeing you there. Isn't the rectory just on the other side of that cornfield?"

"What are you saying?"

"Mr. Tart, I can find out the name of the broker by simply calling my lawyers."

"You could?"

"And I will, but not at the moment. First I'd like to hear what else you have to say and if this is something you've been spreading around Wistfield. If so, then we can discuss it through our respective attorneys. The diocese would provide you with an attorney, would they not? If you were sued?"

"Sued?"

"And my name *is* William Joyce, if you should have your doubts about that. Always has been. That should be easy to check. Try the local police."

"Diocese?"

"Simon, Simon, when I buy something I merely call my lawyers and say 'Buy it.' I can't imagine getting any more involved than that. Could you?"

Joyce had circled Tart and now stood between him and the door.

"You can't imagine how intrigued I am, though, to know what could have possessed you to think otherwise."

Tart opened his mouth but nothing escaped.

"*Have* we been spreading these thoughts to others. I'd really like to know."

"I . . . I . . . don't remember."

"How convenient. Well, since you seem suddenly at a loss for further slander, might I consider this interview at a close?" Joyce swung the door wide.

This was not how the interview was to go. Something had gone wrong and Tart was at a loss to explain why he felt so afraid.

"Mr. Tart?"

Tart's feet felt like lead. The mere act of lifting one of them was excruciating. All this talk of lawyers and lawsuits and, Heaven forbid, the diocese, confused and alarmed him. He wasn't quite so sure of himself anymore. The doorknob was in his hand before he realized it. Rushing from the cottage he stood lost in the driveway, looking this way and that, disoriented in time and space. His eyes fixed on Winston Wyc and Dr. Wetmore standing on the front portico of the main house. That's right. Dr. Wetmore had accompanied him to the house. He stumbled in her direction. Miserable and shaken, he needed the support of someone he knew and liked. Someone who understood him. Almost, but not quite, he considered the use of blasphemy.

Chapter 15

From the basement, Winston could hear voices and footfalls above him. One of the voices was that of a woman.

"Oh, there you are." Paul Grimes greeted Winston as he came up through the cellar door. Grimes and Ed Worth stood like sentinels on each side of Janice Wetmore, who looked like a small forest in her grass-colored overcoat, a lime green ribbon wrapped around her hat. She pulled her arm away from Ed Worth.

"*If* you don't mind."

Grimes shook his head at Ed. "This . . . lady says she knows you and that *you* told her you'd take her on a *tour* of the house." It was more a question than a statement.

"Hi, Janice." Winston had hoped the feminine voice was Erika's. "I . . . yes, I . . . I guess I did. This is a good friend of mine."

"Oh." Grimes seemed disappointed. "A little early for guided tours, isn't it?"

"If I'm in the way . . ." Dr. Wetmore made a half-hearted motion toward the door.

"No. I mean . . . well, I *had* told Dr. Wetmore . . .

excuse me . . ." Winston tried introductions. Sullen looks were exchanged.

"Yes, well, Dr. Wetmore is a local historian of sorts, and I had mentioned to her that she might want to see the house before its renovation and then after."

"I see," said Grimes, still not entirely mollified. "You should warn us beforehand, Winston. I . . . we get nervous when we see someone wandering around that we don't know. Insurance reasons."

"I'm sorry," said Winston.

Grimes suddenly smiled. "Nothing to be sorry for. We'll meet again on the grand, finished tour, I suspect. Enjoy." Grimes motioned for Ed to follow him out.

Winston waited until he was sure that they had left the house.

"What in the world are you doing?"

"Come up for my tour."

"I don't remember mentioning any tour."

"You don't? Funny, I thought for sure you said this morning would be good. Anyway, what difference does it make?"

"None, I guess. Where's Skippy?" Winston had visions of Skippy replanting flower beds.

"Left him in the car. That fellow doesn't seem to like trespassers."

"I wouldn't worry about it."

"I've spent a great deal of time thinking about this house lately."

"You and Simon worried about the Berry boy?"

"Simon more than me. I have my own idea."

"Oh yeah? What's that?"

"It only makes sense once we find out who the

fifth person was on the hunt committee. What if it was *that* person who held a grudge?"

"Interesting. It seems to me somebody in this town would remember who that person might be."

"It would seem so, but thirty-three years is a long time. Most of the people who would have cared about such a thing at the time are now dead. Jack will have the information in his records. Gladys, his housekeeper, says he's in New York until late tomorrow or early Friday."

Paul Grimes could be heard directing Ed Worth just outside the window.

"How about that tour?" said Dr. Wetmore.

"Follow me." Winston guided Dr. Wetmore through the house, showing her what he'd have to change, pointing out the more interesting details and explaining how certain of these details can help date a house.

"See the molding on this door. It was hand planed on the actual framework. Applied moldings weren't used until around 1835, when woodworking machines were introduced, and even then it took a while for local carpenters to have access to the ready-made mouldings.

"These Norfolk thumb latches became very popular around 1820 and were used in many country homes until the earthen doorknob with cast-iron box superseded it. There's a nice one on the kitchen door."

"What's this tell you?" Dr. Wetmore pointed to a piece of lath visible in a hole in the wall.

"That's lath and it was made by a circular saw. See the circles the blade left in the wood? That would mean the house would have to date after 1825 or thereabouts, when mills started cutting it

123

this way. The older, riven lath wouldn't be as uniform as these pieces."

"Riven?"

"Cut by hand with a frow and mallet."

"I'm impressed, Winston."

"It's fun. The house is like a big mystery that offers you clues as to its age. You put all the clues together and come up with a date you hope is right. I'd say this house was built between 1825 and 1840. Many times, though, you have to remove the facade to find the original house. It can be quite a surprise sometimes to see what lurks below."

Dr. Wetmore went over to an open window.

"I wish our mystery offered up its clues so readily. Nice view." She ran her hand over the sill. "We can see the cottage from here. You had time to find anything on the Berrys yet?"

Winston glanced out at the cottage. "Haven't had time to look. Whose car is that next to the house?

"That's Simon's old Ford."

"It is? Wonder what Simon's doing up here?"

Dr. Wetmore kept her eyes trained on Joyce's cottage. "Having a talk with Bill."

"About what?"

Dr. Wetmore walked back toward the front hall. "I'm afraid Simon's theory centers around Bill."

"Wait a minute. Simon doesn't think Bill Joyce is this Berry person? Really, Janice, I don't think Bill could hurt a flea, much less hold a grudge for twenty years."

"That's not what Simon says. Sometimes the meekest looking people can turn out to be the most bloodthirsty."

"Spoken like an avid mystery reader. Simon's not

in there right now accusing Bill of being the killer, is he?"

"Simon's a little more tactful than that, Winston. He said he'd feel out the situation and make a move if his theory seemed appropriate."

"And we're here if Bill turns into a raging maniac and tries to kill Simon . . ."

"Simon's to signal us from the window."

"But what if he doesn't have time? What if Bill is stuffing a rabbit's foot into Simon's mouth right now?"

"Quit trying to scare me. Simon will be all right."

Winston could tell Janice wasn't all that sure anymore.

"Shouldn't we be nearer the cottage in case something happens?" Winston was having a difficult time suppressing a smile.

"Probably." Dr. Wetmore wouldn't look at him.

Suddenly Ed Worth stood in the doorway, a frown on his drawn face. "Am I interrupting?"

"No, of course not. I think the tour was just ending," said Winston.

Dr. Wetmore went to speak and didn't. Winston thought he heard her teeth click shut.

"I'll walk you to the door."

"Thanks for the tour. I know how busy you must be, Mr. Wyc."

"No problem, Dr. Wetmore."

Winston and Dr. Wetmore came out on the front portico just as Simon Tart came racing out of the cottage. The vicar appeared upset. Noticing them on the porch, he hurried up the hill in their direction.

"What in the world is the matter, Simon? You

125

look a fright." Dr. Wetmore came down the steps to meet the vicar.

"I'm going to be sued. The bishop will have my head." Tart's hands patted at his chest as if to calm a rapid heart.

"Sued? What are you talking about?"

"I don't know. Everything was going along just fine, just the way I'd planned, and then all of a sudden Bill Joyce was threatening to sue the diocese."

"Heavens! What did you say to provoke him?"

"Hardly a thing."

"You didn't accuse him of anything, did you?" said Winston, who had come down to join them.

Tart set his round face into a mask of defiance. "I suggested a few things, some thoughts I had concerning these local . . . problems, but I did not specifically single him out."

"But you did imply . . . ?" Winston cocked his head.

"Janice, the evil in that room could be cut with a knife. Oh, goodness, what made me use that imagery?"

"Calm down, Simon. Tell me what happened."

Tart looked about him. There seemed to be just the three of them.

"I happened to mention to him . . ." Tart glared at Winston, ". . . that I had tried to find a record in the town hall covering the sale of the Berry property to him. It upset him. He was obviously shaken by the fact that I had been doing a little detective work."

"No kidding." Dr. Wetmore leaned in closer. "You hadn't told me about that."

"Well, I thought if Joyce was really a Berry, why would he sell himself the house except to throw off any suspicion, and when I tried to find evidence of the sale I found nothing."

"Really?" Winston's interest was piqued. "Maybe the records are kept elsewhere."

"Where?" asked Dr. Wetmore.

"Is there a county seat?"

"That would be New Holland," said Tart. "I hadn't thought of that."

"Records of property sales are kept in the county courthouse *and* the local town hall. It's possible they were never filed in Wistfield. An oversight?" Winston shrugged.

"Or not filed for a reason," said Dr. Wetmore.

"You can check into it if you want, but I'm maintaining a low profile for a while," said Tart. "I don't need a lawsuit."

"Don't give up yet, Simon. It seems to me you've hit a nerve here somewhere. Why else would Bill be so upset?" Dr. Wetmore stole a quick glance at the cottage.

"Wait a minute. You can't really think that Bill Joyce is the killer, can you? He was with us at the hunt, remember?" Winston shook his head.

"That's true," said Dr. Wetmore. "On the hill."

"Maybe he has an accomplice," suggested Tart.

"Maybe it's an entire cult," Winston remarked sardonically.

"Now, I see no reason to be sarcastic," said Dr. Wetmore, protecting Tart's already bruised ego.

"I'm sorry, but I just find the thought of Bill Joyce murdering anyone, or even plotting a murder, laughable."

The three stood silently watching each other's shoes. Winston could see Paul Grimes come out of the cottage.

"Here comes the architect. Maybe we should carry on this discussion later."

"That's a good idea. Would you like me to come back with you to the vicarage, Simon?"

"No. I wish to be alone and think this all out. I'm sure that I'm right about this. If you had only been in that room." Tart was pointedly ignoring Winston.

"If only I had," said Dr. Wetmore to herself.

"This is certainly a glum little gathering," said Grimes as he approached. "Winston, Mr. Joyce would like to see you."

Tart glanced at Winston and mumbled something to Dr. Wetmore.

"Simon and I will be going. We've taken up much too much of your valuable time, Mr. Wyc."

"Please. It was my pleasure," said Winston a little too elaborately. "You two will come again when the project is completed?"

"We'd love to."

Dr. Wetmore beamed at Mr. Grimes. Turning, she took Tart by the arm and led him back down the hill and past the cottage.

"Strange little man," said Grimes indicating the vicar.

"He's okay, Paul. Just a little eccentric. Nothing incurable."

"Well . . . don't forget to see Mr. Joyce."

Winston watched the car pull out of the drive and then headed down to the cottage. Bill Joyce was seated behind a large desk in his study, smirking to himself. Dressed in an emerald green sport coat over a yellow polo shirt, he looked to Winston like a tall leprechaun who had absconded with his own pot of gold.

"Was that the vicar I just saw you talking to up by the house?" asked Joyce.

"And Dr. Wetmore," nodded Winston.

"How well do you know the man?"

"Met him at the Phillipses' Sunday night after the Bantram thing. You were there. Today was only the second time I've talked to him. He seemed to be upset about something." Winston thought it best to disassociate himself from the whole thing.

"He didn't talk about our little meeting in here?"

"Didn't say a thing," lied Winston.

"Hmmm. I apologize if I'm stepping on any toes here, Winston, but I sometimes feel that religion does curious things to some people's brains."

"Toes feel fine, Bill."

"Good." Joyce motioned for Winston to sit.

"Nice pedestal library table," said Winston, indicating Joyce's desk.

"Very good, Winston. Most people think it's a desk."

"Around 1845, I'd say."

"That sounds about right. The Russian leather top is still in excellent condition. Unusual for a desk this old, I've been told." Joyce moved some papers to expose the leather. "You're an expert on furniture, too, Winston?"

"Hardly an expert. Interiors of old houses usually reflected the style of the exterior. That includes the furniture. You can't study one without becoming familiar with the other."

"Live and learn."

"This piece was here or did you buy it?"

"Believe it or not, I picked it up at a flea market for nothing. It's amazing what people will sell when they don't realize the value of something."

"You're very lucky."

Joyce took a moment to preen. "This is not a criticism, Winston, but you seem to be quite popular."

"Sorry about the intrusions. Friends are always curious about what you're doing."

"And all of them ladies."

"It won't happen again, Bill. I've just run out of lady friends in these parts. Besides, I'm hardly the type."

"Well, you've certainly got the looks, dear boy."

Winston felt himself begin to redden.

"Winston, you should learn to say thank you and not change colors every time someone compliments you. Now, I didn't ask you in here because of this female parade, although I would appreciate a little warning. I'm odd about my privacy. What I need from you is some sort of schedule, a timetable, a prophecy if need be regarding when things will be done and in what order. Also, I imagine you'll be going to New York occasionally, and if you do I'd like a week's notice."

"You want a projection."

"That's the word. Something in writing so I can schedule ahead."

"I don't know how accurate I can be."

"That's okay as long as I have some idea. Also, I'm leaving this afternoon. Be gone until Thursday. There's a big furniture auction in Connecticut tomorrow and I'm having James drive me down."

"That should be nice."

The two men stared at each other.

"Did Tart say anything to Dr. Wetmore?"

"About what?" asked Winston.

"Nothing." Joyce pushed some papers toward Winston. "Now I need a favor. While I'm gone could you drive into New Holland and pick up the building permit renewal? You just have to give them this. The address is on the back. I've called them and they will expect you sometime in the next two days. I've let the damn thing go and it expires Friday.

"Well, that's it for now. Oh, wait a minute. Do you have something for Ed to do? He's walking around complaining that he's underused."

"As a matter of fact I do. Last night I drew up some plans for the front door. I'd like to put back the sidelights and the fan window that must have been there originally. He could frame in for that."

"Marvelous, he'll love it. Go over that with him, will you?"

"Sure. By the way, you don't have any pictures of this place do you? Early ones?" asked Winston.

Joyce took a moment to answer. "Not you too?"

"What?"

"I think there's some around somewhere. I'll look."

"It'd help in the details."

"I'm sure," said Joyce.

Stopping in the living room to study the Gothic armoire, Winston could have sworn the piece of furniture took a deep breath. Startled, he took a step backward just as Joyce came into the room.

"Something wrong?" asked Joyce.

"No, no. For a second I thought . . ." Winston felt foolish. "Just admiring this wardrobe. Ta."

Winston left Joyce standing there looking very much like a virescent Cheshire cat plotting all unto himself.

Chapter 16

Winston felt good about the work he had accomplished that afternoon. He'd be ready to take some impressions tomorrow and Ed Worth had started on the front door. In two weeks he'd have enough material for a trip to New York. By then a shot of smog and grime would be needed. In just three days the fresh air and unnatural quiet of the country had started to wreak havoc with his mind and body. That morning he had speculated on the benefits of jogging.

Pulling into Mrs. Cog's drive, he noticed the same man he'd seen spying from the woods at the Joyce estate standing down by the creek that ran alongside the boarding house. Winston wondered if the man might be following him.

"Hi. I'm Winston Wyc."

"Herbert Cog. Call me Herb."

The man whose wife had said knew everything about Wistfield, remembered Winston. The knowledgeable Mr. Cog was tall and reedy, slightly stooped from age. His long arms hung motionless at his sides. Clothing manufacturers always ignore physiques like Herb Cog's, chuckled Winston to himself. The poor man had spent a lifetime with six inches of his arm showing beyond his shirt cuff. Pulled down on his head was a red plaid hunting cap, the ear flaps sticking straight out. Mr. Cog's boyish face shone out from under the cap, a face full of youthful self-possession and good humor. Winston wondered if Mr. Cog's face had changed at all since he was twelve. He realized it had been this youthful countenance that had given the man his elfin quality back at the Joyce estate. Mr. Cog was standing out from the bank in the mud against the stream, and Winston had to stretch to shake his hand.

"Been involved in some adventure up at the Phillips' place, I hear." He held Winston's hand longer than normally appropriate, as if seeking further unspoken information from Winston's grip. "A terrible business. Not the normal sort of event in Wistfield." Dropping his tactile inspection of Winston, Mr. Cog adjusted his false teeth.

"I'm afraid that's all true," said Winston.

"Mother says you're working up at the old Worthwell estate."

"That's right. I'm helping in the restoration."

"Wonderful place. Used to mount Union raids up there when I was younger. Sneak up in the middle of a sunset, a few brave lads and myself, armed to the teeth, and see who was heroic enough to crawl up and touch the house. Indians used to do that. Instead of killing an enemy they'd touch 'em. Embarrass the hell out'a the other warrior. Shame was worse then death to those fellows. 'Course, I doubt if the house was too embarrassed." Mr. Cog found this last statement particularly funny, but his false teeth shot backward with the sudden laugh, abruptly choking the hilarity.

Winston watched in amusement as, with sharp coughs, the man tried nonchalantly to recompose his mouth.

"Your wife says you'd be able to answer any questions I might have about the Worthwell place."

"Could try. Could try."

"Do you know exactly when it was built?"

Staring off above Winston's head, Mr. Cog assumed a lecturing tone.

"Let me see: house begun in 1830, west veranda and south wing added in 1846, east portico in 1860, just before the Civil War. An overly ornamented house. By the late thirties, when I . . . eh, saw the house, it was in need of a lot'a repair."

"Were you ever in the house?" asked Winston.

"No, can't say I was."

"What about the Worthwells?"

"Can't help you much there. Miss Worthwell was the daughter of a General Worthwell, a Southerner who defected with the family fortune to fight for the Union cause and the abolition of slavery. Had gone to school in the North, you see. Harvard. Less gracious historians, though, say that Worthwell was a kook and was in trouble with local authorities in the South for strange religious practices. What that meant, I couldn't say. Probably saw the writing on the wall and wanted to go with the winning team." Mr. Cog stopped to realign his teeth. "His only child never married, kept to herself, and gave the estate to her gardener when she died."

"The Berrys."

"That's right. Samuel and June Berry. They weren't from around here. In fact, you never saw them except in the village occasionally running an errand. Must have had plenty of friends from their old home town, though. 'Bout every coupl'a years there'd be five, six cars show up. Big get-together. That hasn't happened since I was a kid."

"You don't by chance have any pictures of the old Worthwell house?"

"No, I'm afraid not. There's talk around of it having been part of the Underground Railroad, but plenty of houses maintain that nowadays. Gives em a little something. Probably helps resale. I can check the files I have to see if there's more."

"I'd appreciate that."

"Fact, we can look right now if you have the time."

Winston was about to beg off when Mr. Cog, whose boots had cemented into the mud from standing too long, stepped from his galoshes and into the mire with his bare feet.

"Holy hotcakes!" Mr. Cog mud-sucked his feet onto the bank. "Mother'll get a big laugh out of this," he said, wiggling his brown toes. Winston went to retrieve his boots.

"Forget em. No need for us both to get dirty. They ain't goin' nowhere." He gave Winston an exaggerated frown. "We'll do those books later, if that's okay." Mr. Cog headed up toward the house.

"Oh, Mr. Cog."

"Herb."

"You weren't by any chance up at the Worthwell place this morning?"

Mr. Cog looked down at his dirty feet. "Well, yes I was."

"I thought I saw you in the woods."

"Ah-hah. That must have been you in the window."

Winston nodded.

"Funny thing, your being here reminded me it'd been a while since I'd seen the house. Guess some of the kid came out in me. Went sneakin' around a bit." Mr. Cog looked off over Winston's head. "My best friend passed away coupl'a summers ago. We spent a lot of time together. Other men like to go fishing to be alone, or maybe watch birds, but George and me, we'd go off into the woods and look for old foundations, mounds, places people *used* to live. Talk about who they were, what they might have done, where they might have gone. George knew more about this area than I did, and that's saying a lot. Mother said we spent too much time living in the past, but I don't think so." Cog looked down at Winston and smiled. "You'd probably know something about that, you being a historian of sorts."

"Makes perfect sense to me. You'll have to take me on one of those walks some time."

"Pick a day. Mother can pack a mean lunch."

"I bet."

The two men stood watching the water rush and eddy in the creek.

"I should head on in, my feet are feeling the weather."

"We can talk later. I'd like that."

Winston looked over at Mr. Cog's boots standing in the mud, the boots of an invisible eavesdropper to their conversation. He laughed to himself, wondering what Mr. Cog could have been doing in the creek. Mrs. Cog's laughter joined his—a distant, muffled howl from the house.

Chapter 17

Winston had no difficulty finding Dr. Wetmore's brightly painted, salmon-colored house. The only color like it in Wistfield, she had said, and he had to believe her. It rose like a fat lady's blush from the neat, wide lawn nestled on a quiet side street of the village. Dr. Wetmore, wearing a shiny, yellow caftan, stood waiting at the curb. Her hair, seemingly under control for once, was woven into a complex arrangement of braids. From a cavernous bag hanging at her side, Skippy's black nose, ever vigilant now, could be seen testing the evening air for wickedness. As they drove toward Meadowbrook Farm, Skippy kept a watchful eye on Winston's driving technique.

"You get a chance to talk to Simon after this morning?" asked Winston.

"Just briefly. I tell you I don't know what's gotten into that man. Yesterday he was going on about Bill Joyce this and Bill Joyce that, and this afternoon when I called him he said he'd come across something that changed everything. Wouldn't talk about his meeting with Bill."

"Can't imagine why. Who's it now?" Winston shook his head.

"He wouldn't say, but he promised a wonderful dessert for after dinner tonight."

"The latest theory, no doubt." said Winston.

"Myself, I've been on the phone checking to see if anyone might have seen any odd characters hanging about the hunt Sunday, and I must say I've never come across such a cockamamy collection of stories. Harvey Middleton claimed he saw an outlaw motorcycle gang just before the hunt, but it turns out that it was two hours earlier and out near his farm. That's twenty miles away. Constance Little thinks Wistfield has come under an evil spell, just like in some movie she saw last week. And there was . . ."

Winston was aware of the deer grazing in the meadow on his right and was only half listening. He could see the rotary in the distance.

"Isn't the church up here?" asked Winston. He had offered to pick up Vicar Tart as well, since it was on the way.

"Take a right on Coonden Road," answered Dr. Wetmore.

And past the church is Meadowbrook Farm, thought Winston, and the lovely Erika Phillips. He was looking forward to tonight's dinner.

Dr. Wetmore waited in the car as Winston went up and knocked on the vicarage door. After two minutes he knocked again.

"Isn't he here?" Dr. Wetmore yelled from the drive.

"Doesn't seem to be," answered Winston.

"Maybe he fell asleep. I've come by in the early evening before to see him and found him snoring at his desk. His parishioners' sins weighing heavy

140

on his mind, he'd tell me. Let's go in. The door is never locked."

The vicarage was furnished in heavy Early American to complement the Carpenter Gothic style of the house and church. The wide pine floorboards were polished to within a half inch of oblivion and the walls were painted a stark white to highlight the dark furniture. Imitative Grandma Moses-like paintings hung on the walls, along with many old photographs. Winston checked the photos to see if any included the Worthwell estate. Several Americana *objets d'art* were carefully positioned around the room. Winston particularly liked a set of hand-painted pockmarked ducks that must have graced an early shooting gallery.

Tart was not in his study. As Dr. Wetmore went through the many photographs laying on Tart's desk, Winston admired a Windsor settee and behind it, on the wall, photos both old and new of people beagling.

"Simon likes old photographs," said Winston.

"He collects them," said Dr. Wetmore. "He has files full of them. It looks like he just got in a new batch."

"I wonder where he is?"

"He might be in the church. Let's check." Dr. Wetmore whistled for Skippy, who came running in from the kitchen.

Winston stood in the fading light looking up at the church. The sharply pitched roof and vertical siding drew the eye upward to the tall, slender bell tower that graced the peak. The belfry was open to the elements, and Winston could see the large brass bell within.

"It's really an exquisite example of Carpenter Gothic. Look at that detailing."

"I've looked at it every Sunday for thirty-five years. Let's find Simon."

The church was entered through a small narthex that supported the bell tower. The bell rope hung idly by the entrance. Winston had an urge to pull the rope. Simon would surely come running then. The interior of the church was a single long nave with a raised choir at the far end flanked on the right by a small organ and on the left by the pulpit. A low communion rail separated the congregation from the simple wooden altar. The room had the warm, varnished look and feel of a place tenderly cared for over many years. The hand-hewn collar beams and bracing and the rafters and wainscotting were still unpainted oak, as handsome now as in the 1850s, when the building was constructed. The aged wood and leaded stained glass windows lent the small room a solemnity hard to find, or imagine, in a modern structure devoted to the same Christian worship. The worn pine pews bore silent witness to the empty church.

"I'd say he wasn't here," said Winston. "There's no place to hide. Maybe he already left."

"Could be. I didn't see his car. I'll check the sacristy."

To the left of the pulpit an arched door led into the sacristy. Winston bent down and picked up a large Bible that lay open on the floor.

"Must have fallen from the pulpit," said Winston.

"Possibly . . ." Dr. Wetmore looked doubtful.

The sacristy obviously doubled as dressing room and storage space and it was a mess.

"What zephyr went through here?" marveled Winston.

"This doesn't look good," said Dr. Wetmore.

Second inspection of the room showed it was more than just the victim of untidy housekeeping. There were signs of a struggle. A clotheshorse had been turned over, two pictures had fallen from the wall, and glass lay shattered on the ruffled carpet. Skippy barked twice and bounded through an open side door.

"Is that usually left open?" asked Winston, who was already sensing the worst.

"Not that I know of." Using her finger, Dr. Wetmore lifted some blood off the bottom of the doorjamb. "This blood is still moist."

Cautiously the two investigated the back lawn of the church. Tire tracks were evident in the wet grass. Tart's old Ford stood in the shadows.

"I think Simon might have finally come up with the right theory. Only problem is, he must have told the wrong person."

Dr. Wetmore was silent. Winston wasn't sure in the dark, but he thought he saw the glistening of a tear on the doctor's cheek.

"Janice, he's probably okay. Certainly kicking. If our killer had wanted to kill him, he'd have done it here."

"We don't know it was the killer, Winston. It might have been some thief after the church silver."

"That's it." Winston went back into the sacristy. Lying on the floor was Tart's black cape. Winston bent down and picked up the corner of a torn photograph.

"Wonder where the rest of this went," he said to himself, not finding any more of the photo among the debris. "I think it's time we called Captain Andrews."

Chapter 18

Winston, who was peering through the window above the sink at the two policemen standing in the door of the church, noticed Captain Andrews giving him looks of frustration. The captain had been questioning Dr. Wetmore and Winston in the vicarage kitchen for what seemed to Winston an eternity. Winston had been waiting for the pickup truck brigade, but it had never materialized. Not even a fire truck. At this point, Winston would have welcomed the carnival bustle of the Phillipses' cornfield.

"And what about you, Mr. Wyc? You full of theories too?"

"Can't say I am, Captain."

"Doctor, you and your missing friend should have notified the police the minute you suspected anything. This isn't 'Mystery Theatre,' it's the real world."

"I realize that, Captain Andrews." Dr. Wetmore was grim and tight-lipped. Whatever her first rush of emotion, Winston noticed she was now under studied control.

"Now this doesn't seem to follow the other *modus operandi*, but we never know. We got no vicar and there's no good luck charm. I think the vicar came across something that shed light on this thing and pursued it on his own, thinking maybe he could wrangle a confession out of somebody. Who knows? He's missing now."

"You will look for him?" asked Dr. Wetmore.

"Of course, Doctor. We've already started. Do you mind if I have Sergeant Miller take you home? I want to talk to Mr. Wyc here for awhile."

Without waiting for an answer, the captain left the kitchen. From the window, Winston watched him cross the lawn to where several men stood smoking in the night air. Winston turned to Dr. Wetmore.

"You okay?"

"I'm all right. Humans are plagued with optimism. As long as I don't know for sure what's happened to Simon I can only imagine him alive and well. I'm afraid I've acted something of a fool."

"Don't blame yourself. Unless it directly affects you, danger always seems so abstract. It's an attitude you become quickly familiar with living in New York. A type of protection."

"I wonder what the captain wants to talk to you about that he can't say in front of me?"

"I've no idea. Did you get hold of Erika when you called?"

"Yes, I did. She wanted us to come up after the captain questioned us, but I don't think I have the energy. I'll have Mr. Miller take me home."

Captain Andrews came in from the outside.

"The sergeant will take you home now, Dr. Wetmore. And please, if you think of anything else, give me a call."

"I'm properly chastised, Captain. Not to worry."

As Dr. Wetmore collected her bag, arranging the

sleeping Skippy so his nose stuck out just so, Captain Andrews took the time to make a phone call to police headquarters. Winston ignored the captain's conversation, instead helping Dr. Wetmore with her bag.

"Not till Thursday." Captain Andrews' voice rose into the phone. "Damn. Okay, Hardesty, thanks."

As the captain hung up the receiver, Dr. Wetmore turned back into the room.

"Oh, there is one thing, Captain. Seeing you on the phone just now has jolted my memory. Before Simon hung up on me this afternoon he said something strange. I've just now remembered it."

"Yes?" said Andrews.

"He quoted something. Let me see . . . it went like this: 'The tongue can no man tame, it is an unruly evil, full of deadly poison.' At the time I thought he meant I should keep my mouth shut, but now I don't know. Maybe he was giving me a clue of some kind." The idea seemed to revitalize the doctor. Her face took on some of its old glow.

"I couldn't tell ya, Doc. Sounds like it's from the Bible or something. Tell it to Sergeant Miller on the way home and have him write it down."

Dr. Wetmore gave Winston a long look and then shot out the door, letting in a gust of cold air.

"She's something," said Winston.

"Yeah, she's something, all right. But what?"

"It's getting cold," said Winston, shutting the door.

"October's been unseasonably warm. 'Bout time fall got here." Captain Andrews sat at the kitchen table. "Have a seat." It wasn't a request. "How much of this did you know when we had our little talk at the Cogs's?"

"All of it."

"I see." Andrews took out a plastic ziplock bag that held the torn piece of old photo. He played with it as he spoke to Winston. "I can understand you being new here and maybe a little confused in your loyalties, but this might not have happened if you'd spoken up then."

"Don't rub it in, Captain. I'm more than aware of the consequences of my silence. At the time I didn't take it very seriously. Their suspicions seemed so far off the mark. You'd have heard about it soon enough."

The captain sat silent for thirty seconds.

"You think he's dead?" asked Winston.

"I don't know. The men actually looked for a rabbit's foot but didn't find one. The reason he ain't dead is anyone's guess. Maybe there was more info the killer needed. There's the chance it's something else entirely. I just don't know." Andrews studied the packet. "Let's take a look at those photos on Tart's desk."

The two men walked in silence back into Tart's study. As the captain thumbed through the photographs, Winston studied the pictures on the walls.

"Look at these, will ya?" asked Andrews. "You're the historian. Any of these pics tell you anything? I draw a blank."

Winston slowly went through the photographs. They appeared to be of Wistfield in the thirties or forties. Not that old. "Nothing." Winston couldn't see any connection in the pictures with the murders. "Maybe there was a photo here of the hunt committee from that time."

"That's what I was thinking. Tart might have recognized the fifth member." Andrews stared at the wall photos. "This committee stuff is the first real lead we've had. Too bad I didn't know about it sooner. Earlier, just after I got here and the doc told me of the committee possibility, I had Sergeant Hardesty call Mr. Glenn in New York. I just talked to the sergeant on the phone. Said Mr. Glenn can't get up here until Thursday. Says the files are a mess. I could get a search warrant and enter the house, but . . ." The captain shrugged. "It's gonna be very interesting to see just who those other committee members were. The Berry angle doesn't seem right to me. Course, you never know. You got anything else you might want to add to the doctor's testimony while she ain't here?"

Winston shook his head no. Back in the kitchen the two men put on their coats.

"What about the knife we found in James Bantram? Was that traceable?" asked Winston.

"Not yet. Our forensic guy says it's a real antique dating from the Civil War. We've no idea where it came from. We've been checking with collectors and museums. You know of anyone around here collects that sort of stuff?"

"Can't say that I do."

"Listen, anything come up you got my card. *Anything.*"

"You've got my word on it."

Winston stood outside in the cold breathing in the crisp night air, using it to purify his system. If Simon Tart was dead, he would feel responsible. Suddenly he was no longer playing silly games with a couple of old crazies. He liked Dr. Wetmore and it hurt him to see her anguish over Tart's disappearance. Outside the circle of light that radiated from the vicarage porch was total darkness. Winston realized he had never seen a night so complete. In New York there was always illumination coming from somewhere. Here, the many stars overhead shed no warmth or light on the blackness of the countryside. Simon Tart could have stood five feet outside the circle of light and Winston would not have seen him. Anyone could be standing there. Winston shuddered and quickly got into the Volvo."

As Winston came to a stop in front of the Phillipses' house the front door opened and Erika appeared.

"Everything okay?" Erika spoke softly.

"Not really."

Standing at the foot of the columned portico looking up at Erika, Winston experienced the same feelings he had at their first meeting: the world falling away, leaving only them and the steady distance between them. She was even wearing her jeans and flannel shirt—a soft, rangy cowgirl with pale, probing eyes. Winston was very glad this woman existed. In all this roughness hers was a gentle hand, a balm to soothe his mind. Winston started slowly up the steps. "I've been made to understand that the master of the house is out tonight."

"I'm afraid so. That bother you?"

"Not yet."

"Oh . . . well, we'll have to work on that." Erika gave Winston a lingering, quizzical look. Suddenly she turned into the house. "There's plenty of food left. Janice go home?"

"Yeah. The night's been a little harrowing for both of us." Winston followed Erika into the large foyer, which now echoed with the heavy silence of an empty museum. In the kitchen, Erika motioned for Winston to sit at a stool and began pulling covered dishes from the refrigerator.

"Mind eating in the kitchen?"

"Not at all."

"Hope you're hungry. What exactly happened to Simon?"

"How about a drink first?"

"You got it. Name your poison."

"Scotch. Your best stock, thank you." Winston hadn't realized how hungry *and* thirsty he was. Relating the events of the evening, he understood suddenly how really serious the whole situation was and that Dr. Wetmore might be in considerable danger herself. Whoever this maniac was, he would go to any extreme to protect his identity.

"My big concern now is Janice. She had this look in her eye tonight that said 'I'm going to get this madman.' It's not what she should be doing. This killer is ruthless, and another elderly lady isn't going to make much difference to him."

"It's good that Captain Andrews and the police are finally in on this hunt stuff," said Erika.

"You talk to your father yet about who the fifth person might have been?"

"Not yet. He's still down at his brother's place in Connecticut. Be back Thursday for my opening. I can ask him then."

"Maybe you should call him."

"I can't. He's holed up in a cabin up on a mountaintop drinking Rebel Yell and playing cards. The rule is no phone. I guess I could get a message through somehow."

Erika prepared herself a plate of food and sat opposite Winston at the counter. They ate in silence.

"I guess I'm not very hungry," said Winston finally.

"I'm glad you're here. I'm not often frightened, but this whole business gives me the creeps."

"I don't think you have anything to worry about." Winston looked up and caught her staring at him, a soft, amused smile on her lips. "Of course, if you'd like me to . . . stick around, I could do that. We could put a cot by the door."

Erika swung her head slowly from side to side. "No cots."

"I could act as sentry. Use a small howitzer from your father's gun room."

"All locked up. I've no idea where he keeps the key."

Placing his fork on his plate, Winston finished chewing, wiped his mouth and sat back on the stool. "I was made to understand by a certain lawyer friend of yours that you were part of a well-thought-out program. Spoken for, as it were."

"What do you care?"

"I'm not into games."

"Games? Remember that first day we met and I was so mad? I'd just come from a meeting with my lawyer friend and my father about a proposal. Jack had consulted with Father before coming to me. Father thought it a grand idea. They corralled me in the music room, asking me together, like the whole thing was some kind of damn merger."

"What did you say?"

"I was so stunned I said I'd think about it. What do you think?"

"I think you should ship the asshole."

"I was hoping you'd think that way." Erika rose from her stool and switched off the overhead light.

Winston was aware of Erika's tongue as she came around the counter toward him. Just the tip rested on her lower lip.

"You have a wonderful mouth," said Erika.

"So do you, but I'm afraid mine's all greasy."

"Let's see."

Their lips and then their tongues touched—an unhurried, gentle exploration.

Lifting her head, Erika ran her tongue over her lips. "Needs salt."

The dark of the kitchen closed in around their awkward silence.

"How about a special after-hours tour of the house?"

"I like tours."

Taking Winston by the hand, Erika led him from the kitchen through the foyer and into the piano room.

"The music room. As you can see, it's an octagonal room, which allows for perfect acoustics. Not that there's been a recital in here since I was a little girl. Note the painted ceiling. The scenes are those of an idealized Wistfield."

"It could be more ideal? And when were you a little girl?"

"Very briefly. There's a picture on the piano to prove it."

"I know. I've seen them. You look old in this one."

"That's my mother."

"Really? It could be you."

"It's true. My mother and I were like twins. It used to astound people who didn't know us."

"What happened to your mother?"

"She died five years ago of cancer."

153

"I'm sorry."

"Even now I can come across something of hers stored in a drawer or closet and get all weepy. Silly." Erika brushed dust from the picture. "Where were you brought up, Mr. Wyc?"

"Brooklyn. Behind the Con Ed smokestacks in Greenpoint. A long way from hunt country."

"Sounds bleak."

"Not too bad, really."

"I don't mean it that way. I'm aware I've been privileged. I know that."

"It was a Polish community, warm and neighborly. My father was Polish. His father's name was Wycowski. Pops thought Wyc would win him a better place in the New World. My mother was Irish. A Cronin. She came from Vinegar Hill, twenty blocks away. It was a long twenty blocks in those days."

"Here's the game room. You don't sound like you come from Brooklyn."

"My mother used the address of relatives in the east eighties so I could go to school in Manhattan. I did my graduate work at NYU. And you?"

"Ethel Walker and Bennington. Father thought there'd be no boys about. Was *he* wrong."

"My mother worked hard to make sure *I* stayed away from the neighborhood 'baggage,' as she called my friends. She didn't want me to become a Brooklyn butcher."

"Like your father?"

"You got it." Winston remembered those arguments—his father upset and embarrassed because his own wife thought the son should be something better than he was; his father standing there, his bloody apron wrapped neatly and tucked in a brown

154

paper bag for his wife to clean, the bag beginning to stain.

"Nice collection of firearms."

"Some are very old. Belonged to that gentleman up there." Erika pointed to a portrait hanging over the fireplace. "Colonel Ezra Phillips. Looks a big pain in the ass, doesn't he?"

"I like the fireplace. Italianate." Winston plopped into a chair. "Sorry, I can't concentrate. I can't stop thinking about this murder business. I've spent my whole life in New York, the capital of murder and mayhem, and I've been real lucky, I guess, for in all those years I've never seen a dead person. Only people who looked dead or wanted to be dead. Now here I am in this rural America fantasyland for three days and already I'm way over the limit on the number of murdered dead people you're supposed to see in a lifetime."

Winston sat looking up at Erika as she came over. He said nothing as she took him by the hand and led him out of the room, up the curved staircase, and into a large room at the end of the hall.

"Last stop on the tour. The four-poster bed was my great grandfather's. It's a camp bed used by officers during the Civil War. He would actually take it in the field with him."

Erika stood silhouetted at the laced window unbuttoning her flannel shirt. Feeling like he'd stepped into a dream, Winston stood hushed, not wishing to destroy the illusion.

"Sometimes, just before I fall asleep, I can hear what sounds like cannon fire in the distance. But you can only hear it from the bed."

"I've never heard cannon fire."

Outside, on the other side of the world, a beagle howled against the coming of winter.

155

* * *

Waking suddenly, Winston experienced the disorientation of being in the wrong bed. The doors and windows had been rearranged, the bedside lamp exchanged for another. Sitting up, he was surprised by the form hugging itself at the near window. It took a moment for him to recognize the profile as Erika's, and then the evening rushed back over him, a lingering, warm-flanneled night of lovemaking and few words. Winston relaxed back against his pillow.

"Anyone out there?"

"Just lots of moonlight and a pheasant." Erika's voice fogged the window.

"Sounds exotic."

Moving back to the bed, Erika stood looking down on Winston, her eyes in shadow. "Not really. Jack owns the land next to ours and raises them for hunting. They wander over all the time." Slipping under the covers, Erika shivered up next to Winston. They lay in silence while Erika's body warmed.

"The poor bird looked so frightened. It would take a few steps, stop, look around at every shadow, and then repeat the same ritual a few steps later. It must be horrible to live a life so full of danger."

"Does a pheasant actually look at the danger that way or is it merely a reflex?"

"I was thinking that's where we might be heading. Always looking over our shoulder."

"What are you talking about?" Winston fought the urge to go back to sleep. He concentrated on the perfume of Erika's hair.

156

"Early morning rambles. I guess these deaths have me spooked."

"Uh, huh."

"Don't go to sleep, Mr. Wyc." Erika pinched his chest.

"Owww. Winston. The name's Winston."

"Why did Mr. Wyc become an architectural historian?"

"I don't recall."

"Yes, you do. Talk to me."

"I grew up loving the older buildings of New York. Their dignity, their charm, their . . . their history. As I got older, I realized they were disappearing, being replaced with ugly, cost-efficient structures that had none of the style or grace of the older buildings. I wanted to save them."

"So you've come to the country to renovate rich people's homes."

Rich people's homes. His mother had always wondered out loud about the lives of the rich. Would walk him as a young boy past the houses and apartment buildings of the wealthy around Central Park, on the side streets off Fifth Avenue, whispering to him about the fancy interiors, the exquisite furniture, and the servants. Winston knew it was those very walks that had first sparked his interest in architecture.

"I'm in a brief exile at the moment, but I shall return." Winston yawned. "Actually, I thought the country might be the perfect place to put some notes together and write a book and get some sleep. And make some money."

"Would you do me a favor, Mr. Wyc?"

"Only Winston does favors."

157

"Go back to New York and save a few buildings."

"What?"

"You were in that cornfield. I think it's dangerous for you up here."

"Don't be silly."

"Please. For me."

"I'll think about it."

"The sun comes up in just a few hours."

"Don't tell me that. I need to sleep."

Winston pretended to close his eyes. Watching Erika, he could see in the fading moonlight a single tear glisten at the corner of her eye, beginning a slow tracing down her face and onto the flannel sheet.

"You okay?" Winston cradled closer.

"I think my life is about to get complicated. I'm not sure it's what I need."

They lay in silence watching the sunrise slowly paint the wall with a new day.

Chapter 19

Winston stood in the Cogs's kitchen door looking down at Amy Cog and Janice Wetmore. The plastic cuckoo clock on the wall chirped three o'clock. An assortment of homemade confections were arrayed before Dr. Wetmore like sweet offerings. The doctor was staring at her cup of coffee with a look of bewilderment.

"Ladies, how are we this afternoon?" Winston avoided Dr. Wetmore's inquiring grin.

"Something wrong with the bed, Mr. Wyc? Maybe it's too comfortable. We could fix that." Mrs. Cog gave Dr. Wetmore her sly smile.

"The bed's fine. I fell asleep at a friend's house. Watching TV."

"You look like you fell asleep ten minutes ago. Come on in, I'll pour you a cuppa."

"No shock therapy, thanks. I had a cup of coffee at work this morning. That's my limit for the day. If nobody minds, I'm going to take a little afternoon nap."

"What's that supposed to mean? Shock therapy," asked Mrs. Cog, always on the alert for the innuendo.

"Nothing," said Winston. "How was your night, Doctor?"

"I couldn't sleep. I spent the whole night thinking about Simon and how I could find him."

"I don't think that's a good idea. Why don't we just let the police handle this from now on?"

"That's what I told her," interjected Mrs. Cog from the stove. "She's going to wind up missing herself if she's not careful. I told her to take a vacation." Mrs. Cog addressed all this in a stern voice to her coffeepot.

Winston gave Dr. Wetmore a look of entreaty.

"Don't you start too. I can do this by myself if you like."

Winston could see that Dr. Wetmore was not going to be stopped easily, and he was too tired to argue. He might have to turn her in to Captain Andrews.

"What is it you intend to do?" he asked.

"Simon had said to me that he thought it was someone who had moved into the area in the last two years. It was just about two years ago that all this trouble began. Amy and I have been going over just who that might be. There's quite a few, actually. Mostly weekenders, I'm afraid, who we don't know anything about."

Winston found that hard to believe.

"There's Ms. Bartle the schoolteacher, but we ruled her out."

"Schoolteachers can't kill people?" asked Winston.

"Ms. Bartle plays organ at the church."

"Well that certainly rules her out."

"Don't be snide. There's two who you know."

"And who are the two unfortunates?"

160

"Jack Glenn and Bill Joyce. Jack bought his place about two and a half years ago, but that's close enough for us, and Bill's been here just under two years."

"For us? I thought you tried to talk her out of this," Winston admonished Mrs. Cog.

"Just listen to what she has to say, fella," said Mrs. Cog.

"I can't imagine either one of them being the killer, although Amy's not so sure, so I'm going back to *my* original theory, which is we have to find out who the fifth person was on the hunt committee. I think that's our culprit."

"I'm with Mrs. Cog on this one. That Jack Glenn has a surly look to him."

"That smacks of a little jealousy, I must say," said Dr. Wetmore. "She was actually leaning the other way."

"Bill Joyce? I can't see it," said Winston, yawning.

"I think you're right," said Dr. Wetmore.

"Well, that's a complete turnaround," answered Winston.

"I don't like that Bill Joyce," growled Mrs. Cog. "There's something not quite right about a man who doesn't work. Also, he wouldn't allow Herb in his house to look for the Underground Railroad. Said it didn't exist. Well I know that's bunk. My grandfather said he'd *seen* it."

Suddenly Winston was very tired. This whole conversation was bunk as far as he was concerned. He didn't see how Jack *or* Bill could be the killer. They were both out of town when Simon disappeared. The police had talked to Glenn in New York late yesterday and he knew Bill was in Connecticut until tomorrow.

"Here's my two cents worth," said Winston. "I think Simon found a photograph with the culprit in it. How he knew it was the culprit I haven't the slightest idea, but the photo told him something. He got in touch with this person and the rest we know about. Since it was an old snapshot, it would have to be somebody who's been around awhile. That would tend to support Janice's theory."

"Good thinking," said Dr. Wetmore. "Simon told me himself that Bill was off the hook."

"That's not exactly what he said. You told me he said that what he'd found changed things. That's not the same thing," said Winston.

Dr. Wetmore thought about that. "True, but he implied Bill was no longer a suspect."

"Uh huh. Speaking of suspects, what ever happened to Hugh Bantram and that gardener who got fired? Weren't they on the list?"

"Barney Potter wouldn't hurt anyone," said Mrs. Cog.

"Barney's been in the hospital since last Saturday. He took that firing pretty hard. And Hugh's a complete basket case. I forgot to mention it, but I went to talk to him yesterday." Dr. Wetmore rearranged a cookie on her plate.

The three stared at the table.

"Look, I've got to get some sleep. My advice is not to do anything." Winston stood ready to go upstairs.

Dr. Wetmore also busied herself with leaving.

"You go ahead. Maybe you'd like to join me early tomorrow and go up to Jack's house. Take a look through those old hunt files. Jack's in New York until late tomorrow. I've already talked to his housekeeper, Gladys. She's an old friend of mine and said she'd let me in. No possible harm could come to me up there."

"Now wait a minute. You're talking about breaking into Jack's? Think I'll take a pass, thank you," said Winston. "You're going to get into trouble with the law. Captain Andrews and the boys will take a look at those files when Jack gets back. Why can't it wait?"

"The police are waiting for Jack. That means they probably won't look at those files until late tomorrow or Friday. Who knows what will have happened to Simon by then?"

Dr. Wetmore looked so somber that Winston couldn't argue with her. "Would you do me a favor, then? Once you look at the files call Andrews. Will you promise me that?"

Dr. Wetmore hesitated.

"If you don't say yes I'm going to make a citizen's arrest this very moment."

"You don't look like you have the energy to arrest a dead squirrel," offered Mrs. Cog.

"Whose side are *you* on?" groaned Winston. "Look, I've got to get some rest. Could you call Mrs. Cog here when you get done and let her know you're okay? That would sure make me rest easier. You wouldn't mind, would you Mrs. Cog?"

"Not at all. Information central, that's me."

"I could do that," said Dr. Wetmore. "And I'll call the police."

"Promise?"

"Promise."

"Great. Now if you'll excuse me."

Winston left the two ladies planning the phone call while he went upstairs to shower and fall into bed. As soon as Janice took off he would call Captain Andrews and have him keep an eye on her. Wherever Simon was he would wait until the police found him. Winston reasoned the worst about the vicar, but he just couldn't bring himself to say anything to Janice. He hoped he was wrong.

Figuring he'd lie down for just a few minutes before taking his shower, Winston thought back on last night. Erika had said this morning she'd be working late at the gallery today in preparation for tomorrow's opening and that he should drop by later. I should get a board for this bed, he thought. It's much too soft.

It was his last thought before falling into a deep, velvety sleep.

Chapter 20

Dr. Wetmore had lied about Gladys letting her in at Jack Glenn's house. Gladys had said she wouldn't be there because Jack didn't like anyone in the house when he was in New York. She lied because she knew Winston would never allow her to go up by herself. He would want to wait for the police to investigate the files and . . . well, that wasn't fair, she thought. Once she had the name, finding Simon would be easy. She'd let the police do that part.

Having risen early, Dr. Wetmore put on her darkest jogging attire and limbered up for the break-in. She wanted her mind and body at peak form for the adventure. No telling what might happen.

Never having been to Jack's house, Dr. Wetmore wasn't sure whether she'd be able to break in. She'd never forcibly entered a house before and was frightened and excited at the same time. The exigency of the situation was justification enough in her mind, and she couldn't believe that if Jack did happen to find out he wouldn't just accept the reasons and let her go. Heroines in all the mysteries she read did far worse things to solve otherwise baffling crimes.

Jack Glenn's house sat at the end of a long drive.

A large, center-hall colonial, it had been built in 1790 by the owner of the local iron ore yards. The stagecoach line from Albany to Hartford had run right past the door at one time, but the only indication left was the last half of Jack's driveway, which ran straight and flat up to the house and some way beyond.

Dr. Wetmore parked at a small turnaround a little distance from the house. Checking to make sure no other cars were evident, she took a deep breath and with Skippy under her arm went straight up to the front door and rang the bell. If anyone was home she would find out about it now and not later, while skulking around the interior of the house. At the front step she could still come up with a plausible excuse for her presence. Once inside it might prove more difficult. No one answered her ring. For the heck of it she tried the door, but it was locked.

I never lock *my* door, she thought. Placing Skippy on the ground, she made her first circle of the house. The back door and all the windows were locked. There was also no evidence of a security system, although she couldn't be absolutely sure of that. She circled the house again. Off in the direction of the barn a dog barked. She froze. What if there was a vicious watchdog? Skippy, who'd already disappeared around the corner, would have welcomed a burglar, and the fact that people kept dogs that didn't hadn't occurred to her.

When no slavering mongrel appeared, she cautiously moved out of sight of the barn to the other side of the house.

Looking for Skippy, she found him inspecting the basement window closest to her.

"What have we found here?" Skippy clawed at the

basement window, emitting a low growl. Dr. Wetmore inspected the rusted window on her hands and knees. To her delight, she found the window was unlocked and wide enough to allow entrance. Pushing the casement aside she peered into the darkness.

"I'm glad I wore my older jogging outfit, Skippy. This basement looks a mess."

After some difficulty Dr. Wetmore dropped to the basement floor. Skippy landed beside her with a sharp yelp. Brushing the cold, damp dirt of the floor from her hands, Dr. Wetmore peered into the dimness. A feeling of terror and excitement gripped her. She wondered if burglars experienced this same sensation when entering a home illegally. Maybe that was part of breaking in, part of the reason most second-story men go back and do it again. Her heart racing, Dr. Wetmore slowly climbed the creaky wooden stairs that led directly into the kitchen.

Dr. Wetmore wasn't particularly fond of Jack, but she had to admit he kept a tidy home. The choice of furniture was thoughtful and in keeping with the house, not like some homes she'd been in, where newcomers from New York brought with them styles more appropriate to spaceships or science fiction movies than to carefully tended survivors of the past.

An illegally entered house is an echo chamber that takes the slightest noise and magnifies it a hundredfold. Dr. Wetmore kept stopping and calming her heart as she crept her way through the house to the study, where, she reasoned, Jack would keep the files. She kept expecting someone to jump out at her as she peered into each room. Skippy had refused to leave the kitchen, becoming suddenly very skittish. She had left him shivering by the basement door.

Off the entrance hall she found Jack's study, an interior designer's conception of what the well-heeled single man would want in *his* room. Dark wood and burgundy leather seemed to cover everything, from walls to furniture. Even the shelving uprights were upholstered in leather, tacked to the wood with silver studs. Mixed in among the framed hunt scenes, animal trophies stared down from the walls, and over the fireplace hung a portrait of Jack himself—dressed in his hunting pinks and holding a whip. There was a look of studied disdain on his brooding face; the eyes seemed to follow Dr. Wetmore as she began searching the room. Why did portraits always have to do that? she thought, wishing he would stare at something besides her.

Against the wall opposite the door stood an oak cabinet with the words "Hunt Committee" stenciled on the wooden drawers. Dr. Wetmore began opening and inspecting the contents. The third drawer held a collection of leather-bound notebooks inscribed with different years.

After a hurried and enthusiastic search, she realized the year 1954 was missing. So was the year 1955. Had Captain Andrews been here? Had . . . Dr. Wetmore looked apprehensively at the door . . . the killer been here? The house suddenly seemed too quiet. She could hear a nuthatch scolding a squirrel outside the window. Moving slowly toward the door, she noticed what appeared to be a pile of journals on Jack's desk. Reaching from a distance, she picked up the top journal, reading the date 1954. She could hardly contain her excitement.

Standing at the desk, she turned the cover and began reading the first page. At the top of the second page she found the list of committee members. Florence Perkins—President, John Hardwell—Treasurer, James Bantram, Cynthia Hall . . . and . . . she couldn't believe it . . .

Skippy came tearing into the study. Seeing his mistress by the desk, he took up a position behind her and began barking.

"What is it, Skippy? Stop that!"

Kneeling, Dr. Wetmore tried calming the barking dog. Maybe he was . . . Suddenly she was aware of someone other than the painting staring at her. As if the portrait had come alive, the flesh-and-blood Jack Glenn stood framed in the study door. Dr. Wetmore almost sat on the floor. Rising, she placed the journal back on the desk, her face frozen in an awkward smile.

Looking around the study for accomplices, Jack came slowly into the room.

"What a surprise, Doctor. Gladys must have left the front door open. It's unlike her. I see the police aren't the only ones interested in the hunt journal from 1954."

Dr. Wetmore could only nod. It had never dawned on her that Jack might actually appear, so she was unprepared to offer him any reasonable excuse for being in his home. The fact that he had come up from New York early to find the same notebook she now held clutched to her chest didn't augur well. Skippy, who had taken refuge under the desk, issued a series of low growls.

"Yes?" said Jack, who now stood facing Dr. Wetmore on the other side of the desk. She had never realized how big he was.

"I'm trying to find Simon Tart."

"And have you found him, Doctor? Was he behind the wall cabinet? Maybe the Hitchcock chair?"

"I didn't expect you up until tomorrow . . . and . . ." Dr. Wetmore wasn't sure how much information she should impart to this man.

"Why don't you have a seat, Doctor. I think we should have a little chat."

Dr. Wetmore sat down, not so much because she wanted to but because her legs suddenly felt incapable of supporting her.

"And could you get that dog to stop moaning? He seems to think I mean to harm him in some way. Let him know that's not the case, could you do that?"

Glenn reached over and took the journals from the desktop. Pulling up another chair, he sat opposite Dr. Wetmore.

"Now. What have we learned?"

Chapter 21

Winston woke even before the sun rose outside his window early the next morning. At some point in the night he had removed his shoes, but they were the only thing. He felt and looked like one of those crumpled winos he always saw holding up a gutter down in the Bowery. Sitting on the edge of the bed, he tried remembering what day it was and if he was still in the country. The room certainly was from another experience. Perhaps a hot shower would make all well again.

Showered and shaved, Winston stood on the Cogs's porch inhaling the morning dew and feeling like he'd just inherited the earth. A curling fog crept back toward the creek, shrinking before the sun's early rays. Winston had never heard so many birds. He would have to take up bird watching while in the country; it seemed such a country thing to do. Up early every morning, a healthy breakfast of oat flapjacks on the porch while he astutely identified the many species of feathered songsters, maybe a little exercise.

Good luck, thought Winston as he shut the door to the Volvo and prepared to go to work. What is it about the early morning that deranged a person?

Maybe the left side of the brain doesn't completely awaken until the sun has reached full circumference, allowing the right side to mislead us with unnatural desires. Everything seems so verdant, so new, so moist. The day has thirty-four hours and we have nothing to do. Winston laughed. He had almost braved a cup of "shock therapy" but thought better of it. He didn't want to upset any sleeping brain molecules by sticking them with Mrs. Cog's caffeine electrodes.

And then maybe it was a woman named Erika who filled him with such intensity. As he drove along the empty roads, his memory traced the curve of her hip, her spine, her lower lip. Erika was his new day and tonight he would see her again. Thank goodness Bill was gone until later. Winston didn't want anything to destroy this feeling. As he parked beside the house, his bubble burst with the emergence of Ed Worth from the front door, his gaunt face shiny in the morning light.

"You ever go home, Ed?" asked Winston. He realized he had no idea where Ed *did* live.

"Best time to sharpen my tools." Ed Worth managed to say this without an offending sneer.

"I bet." Must be early for Ed, too, thought Winston. "Door's looking good," said Winston.

Ed shrugged.

"I'll be inside if you need anything." Like the day off, said Winston to himself.

Sitting in the back parlor staring at the blueprints, Winston realized he didn't want to do any work. The emptiness of the house depressed him. He felt restless and a little sorry for himself. Ed Worth had put him in a bad mood.

Rising, Winston went over to the cellar door and

peered down into the darkness. The forms pressed yesterday should be removed and dusted with talc. A little work would get him feeling good again. Or would it? An idea came to him. Maybe he'd look for evidence of the Underground Railroad. Mrs. Cog seemed pretty adamant that it was in the house. People who got involved in smuggling slaves to Canada usually developed fairly sophisticated hiding places. It *was* against the law. Winston would spend a few hours searching for signs that the house might have been used as a stopover. Again the day became filled with promise and maybe a little fun.

Three hours later, Winston sat on the lawn outside the basement door beginning to think Mrs. Cog, or rather her grandfather, was wrong. The attic had been gutted and newly insulated with no evidence uncovered of any hiding places. With careful measuring, Winston dismissed the existence of secret rooms. Exploration of the basement had produced nothing but cobwebs, dirty knees, and a bump on the head. Winston could hear Ed Worth pounding in the front of the house. He wondered briefly if Ed might have come across something, but he quickly dropped the idea of asking him.

Down the long incline directly before Winston stood the cottage, its rear wall backed into the hill. Winston traced the outline of the bungalow with his eyes, lazily taking in the garden and the shingled shed roof. The front of the cottage had been stuccoed while the side walls remained fieldstone, blending easily and naturally into the hill. *Into the hill*, thought Winston. Jesus, that's it!

Suddenly Winston was up and running down the slope. He supported himself on the doorjamb to catch his breath. Bill wasn't expected back until later that day and Ed Worth was busy being a good carpenter. Who'd know if he took a little look around? Winston tried the door. It swung open. He hadn't really expected it to be unlocked and was surprised to see it open, inviting him in. The Fates were with him. A quick look around and he was inside, the door shut behind him.

Winston was familiar with the interior, having spent his first night here. The dampness of the place and its damaging effect on the furniture had bothered him. Now he knew why it was so damp. The cottage fronted on a cave, or at least a deep impression in the earth. All he had to do was find the entrance. A thorough search revealed that the floors were complete and without seams, as were the walls. The kitchen cabinets held nothing but cans and cookware, no secret passages.

Winston sat back down in the living room, going over his options. Bill's study was in the front, away from the hill, so it wasn't there. The bedrooms were . . . Winston smiled. Of course. Right there in front of him all the time. Against the back wall stood Pandora's box, the root of all evil, Bill's grotesque armoire that hugged the rear wall and had spooked Winston the other day because he thought it had taken a breath. What he had heard was air escaping from within the earth.

The heavy doors were locked. Winston needed to find either the key or a pry bar. A key was preferable. Explaining the damaged doors to Bill might be difficult. Which brought up the question of why Bill might have lied about this cave, saying to Mrs. Cog he knew nothing of its whereabouts. Of course, maybe the cabinet held coats and broken umbrellas, but Winston was almost positive there was more behind those doors than just a wooden back panel. He ran his hands over the top rail in search of a key. Nothing. Bill's pedestal desk was a possibility.

None of the side drawers held the key, and the center drawer was locked. Getting on his hands and knees, Winston explored the underside of the desk. He was lucky. The glide rails were exposed and fastened with only a few screws. Take them out and one side of the drawer would drop down, disengaging the simple mortise lock. Ed would have a screwdriver. As Winston went to leave the study he remembered something. These pedestal desks usually had hinged ends that folded outward, remaining open and supported by a stay-joint near the bottom of the panel. Portfolios and large drawings were stored in these recesses. This desk had the wide side pilasters that indicated such a storage space.

Once again Winston searched under the desk on his hands and knees. The ends were disengaged by pulls that were located near the . . . and there they were! Winston gave each a yank. The end panels dropped open.

Winston had pulled out what appeared to be old floor plans of the estate when he heard the front door of the cottage slam shut. Quickly he replaced the prints and closed the ends. He was casually sorting through the papers on top of the desk when James entered the room. The chauffeur was very surprised to find Winston staring back at him.

"What in the . . ." James stopped still.

"Hi, James. Sorry to startle you. Mr. Joyce said he might leave some old photographs of the original house here on his desk for me. If he could find them, that is. It appears he had no luck."

"Photographs?" James had quickly regained his surly composure. He stood staring as if Winston had soiled the study in some way.

"Yeah. Old snaps. They're not here, though." James made Winston uneasy. Even during their first meeting in New York the man had intimidated him. "I thought Mr. Joyce wasn't coming back until later today."

"Mr. Joyce went ahead to Boston. I came back last night."

"He's not coming back today?" Winston wished James would stop staring at him in such a churlish manner.

"I'm to pick him up later at the train station. Shall I tidy up in here, Mr. Wyc?"

James's offer was a dismissal.

"Sure." Winston hesitated. "You know about the furniture, James?"

"A little. I sometimes assist Mr. Joyce in his purchases."

"How much of the furniture was here when the house was bought?"

"A lot. Most was in poor condition."

"Was this desk here?"

"I believe it was."

Very interesting, thought Winston. Bill claimed he bought the desk at a flea market. He wondered if he should take the chauffeur into his confidence and ask about the possibility of a cave.

"You've worked for Mr. Joyce a long time, James." Winston casually inched toward the door.

"A long time, Mr. Wyc."

"I see." James had emphasized the word *long* a fraction too hard. James was obviously too much a company man, and Winston decided to let the issue rest for the time being.

"Well, I'll get back to work. If you'll excuse me."

Winston had to gently push his way past James, who refused to budge an inch from the doorway. The tension in the man's body was disconcerting to Winston, but he couldn't help stopping and giving Pandora's box one more look.

"James, you ever hear tell of a cave somewhere on this property? Maybe a hidden cave used for hiding slaves during the Civil War?"

James stared at Winston but he didn't look over at the armoire. Winston had hoped the man would betray himself with a nervous glance. No such luck.

"I've heard rumors about the Underground Railroad here. Mr. Joyce even looked for it when he first arrived here, but nothing was ever found."

Winston nodded, hesitated, and then hurried from the cottage and back up to the main house.

Having been caught in the act of snooping, Winston suddenly remembered Janice Wetmore. He had thought of calling Captain Andrews yesterday about keeping an eye on her, but he had fallen asleep. He hoped she hadn't done anything foolish yet. He would get in touch with Mrs. Cog first and see if she had heard from the doctor. If not, he would call the police.

Chapter 22

Dr. Wetmore was still cleaning the ink from her fingers when Captain Andrews came into the room, giving her his best glare. Dr. Wetmore would not be intimidated. It may have been illegal to break into Jack's house, but it was all for a good cause and she would not be made to feel ashamed or repentant. If she had to do time then so be it. Older women than she had gone off to jail and done their punishment and come back into the world to live rewarding lives. The key to one's survival was knowing that in the eyes of the public one was right and that sometimes the laws had to be bent to achieve a greater good.

"First time you've been fingerprinted, Doctor?" Andrews sat down opposite Dr. Wetmore.

"The very first, Captain. Thank you."

"It seems it might not have been necessary. I had a long talk with Mr. Glenn and I think he's ready to drop charges if you promise to stay clean and not interfere with things anymore. He realizes you were acting only with good intentions."

"That's decent of him, Mr. Andrews, and you can tell him I'm always clean." Dr. Wetmore had to shift gears slightly, being a little disappointed she was not going to jail.

"Yes, well . . ." Andrews pushed some papers across the table. "Just sign these and you're free to go. With one stipulation."

"What might that be?" Here it comes, thought Dr. Wetmore. Community service.

"You're to be confined to your home from five in the afternoon until eight the next morning for the next month. It's mentioned in the papers there: page two."

Before Dr. Wetmore could protest, a young officer knocked and entered the room. "Phone for you, Captain. It's a Mr. Wyc."

"Thanks, Kevin. Switch it into here."

Smiling at Dr. Wetmore, Andrews pressed a button on the phone next to him and waited.

"Your friends must be looking for you, Doctor. Nice to be loved, heh?"

"Mr. Wyc knew nothing of my venture."

"I bet. Oh, hi, Mr. Wyc. The second half of the comedy team Wetmore and Wyc is right here. Seems she wandered into the wrong house. Of course you wouldn't know anything about that. Uh huh. Uh huh. No, she's fine, although I think she's upset we're not booking her. Sure you can talk to her." Andrews handed the receiver across the table to Dr. Wetmore. "Mr. Wyc wants to make sure we're not torturing you."

"Hi, Winston. No. No, I'm okay, but listen to me. Give me a call at home in a few hours. Yes? You do? That's okay, I have my car here. Thanks." Hanging up, Dr. Wetmore sat staring at the release forms. Captain Andrews wasn't saying she couldn't go out during the day, and since she rarely left the house at night anyway . . . besides, this document probably wouldn't float in two inches of strap molasses, much less a county court.

"I agree to the terms," she said reluctantly. Better to let him think she didn't like the offer.

"A sensible response, Doctor. I couldn't help but note, though, a certain enthusiasm on your part when discussing the hunt committee with Mr. Wyc just now. This is the last warning. If I find you further interfering in any way with this investigation I'll not be so good-natured next time." Captain Andrews spread his hands for emphasis. "I only say this for your own good. You find out *anything*, you give *me* a call." He gave her another big smile. "The officer who brought in the phone message has the keys to your car. Please drive carefully."

Dr. Wetmore sat in her car, letting it warm up. She thought back over the name she had found in the journal. The fifth person on the committee had been a Julia Westcliff. It had taken Dr. Wetmore a full hour to remember who Julia Westcliff was, and when she did she also remembered that Julia had been dead for five years. This unwanted information had placed her back on square one. She was going to have to look back over her list of recent newcomers.

Dr. Wetmore was more than half way home before she noticed the patrol car following at a discreet distance.

Chapter 23

Winston decided to walk the half mile from the Cogs's boarding house to Erika's art gallery in the village. The evening air was cool, and a quick walk would give him energy and time to think. Dr. Wetmore had called to say she was under house arrest and wouldn't make the opening. Winston didn't get the impression it upset her too much. She had been even less enthusiastic about the discovery of the fifth committee member, inasmuch as the revelation all but destroyed her theory that this member might be the killer. The fifth person had been a Julia Westcliff, who thirty years ago had married a Fletcher Phillips. The mystery committee member had turned out to be Erika's mother. What that meant neither he nor Dr. Wetmore knew, except that if the members of the committee were the only targets, then the killings were over. If that was the case, then the killer might never be caught; having accomplished the mission, he or she would probably take a low profile or disappear altogether. Dr. Wetmore had hung up saying she would call Erika. The subject of Simon Tart hadn't come up.

And Bill Joyce was coming up short on the truth meter. There was a possibility he'd lied about the desk and the wardrobe. Why did he say he'd bought the desk if he hadn't?

And if something was hidden behind that monstrosity in his living room, then why wasn't he being up front about it? Maybe Simon had been right about Joyce after all, and if not, then Joyce was certainly up to his neck in his own little mystery. Winston wondered if Bill had actually gone to Boston. If he was back he would more than likely be at the opening.

Winston was surprised to see a very large crowd standing outside the art gallery. Erika had mentioned in passing that the artist was from New York and was well-known, but this looked like opening night on Broadway. Once within the throng, Winston could have been in Soho attending a hot new gallery opening. Many of the crowd were younger then he was, dressed all in black, their limp, colorless faces accented with splashes of bright hair tints. They didn't seem to be present to attend the opening so much as to attend one another. Everyone appeared so nonchalant that Winston was certain that at some predetermined moment they would all collapse in a fashionable heap on the wet grass. He remembered Rheingold College was near and wondered if this accounted for the presence of the hopefully chic. Others in the crowd looked familiar and more homegrown.

Weaving his way to the door, Winston presented his invitation and squeezed through into a small anteroom where coats were taken and noses could be powdered. Double doors led into the gallery showroom, a large, open area with a high ceiling topped by an immense skylight that tonight gave those inside a panoramic view of the stars. Winston was impressed with the professional nature of the gallery. Wistfield and its rural atmosphere might have been a thousand miles away.

The room was packed with people holding plastic cups of white wine discussing everything but the art on the walls. Peering over the many new coifs, Winston noticed Erika holding court over to his left.

"Winston, I'm glad you made it." Erika gave his hand a quick squeeze.

"I didn't realize the entire county and most of New York was to be here."

"It's a good turnout. Jules is a very popular artist."

"How did you get him to open in Wistfield?" asked Winston.

"It was definitely not a career move. He's an old friend from Bennington and the paintings aren't new. He wanted to help me and the gallery."

"Doesn't sound like a New York society artist to me."

"He's not all that altruistic. There are some local people and plenty of weekenders who can afford to buy his paintings." Erika leaned closer into Winston. "I got a call from Janice before coming over tonight."

"About your mother?"

Erika nodded. "I already knew. My father had called earlier to wish me luck on the opening and I'd asked him about the committee. He told me."

"What do you think that means?" asked Winston.

"I've no idea. I've had no time to think about it."

From out of the crowd came a ridiculously thin, middle-aged woman with a huge blonde bouffant hairdo. She looked like a stylish bottlebrush.

"Erika, sweetheart. God, what a mass! It's *wonder-*

ful! Of course, no one here knows the first thing about art, but what can one expect in the sticks?"

"Charity, I'd like you to meet Winston."

"How do you do." Charity stuck out a bony hand, an eagle's taloned grip. "Charity Thorndyke. I've known Erika for years. It's my money the dear girl's got invested here. What do you think?"

"I think it's money well invested," said Winston.

"Damned right it is. She's a peach. *Look* at this crowd. I'm going to work the room, dear. I advise you to do the same. Rescue you later." She gave Winston a wide, insincere smile and disappeared into a backdrop of black gowns.

"What a peach. Invest all her savings, did she?" asked Winston.

"Hardly a penny. You'd think she supported the gallery all by herself. I . . . oh, no." Erika looked up at Winston and made a sour face.

"What's the matter?"

A loud *ahem* was sounded. Standing before them was a tall, peregrine faced woman, her hawklike grin beaming down on them, sparrows for the taking. "Let's don't be hoarding *all* the beautiful boys now, Erika." The woman concentrated her gaze on Winston's face.

"Mrs. Goodall, sorry I didn't see you. This is Winston Wyc. Winston, Velvet Goodall."

"Velvet?" said Winston.

"Yessss," said Velvet with a smooth purr. She widened her eyes at him. "I noticed you from across the room as someone I didn't know. What a foolish world, I thought to myself. And what do you thrive at, Winston?"

Winston sought rescue from Erika, who was doing her best to suppress a grin.

"Winston's a historian, Velvet," said Erika quickly.

"Historian? My, my. You seem too young to be into history, Winston."

"Like Merlin, I'm traveling backward in time."

"Lord, don't I wish I could," said Velvet with a loud sigh.

"I was just showing Winston to the bar. Can we get you something?"

"No, thank you, dear. Liquor contains sugar. See you later, Winston." Velvet raised her hand and waved two fingers good-bye.

"What was that?" asked Winston.

"Velvet's okay. She's had a couple of financially successful marriages and I think in her advanced years she's looking for a pretty face."

"To what? Chew on?"

"That's not nice," said Erika laughing. "The bar's over in that direction. I have to seek out a few possible buyers and talk art. Would you mind? I promise not to stay away." She looked rueful and gave him a peck on the cheek.

"I would mind, but I'll be a big boy about it."

"Go have a drink. I won't be gone long."

Winston watched her go and decided a drink would be a good idea. The bar was a small alcove off the main room. Drinks were being served by the same young man who had waited on Winston at the Wistfield Inn. His long blond hair was neatly tied back over his collar and the earring was gone. Standing, waiting for his drink, was Jack Glenn.

"Well . . . Winston, isn't it? Good to see you again." Glenn's tone implied otherwise and he gave Winston's hand an extra crush in case the message wasn't clear.

"Let's see, it's Jack, as I remember. How are you?" Winston tried out a limpish grin.

"I don't complain. Wouldn't help if I did, would it?" Coughing up a mirthless chuckle, Glenn reached back for his drink, addressing Winston without looking at him. "I can't stop thinking about poor James Bantram. Horrible incident. More episodes like these 'good luck' murders and land values will begin to suffer."

"Think so? What a shame, and I was just thinking of investing locally." Winston looked overly concerned.

"Wistfield can be rather expensive, Winston. Now Columbia County, which is north of here, is still quite cheap. Farmers are being forced to sell chunks of land all the time—and at reasonable prices. I'd start there if I were you."

Damned if he isn't threatening me, thought Winston. "Money's no problem. The trust fund kicks in pretty soon and . . . well, you know how it is, my accountant's going to want me to invest. Keep the government off my ass."

"Trust fund?"

"Now, Jack, you're not one of those people who resent it when someone just happens to be born into a little luck, are you?"

Jack was not amused. "How nice for you. We'll bump into each other again, I'm sure."

Watching Glenn push his way back into the crowd, Winston wondered if Jack might have some reason to bump off the hunt committee. Certainly plenty of anger lurking just below the surface in that man, he thought. Had Andrews done a background check on Jack Glenn?

"That's neat. A trust fund." The kid serving

drinks was impressed. "What do you want to drink?"

Winston laughed. "Pal, I can't afford a bus ticket to Albany. Your best scotch, thank you. A little ice."

Drink in hand, Winston wandered back into the gallery intent on actually seeing the art.

"Amazing isn't it?" A man next to Winston spoke directly at a painting, a picture Winston suspected of having been firebombed. "We're only two years apart in age, but I feel I'm looking at the work of a much older, *much* more experienced man." He turned his reddened eyes up to Winston. "What instincts. I'll never have it no matter how I ripen."

"Ripen?"

The man looked away. "Don't you ever wonder if it's worth all the bullshit."

Winston offered a concerned face.

"You're not an artist, are you? Just as I thought. How could you know? The critical indifference is like a psychosledge, hammering away at one's hardsought uniqueness."

Winston nodded and drained his drink.

"And what about one's own indifference? How do you get past that?"

Winston was at a loss for words. The man shook his head and shuffled away. Perhaps to find a bridge, thought Winston.

"Such a gifted revisionist."

Winston turned to his right. The vacuum left by the man had been filled instantly by Velvet Goodall, who leaned her body into Winston's.

"Revisionist?" echoed Winston, looking for a means of escape.

"Absolutely. I call Jules the Mozart of art. I can tell from your face, Winston, that I'm not making

189

myself clear." She covered him in her lavender breath. "As Mozart rewrote music for his time, Jules is reinventing art. My goodness, look at the sexuality and violence in this piece. He's not simply reworking the libido, Winston, Jules is creating whole new symbols of generative cognition. Sometimes while studying his work I actually perspire."

Winston removed Velvet's hand from his left buttock.

"You have me at a disadvantage, Velvet. I'm not quite as familiar as you with this particular artist."

"Shame on you." Velvet raised her hand to signal someone in the crowd. "How would you like to meet the genius himself?"

"Do I have a choice?"

"Here he is," boomed Velvet.

Winston was introduced to a tall, well-groomed man. The man's head and features were oversized but handsome, the hair slicked back to emphasize the prominent brow. The large, dark eyes drew one in, and although Winston was meeting the man for the first time, the intensity of his eyes hinted of shared secrets. Winston wanted to dislike Jules but found it difficult.

"Wyc? That would be shortened from Polish, is it not? I've always admired the Polish people. Their poetry certainly but their courage especially."

"We're a patient people."

"Of course. And art, Mr. Wyc. Are you fond of art?"

"I'm afraid I'm rather ignorant on the subject."

"Winston's a historian," filled in Mrs. Goodall.

"Interesting. Not to embarrass you, Winston, but I've found that most people who plead ignorance

190

are, shall we say, displeased with my paintings. You can tell me what you think without offending me."

"Believe me, that's not the case here."

"Jules is painting churches at the moment," said Mrs. Goodall, offering an explanation for the bomb patterns on the walls.

"I've become deeply interested in art and religion, Winston. That is, religion as myth, not ideology. Something experienced from the heart, not the head. My work explores religion and its original concerns with the natural world."

"I must give it another look."

"The church is merely a metaphor for the mythic experience."

"I see."

"Do you believe in God, Winston?"

"I'm not sure. Do you, Jules?" Winston thoroughly believed in another scotch.

"I find that if we search deep enough, all of us discover the presence of a god . . . or maybe a little devil."

Jules chuckled to himself. "I find both figures essentially human, don't you? The one a projection of ourselves, the other of our enemies."

Jules smiled, sharing another secret that Winston should know but must have forgotten.

"I'm afraid, Jules, that my views concerning . . ."

"Oh, listen, Winston, it's important I talk to this person over here. It's been a pleasure to meet you. Come back and view the paintings when the room is lit by the sun and you have the space to yourself. I believe you'll reconsider."

"Sure. First thing in the morning," said Winston.

Jules chuckled and Winston answered with raised eyebrows and his own enigmatic smile. Mrs. Goodall grabbed his arm as Jules quickly receded into the babble.

"The man takes my breath away. I own two of his paintings."

"That's great."

"There you are! I hate to intrude, but I'm going to steal Winston for a dance."

Erika appeared from behind Velvet.

"Bye, Winston." Velvet feigned misery.

"Bye, Velvet." Winston almost picked Erika up to run with her. "Dance?"

"In the next room is a small band for entertainment. You do like to dance?"

"Sounds like heaven."

Erika led Winston through the crowd and into an equally large but quieter room that was lined with white banquettes. A raised platform barely provided space for a trio playing slow, jazzy dance tunes.

Winston led Erika in among the dancing couples. Reaching for Erika's waist, he gently rested his fingers on the curve of her hip. Erika stepped lightly up against him, placing her arm on his shoulder. They began a slow swirl to the music.

"You dance well," said Erika. "Not many men nowadays give dancing much due."

"Felice and Fernando's Dance Academy gets all the credit, thank you. My mother insisted. She firmly believed a man could only truly win a lady's heart with the perfectly executed dip. Even at ten years old."

"A wise woman, your mother."

"That and my dancing partner, Butch DeLuccio. He taught me balance and swiftness of foot."

Bringing her head forward, Erika spoke closely

into Winston's ear. "Fancy dips not needed with this woman's heart."

"Don't let go. I might very well float to the ceiling."

Just as they curved into the next tune, Jack Glenn tapped Winston on the shoulder.

"I think I'll take over from here." Jack managed a smile.

"Sure thing." Winston reluctantly backed away. "The night is full of dances."

While watching Jack bounce Erika to the other side of the room, Winston noticed out of the corner of his eye that Velvet Goodall was moving in his direction. Quickly and almost at a crouch, Winston made his way to the bar. With drink in hand, he decided to look for Bill Joyce. After ten minutes he realized Bill wasn't in attendance and headed back to the dance area. Erika and Jack were gone.

Winston casually wandered back into the gallery, but still no Erika. He tried the anteroom. Velvet Goodall appeared before him, draped in a fur coat.

"Winston, you're still here. I must say I was surprised to see Erika leaving with that Jack Glenn fellow. I wanted to tell her what a gorgeous time I had and she just scooted right by me. I imagine she'll be back." Velvet gave Winston a shrug.

"Of course."

"Come see me for tea. I'd love to show you the paintings of Jules's that I own."

"I'll do that."

Winston watched the crowd thin out for twenty minutes before getting his coat and heading out into the cold night. Erika and Glenn were not outside. Winston even checked around the corner of the building. Back on the main street, Winston gave the Wistfield Inn a long consideration, but the lights went out just as he stepped off the curb in that direction.

The walk back to the Cogs's was a long one. Alternating between anger and concern, Winston avoided Wistfield's two street lamps and headed away from the village. Until he heard from Erika, Winston was going to think the best. Or try to.

The air was turning sharply cold. Trying very hard not to feel sorry for himself, Winston hunkered down into his jacket and, passing the Cogs's, crossed the wooden bridge into the fields behind the boarding house. The damp grass, hardened by the cold, crunched underfoot like breaking crystal. Winston stared up at the black night sky with its bright three-quarter moon and thought back over the last five days. He was in the middle of an adventure, no doubt about it, but what part was he playing, the hero or the buffoon? Erika seemed to like him, her actions certainly indicated such, but he didn't really know her or she him. She and Jack had a whole history, a past that was woven into the fabric of Wistfield, a place he didn't belong to or fully understand. The winter would end and he would go back to New York City. He wasn't going to move to the country and Erika had family and gallery here; she certainly wasn't about to uproot and come join him. Maybe they were fated to an epistolary romance like in the old days, with scented letters and purple prose. Or a Christmas card once a year. Or nothing.

Crossing back over the bridge, Winston stopped to stare into the icy water. This weekend he would drive down to the city and deliver some molds to the Rinaldi brothers. He needed a dose of normal civilization. Who could possibly survive in a place where the bars closed at ten o'clock? If he was lucky he might even get mugged.

The chill air began to hurt Winston's nose. Hurrying, he paused at the Cogs's front door to listen, hoping that his landlady was abed and not lurking in the hall with a plate of butter cookies and a glass of warm milk. Finding the coast clear, Winston quickly climbed the stairs to his room. Sitting at his window in the moonlight, he thought of pheasants and cannon fire.

Chapter 24

Winston woke late. No dewy lawn greeted him as he stumbled out on the porch this morning. No happy thoughts of bird-watching and a life in the country. The sun was up but the day was cool. Mrs. Cog had said something about the chance of first snow that evening, but Winston hadn't really been listening, his thoughts were on work and the fact that if he didn't start producing Joyce might fire him. Besides, he needed to concentrate on something other than Erika.

Winston parked by the main house. The towering maples in the front lawn were beginning to drop their leaves, exposing the scaffold around the house. The metal webbing and the fallen leaves gave the house an uninhabited and forsaken feeling. Joyce's vision of carriages and swirling dancers was a long way off, and Winston couldn't see this soulless house ever being warm or full of happiness. Whatever strangeness the Worthwell people had brought with them from the South was still very much a part of the place, and until the house had been lived in and loved for a long time that feeling was going to persist. Bill didn't seem to have the right goals or ideals. And what about Bill?

Winston could hear hammering in the house. Maybe he'd ask Bill about the armoire and get an answer this morning.

Solving that puzzle would be one step in putting his mind to rest.

Ed Worth was in the dining room area constructing something out of sawhorses.

"Hi, Ed. Seen Mr. Joyce?"

"Not here."

"I can see that. Is he down at the cottage?"

"Nope."

"Did he leave a forwarding address?"

Ed wasn't amused. Lively banter confused him.

"Didn't come back yesterday. The chauffeur went to get him."

"All the way to Boston?"

"Boston?"

"At the train station?"

"Don't know." Ed went back to his business.

Winston wandered back into the kitchen area where the work prints were spread. Certainly James hadn't driven to Boston to pick up Bill, Winston reasoned, so they might be back soon, the train station being only a twenty-minute ride. This would not be the time to explore the cottage. Settling down to the prints, Winston planned out a day's work and wondered how he could approach Bill about the armoire.

At ten minutes to noon Winston came down from upstairs and back into the dining area. Ed had put together a makeshift table.

"What's this for?" asked Winston.

"Sitting at."

"I can see that, Ed, but who's going to sit at it? Bill expecting guests?"

"Maybe. I just do what the boss tells me to do."
Ed gave Winston a funny grin.

"Look, Ed, if Bill shows up I've gone to get some lunch and renew the building permit in New Holland. Tell him I'll stop back in later."

Winston took Ed's blank stare as confirmation and went out to the car.

Actually he wouldn't be back to Joyce's this afternoon, because after New Holland he'd planned on heading over to Meadowbrook Farm and a talk with Erika. He needed to find out what had happened last night and he didn't want to hear about it over the phone.

Never having driven to New Holland, Winston stopped at the Wistfield Mobil station to get directions and fill up the Volvo. As Winston waited for gas, he noticed the house across from the station was for sale. The sign reminded Winston of something Simon Tart had mentioned up at the Joyce house concerning the sale of the Worthwell property. After renewing the permit he'd find the County Clerk's office and spend some time in the Registry of Deeds, since the two would probably be in the same building. Maybe he could corroborate Tart's findings.

The rural character of the road to New Holland changed abruptly, and Winston found himself driving past hastily constructed condos that might last another ten years. The builder's imagination had been limited to simple rectangles. These were followed by older, two-story wooden structures that reminded Winston of mill houses he'd seen near Yonkers. Tired porches, peeling paint, and drooping storm window sashes were the style with these homes; even the toys on the porches looked broken.

The road had been widened considerably in anticipation of an increase in traffic that, from what Winston could see, had never materialized. These homes had sacrificed their front yards for a prosperity that had never come.

New Holland had at one time been a thriving city on the Hudson River. Centrally located in the Hudson Valley, it had served as an important hub for the warehousing and dispersion of goods brought up the river from New York City in the south and down from Albany in the north. As an early center for trade and local government, it had attracted men who could spend money on large homes and handsome buildings of commerce. When the railroad surpassed the river as the main artery for transporting goods, it also bypassed New Holland, leaving the town to die a slow economic and commercial death. An effort in the sixties to revive the community had been thwarted by the proliferation of giant shopping malls out on the main thruway, pulling shoppers and much-needed revenues out of the town's center. Today New Holland had the look and feel of a city in need of a coat of paint—and maybe someone who cared enough to paint it.

Winston parked in a lot off the main street and went looking for the town hall. It was not hard to find. The town and federal offices in New Holland were housed in a Greek Revival structure that rose heroically, if somewhat self-consciously, above a cheerless street lined with dingy storefronts and boarded-up buildings. At one time it must have stood alone, reasoned Winston, a wide lawn surrounding the exterior, but now the only suggestion of greenery was the weeds that pushed apart the asphalt parking lot.

Winston liked government buildings. Many had been built in the nineteenth century or early twentieth century, when municipalities took great pride in their government offices, wanting and giving those building a facade based on the Classic Revival movement, an architectural approach that borrowed freely from pure Roman and Greek forms. The buildings were ordered and solid and, if occasionally a little grandiose for their surroundings, nonetheless suggested to the community a secure and unbroken link with a heroic past. Behind those wide stone steps and towering columns could only be the most important of men and transactions. Nowadays, town office buildings might be functional, but they looked for the most part like they were constructed out of Leggo sets, with no insight as to form and with but an afterthought of classical architecture smeared on the front.

Winston picked his way around the homeless and unemployed who were using the wide granite steps of the office building as a source of warmth, the stones acting as a passive solar heater, and made his way past the massive Ionic columns and in through the entrance. In contrast to the scene outside, Winston watched men and women inside hurry about carrying various amounts of paperwork, all appropriately dressed in dark suits and intense expressions, their busy shoes tapping out a rat-a-tat-tat that echoed noisily throughout the high-ceilinged marble foyer. Against the wall opposite the elevators men cornered other men, pressing for favors or information, their lowered voices a garbled basso underscoring the percussion of the shoes. Winston read through the directory. Building permits were issued on the second floor.

A thin woman, her elderly face inappropriately circled by a fluffy, Farrah Fawcett-style hairdo, looked up from her desk.

"Hi," smiled Winston. "I'm here to pick up a building permit extension."

"Oh yeah? What's the name?"

"William Joyce. The town is Wistfield."

The woman ran her finger down a computer printout posted on a wall to her right. Rising, she disappeared into the files behind her. Almost instantly she returned.

"Boy, you're cutting it close here. The old one expires today."

"I know."

"Just sign here, please. The fee has already been paid."

"Thanks."

"Think nothing of it."

"If I wanted to look at property deeds, where would I do that?" asked Winston.

"You'd want the Real Property Tax Division records room."

"Where's that?"

"In the basement. Take the elevator to B1 and take a right."

"Thanks again."

"Think nothing of it."

In the Real Property Tax Division room a long, high counter acted as a fence between Winston and the clerks on the other side. It was a few minutes before one of the clerks noticed him. Winston always wondered if there was a required time span that clerks had to observe in government offices when it came to assisting the public. Reluctantly a woman rose from her paperwork to see what Winston wanted. She appeared to be the same age as the previous clerk, but instead of a Farrah Fawcett haircut this one sported a cap of tight, ice-blue curls that didn't look quite real to Winston.

"What can I do for you?"

"Sorry to bother you, but I want to check on a land sale."

"Yeah?"

Winston and the lady stared at each other. Winston cleared his throat.

"How do I do that?"

"Well, you've come to the right place, anyway." The lady gave Winston a thorough looking over before proceeding. "You know where this sale took place?"

"Wistfield."

"You know the name of the grantor?"

Winston hesitated.

"The grantor is the seller. The grantee is the buyer," the woman explained.

"I know the name of the grantee."

"Well, that'll help. You go down that end of the counter and on the right is some shelves. Find the book labeled 'W' and run your little finger up and down the lists . . . You know about when this sale took place?"

"About two years ago."

"Two years ago. Hmmmm. That's the next set of shelves down. Find the year 1987 and put that finger to work again. Once you find the grantee's name, last name first, you'll find a deed number and a date. Got that?"

Winston nodded.

"You bring that number and date back to me, dearie. Think you can handle all that?"

"Gee, I don't know."

"Getoutahere."

Winston headed down the counter. The books were oversized journals that looked like ledgers out of a Dickens novel. A cloud of dust rose as Winston settled the ledger on the counter. Winston laughed to himself. These journals always came covered in dust. No matter that they'd been cleaned only two minutes beforehand, the dust reappeared instantly on the leathery bindings—a fine, powdery moss produced by the ledger itself. The thin, silky paper crackled as Winston turned the pages.

Luckily there weren't that many filings for either 1987 or '88. Winston went back to 1986. The name William Joyce could not be found as a grantee in any of those years. There was no Mr. Berry as grantor. As far as the Tax Division was concerned, a sale had never been registered that involved the Worthwell estate.

"Excuse me," said Winston.

"Find that deed number, dearie?" The lady didn't bother to rise this time.

"No, I didn't. I was wondering if there is ever a time when a name might not be filed here. In those ledgers."

"Could it be filed under a corporation?"

"Maybe, but I don't think so."

"It might not have been filed if there was some legal problem. Of course, two years is a long time. It'd have to be one heck of a legal problem to go on longer than that."

Winston gave the mystery some thought. Had Bill been the front for some corporation or did he own a business that bought the property? Bill didn't seem embroiled in any major legal tangle. He wasn't the type of man who could easily hide such a problem. Had Simon Tart been correct in declaring that the estate had never been sold?

"Where can I find the local survey maps?" These maps would tell Winston who was presently registered as owner.

"That's usually Betty over there, but I'll do the honors. See that big map behind you on the wall? Pick out the section that has the land you want to check and I'll pull the survey. You with a title company?"

"Nope. I'm a historian."

"No kidding. Don't get many of you in here. Just title companies and the curious. Guy buys a piece of land wants to trace the deed back to the original owners. Sometimes it happens. Find what you need?"

Winston gave her the number and watched as the woman and Betty wrestled the large survey folio back to the counter. The appropriate map was found. Winston located the village of Wistfield, and following his finger up the main road took a left out of town and then another left onto Four Partners Road, and then curved to the right up to the Worthwell property.

"It says Berry," said Winston.

"You're right, dearie. It do say Berry. You expecting someone else?"

"Yeah, sort'a. At the moment I'm not sure who I was expecting."

"That's the deed number there. I can look that up if you like. Double-check."

"Could you? I'd appreciate it."

"Someone else claim to own this land? Course, sometimes it doesn't get transferred from the book to here, but since you didn't find it in the book either, I'd be going with this name Berry. Here it is. Deed was last amended back in '56. A Mrs. Berry gave the land to her son, I guess. It says John Berry. Those names sound familiar?"

"Sure do. And that's the last entry?"

"Far as I know, that's who pays the taxes. You want to check to see if the taxes are paid up, I can't do that. Against the law. Privacy and all that. Of course, they publish in the newspaper each year who owes their property taxes, so I fail to see the big deal." The woman contorted her body into a total shrug.

"Wouldn't want to muck with anyone's privacy," said Winston.

"Amen to that, dearie."

Winston sat out on the front steps of the municipal building warming his derriere with the homeless. Simon Tart had been right. The property had never been sold to William Joyce. If indeed that was his name. Simon had thought Bill was John Berry but then had changed his mind, according to Dr. Wetmore. Or had he? And if Bill was Berry then why the front? Was Bill hiding behind this facade so he could enact his revenge without attracting any suspicion? Winston still couldn't see Bill murdering anyone. And what would be the motive? Something to do with the hunt committee? Winston stood to go. None of it made any sense. The murders, a possible cave, the disappearance of the vicar, and now the posturing of one William Joyce. *If* that was his real name. Winston thought of Captain Andrews. He would call from Meadowbrook Farm.

Chapter 25

Meadowbrook Farm looked larger and more beautiful than Winston remembered. As far as he could see, the landscape was partitioned by endless undulating white fences. On the far horizon the Catskills glimmered purple, an appropriate backdrop for such splendor. Beyond the sugar maples that lined the drive Winston could see the distant fields being hayed. The smell filled him with memories of his early teens and of mowing the grass around his own house. He never complained when every Saturday his father fussed over the old Briggs and Stratton, trying with curses and kicks to get it started. Their backyard wasn't very big, but he loved mowing it because of the smell of the newly cut grass. Mom always asked Winston to mow the lawn. His father called it the yard. People with money had lawns, his father would say to his mother; people like us had yards. Mom would shake her head and stomp back into the house. To a young Winston, that perfume of mowed grass had always suggested the large English parks his mother had told him about on their walks, where deer ate from your hand and young couples cut watercress right from the park stream to put in their sandwiches. Winston's mother had come to this country at the age of three, but he had never questioned her on her remembrances.

A woman in a black dress and white apron opened the door. She thought Erika might still be at the farm but she didn't know quite where. If Winston would wait in the music room she'd find out for him. Winston was looking at the pictures of Erika on the piano when Fletcher Phillips came into the room.

"Winston, isn't it? Good to see you again. Cute little devil, wasn't she?" Fletcher Phillips extended a warm hand and even warmer smile.

"Mr. Phillips, how are you? I think she still might be. A devil that is."

"Every time I look at her I'm reminded of her mother. It makes me sad sometimes, but you don't want to hear about that. She was mentioning you over breakfast this morning."

"She was?"

"I'm afraid I wasn't paying much attention. She's down in the kennels if you don't want to wait. That's them with the pointy cupola." Mr. Phillips motioned out the window. "What was it you do again?"

"I'm an architectural historian."

"An architect, heh? Hmmmm." Mr. Phillips left the room deep in thought. Winston smiled after him and went out the patio doors toward the kennels.

Winston peered over the closed lower portion of the Dutch door that led into the kennels. A large open space divided the numerous small stalls that ran up each side. The enclosures were low with small doors that led to an outside run. A young man was using a wide shovel to take cedar chips from a wheelbarrow and toss them into each stall.

208

"What can I do for you?" asked the man coming over to where Winston stood.

"I'm looking for Erika Phillips," said Winston, raising his voice to be heard over the barking of the hounds.

"Come on in. She's with the vet in the back tending to one of the bitches."

"Is it okay to go back there?" asked Winston.

"Sure." The man pointed toward the back of the barn.

Winston peered into the stalls as he passed. Each stall had a bench about eight inches from the cement floor on which the beagles were lying or sitting. The benches were covered in clean hay. In the back was a door that led to a smaller room that had only a few stalls, but they were larger. The noise of the hounds faded as Winston shut the door behind him. Standing in a stall was Erika and a man who looked concerned about the health of one of the beagles. Erika looked up as he came across the room.

"Winston! You're here." Erika gave him a wide smile. "This is Dr. Goodwin. Mac, this is Winston Wyc."

"Mr. Wyc."

Dr. Goodwin was a large man with hands the size and feel of old saddles. Maybe in his sixties. Winston had never seen a face with so many laugh lines. Even relaxed the face smiled.

Winston leaned on the stall supports and listened to them discuss the beagle's problem.

"I'd have a talk with the new man, Erika," said Dr. Goodwin. "If the straw is kept dry this shouldn't happen."

"Yes, Doctor."

"Keep an eye on his work habits. The younger guys tend to be lazy. Think it doesn't really matter. This never happened under old Durkee. He knew how to keep hounds."

"That's true. What should I do?" asked Erika.

"Now don't spread this around . . ." Dr. Goodwin gave Winston a look over his half glasses, ". . . for this remedy is a family secret. Actually, the old fellows always did it but nowadays, with most young vets learning everything from books written by men who learned from books, they've never heard of it. Probably think it was some kind of voodoo, anyway. You aren't one of them young vets, are you?"

Dr. Goodwin leaned toward Winston.

"Not me," said Winston. "I'm all for voodoo."

Dr. Goodwin studied Winston over his glasses before turning back to Erika.

"Where'd he come from?"

"Winston's my new beau. He's a good guy." Erika gave Winston an uncertain smile.

"He must be all right, then." Dr. Goodwin rolled the hound in his hands, caressing its soft underbelly.

"Feed Matilda five or six red herrings a day, plenty of water to drink, and nothing else. Understand? She'll be well in three days."

"Red herrings? Where do I find them?"

"That fish truck out on the highway, claims to come from Maine. He's got them."

"Okay."

Erika and Winston trailed Dr. Goodwin out the door and into the yard.

"You giving the hounds that blood tonic I gave you?"

"Once a week," answered Erika.

210

"Good. Mr. Wyc you take care of this girl or you'll have me to answer to."

"Yes, sir."

Dr. Goodwin gave them both a wide grin, turned, and loped away toward his van.

"Nice guy," said Winston.

"The best. He's the only one left around here of the old school. Some say he never went to college."

"The younger vets, I bet."

"Now that you mention it . . ." Erika forced a smile. "I tried to call you."

"You did?" said Winston.

"This morning, but you'd already left. You're not looking very friendly."

"I waited a long time for that next dance. You could have said something to me before you skipped out."

"I didn't skip out. Jack was being a little out of hand. He said some things that frightened me, threatened to make a big scene if I didn't come outside and talk to him. I didn't want that. I knew too many people there and it was important not to upset anyone. Outside he wanted to go for a ride. A short one. I said okay. I figured I'd be right back. It wasn't a short ride. For an hour he railed about this and that and how I'd betrayed him. When I got back to the gallery you were gone."

"Jack thinks you betrayed him?"

"I told you before, he has this fantasy. Last night he wanted to know when I was going to stop fucking around and marry him. I told him it wasn't going to happen. He blew up. Wanted to know if you were involved somehow, and how you'd better not be because he wouldn't be made to look like a fool."

Erika touched Winston on the sleeve.

211

"Don't you get weird on me. I need you right now."

"I've been pretty depressed all day because of last night. It might take a minute for me to adjust, but I'm not going to get weird." Winston smiled. "Not too weird. How crazy is Jack? Should I watch my back?"

"I don't know. He got irrational at one point, saying I was ruining everything, that his world was crumbling. He scared the hell out of me." Erika took Winston by the hand. They stood in silence for a minute. Erika giggled.

"What's so funny?" asked Winston.

"It's probably why Jack's not a trial lawyer. I can see him threatening to kill the jury if they decided against him."

They both laughed, and Winston could feel the tension between them dissipate.

"I missed you last night. I felt like the kid who didn't get the Christmas present."

"I missed you too," said Erika. "I almost came over to the Cogs's, but I felt funny about doing that. Besides, I was completely rattled by Jack."

"You hilltoppers are a strange crew."

"Hilltopper, heh? Come inside. I have to check Matilda."

"What's wrong with Matilda?" asked Winston.

"Kennel lameness. It's a form of rheumatism. Comes from sleeping on a wet floor. The hound's body is warm and the heat draws the moisture from the cement. That's why it's important to keep the kennel dry."

Winston watched as Erika set out an old army blanket for the hound to lie on.

"You going around telling everyone I'm your new beau?" asked Winston.

"Dr. Goodwin was the first. You unhappy with that idea?" Erika poked Winston in the stomach.

"Not at all."

"I was so happy to see you come through that door. I'm sorry about last night. Lately I've been letting myself coast. For too long it's been the same thing: same friends, same routines, same feelings. Not that that's bad, it's just that I had allowed myself to go numb, not paying attention to my life. When Jack and father proposed to me that Sunday in the music room it jolted me back into the real world. I realized people were expecting me to marry Jack. He would never have asked me if he'd thought for one minute I might say no. Jack has a hard time with rejection. Witness last night.

"That's why I feel so odd about you. I have this sudden . . . awareness and there you are. I come stomping out of the music room and find you in the entrance hall. Good timing, Wyc."

"Winston. That explains the question about my white horse."

"That's right. I thought you might be a knight come to rescue me."

"A rather shabby knight."

"But not too shabby."

Winston held Erika's shoulders.

"Are you telling me I got you on the rebound?"

"First bounce."

"First bounce doesn't count."

"Take it or leave it, Lancelot."

Winston shook his head and laughed.

"You know, I didn't say when the next dance was going to be, did I?"

"No, but I had the definite feeling it was supposed to be last night."

"Ever dance to the music of the beagles?"

"Wasn't that a famous English group?"

Laughing, Erika arranged Winston in a dance position, nestled against him and began to lead him in a slow turn around the room.

The young helper came clanging through the door with his wheelbarrow.

"Sorry."

"It's okay, Tom. Mr. Wyc and I were practicing our beagle-trot."

"Maybe I should bring some dry straw in from the barn."

"That'd be great."

Erika closed the door after Tom. Reaching up, she took her jacket off a hook on the wall.

"Oh, I forgot." Erika took an envelope from her pocket. "This was in the mailbox this morning."

"A letter?" Winston read the note to himself.

"An invitation. Pretty strange, eh?" Erika read over his shoulder.

"The mailman left this?"

"I don't think so. There was no stamp on it. Check who it's addressed to."

Winston studied the handwriting. Carefully he placed the invitation back in the envelope.

"I think Captain Andrews should see this."

"I think you're right."

Chapter 26

Dr. Wetmore parked her DeSoto behind the church to hide it from the road. The police seemed to be leaving her alone during the day, but she thought it best not to take chances. At least she didn't have to break into the vicarage; she knew that Simon kept the spare key under the Saint Francis statue in the doorway garden. Captain Andrews had probably given the house a thorough going over, but sometimes the amateur eye sees things the trained eye cannot, and she was familiar with the house in ways the police would not be.

The interior of the vicarage looked unchanged since Dr. Wetmore had last been there with Winston. Every little knickknack and *objet d'art* appeared to be in its correct place, the many photographs undisturbed on the walls. Having spent so much time in the house, Dr. Wetmore didn't experience the same misgivings and excitement that she had at Jack's. She had left an unhappy Skippy back at her house, feeling it best that he not be with her this time. If someone tried to enter her home while she was gone, they might think twice if they heard Skippy barking.

Relaxing behind Simon's desk, she began a slow

exploration of the drawers in her search of the clippings Simon had mentioned to her over the phone, the ones dealing with the Berrys and their irritation with the hunt committee. Somehow she just knew this whole problem had to do with the Berrys. Simon had discovered the connection and there was no reason she couldn't either. It took an hour, but she found them in a fat file marked "Wistfield Bicentennial." Simon had underlined in yellow magic marker the letter from Sam Berry and the *Roundabout* reporter's article on the hunt committee's gift of books to the library. It was odd to see the old photograph of Flo Perkins and Cynthia Hall. They seemed so young, so vibrant. She was reminded of her own younger days and when she had first come to Wistfield. It was certainly a different village in those days, unimportant and parochial and far removed from the mainstream of the world. Nowadays, although it was an hour-and-a-half drive from New York, some considered it a suburb of the city. Strangers would stop and ask her from the safety of their cars what she thought of the school system. She always told them there was no school system and that children were bussed to New Holland over by the river. That usually caused a stir. Of course, Wistfield had a wonderful school and it would stay that way as long as it remained small and uncongested with enrichment-harassed toddlers from the yuppie homes of New York. Dr. Wetmore gave out a humpf.

None of the clippings added anything to Dr. Wetmore's knowledge, except that the tone of the letter was more aggressively bitter than Simon had implied. Whatever reason Sam Berry had had for keeping the hunt off his land, it was highly emo-

216

tional. Now that all the principals involved were dead, no one might ever learn what that reason was.

Dr. Wetmore glanced through the eight photographs still lying on top of the desk. All were of two or three people posing for the camera in what appeared to be a younger Wistfield. She recognized some of the buildings. Winston thought Simon had discovered the murderer in a photo. How that could be, Dr. Wetmore wasn't sure. For five minutes she sat there staring at the photographs on the wall opposite the desk, letting what she knew float through her mind. Turning one of the photos before her over, she discovered on the back the name and phone number of the antique dealer who had sold the pictures to Simon. Dr. Wetmore was dialing the number before she even knew why or what she was going to ask. A Mr. Shaw picked up on the third ring.

"Mr. Shaw, this is Dr. Janice Wetmore calling from over in Wistfield. I'm an old friend of Simon Tart. Yes. Yes he's . . . eh, doing fine. Of course. I'm calling because of some photographs you sold to Simon recently. Would you remember that sale? You do? Eh huh. Eh huh. Would you remember what exactly was in those nine photographs? You would? I see. Eh huh. Eh huh. I tell you why. I've managed to mix them up with some others and it's important that they be separated out. That would be helpful."

As Mr. Shaw gave a quick review of the pictures an idea began to form in Dr. Wetmore's mind. She waited for the dealer to finish.

"I see. Another question, if I might. Would you possibly remember the faces in these photos? I mean, if I showed you another photo of someone could you possibly recognize them as having been in one of those you sold Simon? Yes. I understand. Of course you couldn't. I'd love to. This afternoon would be wonderful. Thank you, Mr. Shaw. Certainly."

Dr. Wetmore hung up and began calculating her time. If she left now, she could be in Cornwall, Connecticut in forty-five minutes. Well, she would never make it back in time to honor her five-o'clock curfew, but what the heck. It wasn't like she was breaking into people's houses or doing anything wrong. The captain would just have to understand.

Standing, Dr. Wetmore went straight over to the wall opposite the desk and took down a large framed photograph that hung there. Tucking it under one arm, she gave her hair a quick check in the hall mirror, put on her coat, and headed for Cornwall.

Chapter 27

Amy Cog snorted a laugh and smacked her husband's hand as he reached for the cookies she'd just taken from the oven.

"Now what do you think of a wife that beats her husband, Mr. Wyc? Might that be grounds for divorce?"

"Divorce?" shouted Mrs. Cog. "You'd better watch it, Mr. Cog. I might just take you up on it. That new postman's been giving me the eye."

"That little fellow can hardly heft his bag about the village much less give you the kind of bear hugs *you're* used to." Herb Cog gave Winston an exaggerated wink.

"Don't be talking like that in front of the paying guests, Mr. Cog, or you'll be looking for someone else to make you cookies." Mrs. Cog took another swipe at Mr. Cog's hand. "So what is it you want to know about the Underground Railroad, Mr. Wyc?"

Winston had tried repeatedly to get them to call him Winston but they refused. As long as he was a "paying guest," as Mrs. Cog put it, he'd be addressed by his surname. He'd given up asking.

"Your grandfather said he actually saw this hiding place for runaway slaves, or was told about it?"

Mrs. Cog pursed her lips and stared off into the depths of her sink. Turning abruptly, she spoke with authority.

"He definitely saw it. I remember him saying it was a cave. A large cave near the house. Isn't that what he said, Dad?"

"That's how I recall it," said Mr. Cog.

"It wasn't *under* the house?" asked Winston.

"Nope. He said it was near the house but disguised in some way. I don't remember how. I wish I did. Dad here's been looking for that cave for years."

"That's right. As kids we used to try and find it, but we never did."

"Were you ever in the cottage?"

"Sure, but it wasn't a cottage before Mr. Joyce fixed it up. It was a storage shed. Used to keep garden equipment in it. Tractors. That sort of thing."

"There wasn't any big cupboard on the back wall?"

"Cupboard?" Mr. Cog thought about that. "No, don't believe so. The back wall was fieldstone."

"I think that back wall leads to a cave," said Winston.

"How's that?" asked Mr. Cog, sitting up straight.

Winston explained the wardrobe and why he thought it hid the entrance to a cave. Another idea occurred to Winston. "Unless there was another entrance."

"I've never been in the new cottage," said Mr. Cog.

"I *told* you that Mr. Joyce was up to no good. Probably got that Mr. Tart hidden behind that cabinet. That's where Dr. Wetmore should be looking." Mrs. Cog gave a quick nod of her head.

"I wouldn't go that far, but I sure would like to give it a look. If only for historical reasons," said Winston.

"What's keepin' you?" asked Mr. Cog, enjoying a stolen cookie.

"Mr. Joyce and his sidekick there go blank every time I mention it."

"Maybe they don't know about it?"

"I hadn't thought of that," said Winston. There was a chance that James might not know, but Bill would certainly have to. Mrs. Cog hurried from the kitchen to answer the phone.

"It's for you, Mr. Wyc. A young lady by the sound of her."

"Hello." Winston sat on the carpeted stairs in the hallway. "Hi. Yeah, I dropped it off at the police station on my way back here. He didn't call you? That's odd. I thought he would. I told him he should put a patrol car in your driveway at night. Uh huh. Sure, but Mrs. Cog might object. I don't think I'm allowed all-night lady visitors. Will I still get to see you tonight?"

Winston listened.

"It has to be tonight? Do you know who they are? Uh huh. How long will it take? I'm not one to stand in the way of making money. How's this, why don't I meet you there, say around nine? Sure. Till then."

"That reminds me," said Mrs. Cog as Winston re-entered the kitchen. "Some girl from the New Holland *Observer* called earlier. Said she was a reporter. Left her name and number by the phone. Mary Bartlett, I think she called herself."

"I was wondering when the press was going to

catch up with me. We're not supposed to talk to them."

"I told her that. She said she was interested in the history of the area and not the murder."

"I bet," said Winston.

"That wouldn't have been your TV-watching friend on the phone just now, was it?" Mr. Cog gave his wife a sly smile.

"Sure was," said Winston.

"That the Phillips girl?"

"Dad, I told you not to . . ."

"It's okay, Mrs. Cog. I don't think it has to be a secret. Erika and I are big people."

"Well, I know that, but it's none of our business." Mrs. Cog glared at her husband. She turned back to Winston. "And you're right, no all-night visitors. What did you drop off at the police station?"

Winston smiled.

"My TV-watching friend received an odd invitation in the mail today. I gave it to Captain Andrews."

Mr. and Mrs. Cog stared at Winston in anticipation.

"Odd?" asked Mrs. Cog.

"It was addressed to her mother."

"That letter's five years too late," said Mr. Cog.

"It wasn't mailed. Someone placed it there."

"You gave it to the captain. Did it have something to do with the murders?" asked Mrs. Cog.

Amy doesn't miss a trick, thought Winston. How much should he tell her?

"It was an invitation to dinner. Printed by hand."

"Who wrote it?" asked Mr. Cog.

"That's the weird part. There was no address or date, but it was signed 'J. Berry.'"

The three of them sat in the kitchen staring at the cookies.

"Sounds like a prank to me," said Mr. Cog.

"If it is it's one helluva misguided prank," said Winston.

"Maybe the Berry boy *is* in town? Maybe he's . . ." Amy Cog's voice trailed off.

"Exactly," said Winston, heading for the door.

"You going out? Dinner be ready in half an hour."

Winston took a moment to think. "Erika's got a buyer showing up late at the gallery. I'm going to meet her at nine. That gives me a little over three hours . . . Mr. Cog, I'm going to take your advice and go ask Bill about the wardrobe. I've got time and it's starting to bug me. He's been out of town for the last three days and I haven't had the chance. That and the fact that the Worthwell estate, as far as I can find out, was never sold. That makes two big questions he can answer."

"Did you mention that to the captain?" asked Mrs. Cog. "About the sale?"

"Yeah, I did. He said that if Bill was this Berry guy it wasn't against the law to change your name or present yourself as someone else as long as you weren't misrepresenting yourself for illegal reasons. Bill might be acting as a caretaker for the Berry estate or something and pretending to be a gentleman. As long as the estate files no complaints it's not a problem."

"You think that might be the case?"

"Who knows?"

"Well there's certainly plenty of men running around Wistfield nowadays pretending to be gentlemen," said Mrs. Cog. "And the captain doesn't

223

think this is connected in any way with these kill-ings?"

"I don't know how it could be."

"Maybe the answer's in that hidden cave." Mr. Cog poked out his cheek with his tongue.

"We'll know soon enough. I still can't believe the whole situation isn't completely innocent."

"You're probably right. Sure would like to come with you, though." Mr. Cog looked expectantly over to Mrs. Cog.

"You're going nowhere, Herb Cog. You can stay right where you are and eat a good supper. This younger generation is going to die of . . . of anorex-ems or whatever it's called. Taking to the night without a decent meal. Couldn't wait till tomorrow, I bet." Mrs. Cog tried out a series of lesser humpfs.

"It could, I guess, but I have the time right now. I'm too antsy. Tell you what. I'll come back here after I talk to Bill. Give you the lowdown."

"Good idea." Mrs. Cog couldn't resist a little data for information central. "There'll be supper warm-ing in the oven should you decide you want to live past thirty. And Winston."

"Yeah?"

"Be careful." Mrs. Cog gave Winston a quick, tight-mouthed nod.

"Wouldn't want to miss your home cooking. See you later."

Getting into the car, Winston could faintly hear the phone ringing. Wondering if it might be Erika again, he hesitated. Not hearing his name called, and figuring it was probably one of Mrs. Cog's many town spies, Winston rolled out of the drive and headed for town. Rolling the car window up against the night chill, he pulled away just as Mrs. Cog called for him from the front porch.

Driving slowly past the gallery, Winston checked to see if Erika had arrived with the client. The lights were out and the place looked empty. Erika had said she knew who the buyer was and not to worry. Cracking the window slightly, he let the cool air curl around him and thought about what he was going to say to Bill. Something else had been bothering him—and not just the wardrobe or the sale. Something that Ed Worth had said that didn't make sense unless Bill had been there at the house all along.

Winston watched the last rays of the sunset fading in the distance. He thought about his subleased apartment in New York. If he was about to lose his job, he had no place to stay for the next three months. He wondered if he'd be any good at selling art.

Chapter 28

Mr. Harvey Shaw ran a tidy store. The old books, prints, and photographs were kept under glass, and if a customer should request a peek at something, he hovered as a jeweler showing the Hope Diamond might. Mr. Shaw could become visibly upset if two different customers should have the audacity to ask to see something at the same time. He parted with his wares like misers from their money. A thin man of medium height, he had that particular physique peculiar to men who spend their lives standing behind a counter; a sunken chest and round, protruding stomach, as if the chest at some point gives in to gravity and collapses, coming to rest just above the beltline. In the right hands these stomachs can become tools of harassment, and Dr. Wetmore waited and watched while Mr. Shaw belly-pushed a browser around his store and finally out the door.

"I'm not here for the casual shopper, Mrs. Wetmore. My usual clientele is highly erudite and knowledgeable in what I sell. They know exactly what they want before they get here. Your friend Vicar Tart is just such a client." Mr. Shaw attacked a dust mote. "My people have been coming to me for years. I never disappoint."

"Dealing with the general public can be tiring," allowed Dr. Wetmore.

"I take it you speak from experience."

"I was a doctor for forty years, Mr. Shaw. My clients knew exactly what *they* wanted too, except they were mostly wrong."

"I can't even imagine." Mr. Shaw showed just the right touch of personal horror before proceeding. "Now, you had a question about a photograph?"

"Yes, I did. It's an odd request, and I hope I'm not wasting your time, but the vicar and I are trying to identify a figure in one of the prints you sold him, and . . ." here Dr. Wetmore placed the framed photograph she had brought on the counter, ". . . we wondered if you recognized anyone in this print as someone from one of those others."

Mr. Shaw regarded the doctor with a bemused pucker. "Can't you just compare the two photos? That would seem the easiest way."

"I'm afraid the other photo has been lost." Dr. Wetmore tried the declarative approach. It had usually worked with patient's x-rays.

"I see." Mr. Shaw was obviously troubled. He inspected Dr. Wetmore through and then over his half glasses. "How come Mr. Tart isn't here?"

"Vicar Tart is out of town. Family business."

Mr. Shaw gave the photo before him a quick glance.

"I don't see the problem, Mr. Shaw. I'm not asking you to do anything wrong. You have to merely look at this photograph of the Wistfield Hunt Club and tell me if anyone in it seems vaguely familiar. You don't strike me as the kind of man who allows prints to pass casually through his hands. I'm sure each print is regarded with care and remembered

with affection, particularly when sold so recently."
Dr. Wetmore had to stop herself from batting her
eyelashes. "You'll be doing Simon Tart a great service, believe me."

Hesitating for a second, Mr. Shaw repositioned
his stomach and gave the picture another glance.
"The faces are very small."

"You mentioned a photo taken outside the old
Wistfield Inn. That would be the one I lost."

"Ahhh, yes. It was three girls posing in what appeared to be bridesmaids' gowns."

"Three girls?" Dr. Wetmore was disappointed.

"And . . . oh yes, now I remember, in the background stood a man watching them. I remember because the man was obviously annoyed with the girls
in some way . . . as if he didn't like what they were
doing. A large man with a brooding face. He was
standing in the door of the inn."

"Do you see that man in this photo?"

"This is a recent photograph, Mrs. Wetmore.
That man would now be in his eighties or nineties.
I doubt if I'd recognize him."

"Try."

Mr. Shaw registered his displeasure with a sigh
and then held the picture up close to his face, working it this way and that in the dim light.

"Strangely enough, this man standing over to the
side, by the car, could almost be the one except he
looks much too young."

"Which one?" Dr. Wetmore almost knocked the
frame out of Mr. Shaw's hands.

"This fellow here holding his hat."

Dr. Wetmore studied the man closely, shaking
her head.

"Are you sure?" she asked in a small voice.

"Well, no, I can't be sure, but it certainly could be the son of the man in that photo I sold Mr. Tart. But then again, it is a type, isn't it?"

Dr. Wetmore thought at first that Mr. Shaw had made a mistake in the face he'd pointed out, but the longer she stared at the person, the more it made sense. Winston had been right when he talked of having to remove the facade to find the original house.

"Mr. Shaw, you've been a great help. Mr. Tart will be very pleased."

"I certainly hope so. You will have him call me?"

"Of course. Is there a public phone nearby?" asked Dr. Wetmore eyeing the counter.

Mr. Shaw involuntarily looked at his own phone and then quickly away. "I believe you can find one at the general store. That's two stores up the street. They have one of those old types with the closing door. Very private."

Dr. Wetmore thanked Mr. Shaw again and, grabbing her photograph, headed out the door. Two doors up she found one of those new general stores that had been painstakingly modeled to resemble someone's idea of what "ye olde general store" *should* have looked like. The floor was blanketed in one inch of sawdust, the little shavings finding their way into Dr. Wetmore's shoes before she was halfway across the store. She glowered as she passed the perfect fruit and vegetables arranged in strict pyramids, daring you to touch them. Metal signs hung everywhere, evoking a time when a one-inch brownie didn't cost three dollars, penny candy actually cost a penny, and a coke meant soda pop. Dr. Wetmore scowled back at the professor behind the counter who made it clear he was not happy to change her dollar into quarters. Sitting in the phone booth, she picked off sawdust stuck to her stockings.

Mrs. Cog answered on the second ring.

"He's just out the door? Where was he going?" Dr. Wetmore listened while Mrs. Cog told of Winston's proposed evening itinerary. "Is he still in the drive?" Dr. Wetmore waited until Mrs. Cog returned to tell her it was too late, that she'd just missed him.

"Drat!" said Dr. Wetmore.

"Have you heard the latest?" asked Mrs. Cog.

"What's that, Amy?"

Amy Cog told Dr. Wetmore about the mysterious invitation that Erika Phillips had received. Glancing at her watch, the doctor noticed she was almost out past curfew. Captain Andrews probably had the state police already looking for her.

"You say he just left?"

"Just this minute," said Amy.

If Dr. Wetmore went the back way to Wistfield, she would miss Winston by only fifteen or twenty minutes.

"Thanks, Amy. Got to run. Bye."

Winston had to be warned, thought Dr. Wetmore. She could stop by the police barracks, but that would take her out of the way and waste valuable time. She would have to find Winston at the Joyce house and tell him what she knew. The glass booth made an excellent mirror, and Dr. Wetmore hastily braided her naughty hair for the adventure ahead.

Chapter 29

Parking the car at the turnaround, Winston stared up at the dark house silhouetted against the gray sunset. Storm clouds were gathering on the far hills. Mrs. Cog had mentioned the likelihood of snow, and the sky appeared to reinforce that possibility. Winston watched the fading light, uncertain of what to do. The impulse that had driven him from the Cogs's had fizzled and the prospect of actually confronting Bill didn't seem like such a good idea now. Leaves fell from the maples. In the good old days, remembered Winston, people planted a tree at each corner of their new home for good luck. The idea was to plant trees that lasted, which usually meant maples or oaks. It could be a good indication of how large the original structure might have been. *Let's stop playing Professor Wyc*, Winston said to himself. Relieved to see that neither the house nor the cottage had lights on, he decided this would be the perfect time to explore.

Taking a screwdriver from the glove compartment, Winston walked quickly past the main house and down to the cottage. All was in darkness. I wonder where the fellows might be? he thought. Maybe watching me this very minute, ready to jump out and arrest my heartbeat. Winston had felt more relaxed walking through Harlem.

The cottage door swung open. In the dim light the wardrobe loomed massive and sinister against the far wall. Winston sang out "Anybody home?" as he crossed the room to turn on a table lamp near the armoire and quickly inspect the cabinet doors. He was surprised to feel the knob turn and the door come open. Involuntarily, Winston stepped back from the expected cave. Taking in a breath, he cautioned a look into the cabinet, but all that the interior revealed were several outfits of decidedly feminine aspect, if of a somewhat leathery charm.

"Bill, you jaded devil," said Winston aloud. "Maybe I'm wrong after all." Reaching in, he gave the back panel a tentative push. The panel moaned and gave slightly. Winston leaned on it harder. With a gruesome creak the rear of the cabinet slid away from his hand and the silky moist breath of dank air brushed his face.

"Oh, boy." Winston stood staring into the hollow darkness. Was he ready to step into the mouth of the monster? Looking back over his shoulder, he listened for any sound, any movement that might discourage such a rash inclination. He heard nothing to dissuade him. At the bottom of the wardrobe Winston found two large, battery-powered lanterns. Switching on a light, he examined the passageway ahead. The sides of the entrance were covered with rough pine boards going back ten feet. Beyond that it appeared to be dirt. Taking one last look behind him, Winston stepped over the bottom rail of Bill's Pandora's box and entered what looked like a mine shaft. He took care to close the panel in case someone returned. At least they wouldn't discover him immediately.

234

Chapter 30

Dr. Wetmore slowed her heart and her DeSoto as she rounded the next curve, the last one having been sharper than she remembered. Wrapping herself around a tree wasn't going to help anyone. Nonetheless, the road had been empty and she had made good time. Winston would have beat her to the Worthwell estate by maybe fifteen minutes. Concentrating half on the road and half on the immediate future, she thought out what she would do when she got there. On her previous visit, she had noticed a turnoff halfway up the driveway and a hundred yards from the main house. She would hide the car there and cut through the woods to the cottage. Winston had told Amy he was going to confront Bill about some cave or other that he believed was hidden in the cottage. Dr. Wetmore would try to get Winston alone and confront him with what she now knew. Winston was going to be very surprised. They had all been looking in the wrong corners.

A few snowflakes began to fall as Dr. Wetmore pulled her car into the turnoff and just out of sight of the drive. Dr. Wetmore missed Skippy. He would be a great comfort at the moment. She closed her eyes and envisioned him lying by the back door waiting impatiently for her to return. He'd pretend to be mad for a few hours before hopping on the bed and burrowing forgivingly under the comforter. Bed would be very pleasant about now, she thought. Through the trees, Dr. Wetmore could see what appeared to be the lights of the main house. Bundling up against the cold, she switched on her flashlight and bounded into the woods.

Ten minutes later Dr. Wetmore stared through a yew hedge just on the other side of the garden across from the cottage. She had skirted the main house and followed the hedge down the hill. Winston's car was nowhere in sight, but she reasoned it could be parked up by the house. At one point she had seen Bill and the carpenter walking down the drive, but they had disappeared, possibly into the cottage, which was all lit up, the front door standing open. Snow had begun to drift onto the carpet just inside the door. Dr. Wetmore closed her eyes and listened for sounds other than falling snow. The night was sharply quiet.

Bill should learn to trim his peonies back in the fall, six inches from the ground, she chided as she tiptoed through the frozen garden and up to a window. Seeing no one, she eased herself around the open door. The cottage living room was empty. Dr. Wetmore shut the door behind her. Standing statuelike, she once again listened for any noise. This time she could hear something. A faint sound that came from a great distance. The odd thing was the sound didn't come from the outside. She heard it again. It seemed muffled, as if someone was working inside a closed chest. Dr. Wetmore cautiously opened the door to Joyce's study. Finding no one, she explored the kitchen. About to go up the stairs, she paused beside a large armoire that took up much of the back wall in the living room. She ran her hand over the raised carvings of the doors. Serpents and winged lions writhed on the panels, ingesting one another, forming a circle of savage appetites. What a hideous piece of furniture, she thought. It would give me nightmares to have it in my house. One of the doors stood slightly ajar, and Dr. Wetmore ventured a peek inside. Letting out a gasp, she fell backward as a rush of warm air startled her. It had felt like the breath of one of the beasts carved on the doors. Dr. Wetmore sat in a chair.

Calming herself, she studied the yawning wardrobe before her. Other than the stale, trapped air, something else seemed amiss about the piece. The back panel seemed too dark, too . . . Suddenly she realized there *was* no back panel. Jumping up, she gazed into the darkness, feeling for what was not there. She heard the noise again. Deep within the dark, men's voices gently rumbled back up from the bowels of the earth. This was the cave Winston had been talking about! He had been right about its existence. That was probably he, and perhaps Bill, exploring its depths.

Taking out her small flashlight, Dr. Wetmore stepped over the bottom rail of the armoire and entered the cave. After ten yards, she turned to look back at the rectangular opening of light from the cottage. For a moment, Dr. Wetmore realized she didn't want to let go of that warm rectangle, that she should go back into the living room and call Captain Andrews. She heard the men's voices again. What could go wrong? Wasn't Winston here? And she needn't be afraid of Bill. I'll be cautious,

237

she said to herself. I'll proceed slowly and not rush. Whoever is here, I'll check first to see who it is before I let myself be known.

Biting at her lower lip, Dr. Wetmore inched forward, keeping the small oval of light from her flashlight on the ground close to her feet.

Chapter 31

The light playing out before him, Winston probed deeper and deeper into the earth. At two points the passageway was met by smaller, narrower shafts, and Winston wondered if these led to other entrances. The cavity did not appear man-made anymore but a natural phenomenon, like the pictures Winston had seen in brochures of caves one could visit as a tourist. The idea had always seemed silly to him, a subway system with stalagmites. The thick air grew colder. Time had less and less relevance the further Winston moved into the depths. He couldn't tell how long he'd been in the passageway. Suddenly the tunnel widened. Holding up the lantern, Winston exposed below him a large room with what looked like several smaller caves on the far side. At his feet, steps had been chiseled in the rock leading down ten feet onto the cave floor. The room was approximately one hundred feet long and forty feet wide, with the ceiling disappearing into the shadows above. The floor had been leveled and tamped hard. Stored along one side were old trunks and boxes, some broken, their contents spilling out onto the dirt floor. Along the other side some rough tables, chairs, and beds were arranged for use, although the dust on them looked undisturbed for centuries. Shelves hung in disrepair from where they had been stacked into the dirt walls. The dust on the floor, though, revealed many recent footprints.

Winston felt a chill. It wasn't the temperature. The room had the clammy, still cold of a tomb. Slowly descending the stairs, he walked the length of the room, staying in the middle. He explored the caves at the other end. The one on the left was a smaller cave with a pit or hole near the entrance. This hole was covered by a rusting metal grate, while the other formed a niche only a few feet deep. Winston couldn't get his lantern deep enough inside the grate to see what was in the hole. It appeared to be quite deep. He would try to remove the grate later after he'd explored the main room.

Walking back into the main room, Winston stood and watched the shadows made by his light dance above him. This must have been used for the Underground Railroad. The cave had obviously been set up to hide several runaways at a time, and it was perfectly safe. The only problem was that it seemed somewhat off the rail line, if Winston remembered his history correctly. Slaves were smuggled into Canada through Pennsylvania, particularly after the Supreme Court ruled on the Dred Scott case. The ruling made it possible for slaveowners to come into the North and claim their runaways, the court holding that slaves were not citizens of this great land but actually property of their masters. Suddenly no black person was safe anywhere in the States. Although Winston had read of isolated incidents of slaves coming through New York, those reports had never been proved. Of course, smuggling slaves was against the law and not many people were going to admit to it.

Setting the lantern down, Winston inspected one of the trunks nearest him. It was the size of an old steamer trunk and was held shut with a mildewed leather strap. The strap snapped easily, sending up a silky cool shower of dust. Winston was amazed to find the crate full of old Civil War military uniforms and hardware used for bivouacking. One jacket in particular struck Winston's fancy, and he dusted and straightened it out on the trunk next to him. Several rusted medals still clung to the breast, and one epaulet hung by a thread, but the coat was ready to wear. To Winston the boxes were a historian's dream, and no less exciting than had they come from King Tut's tomb. He was so engrossed with the discovery that it took him a few seconds to realize that the noise he'd just heard was the creaking of the back panel on the wardrobe. Running to the steps, Winston could hear the sound of men coming down the tunnel. Quickly crouching behind a crate, Winston turned off his lantern and waited. In the quiet darkness he could hear the muffled voice of Bill Joyce talking to someone, and then a lantern beam danced on the walls. Winston pushed his shoulder so hard into the dirt wall beside him it hurt.

"No one's happy about things, Eddie. Subtlety, Ed, that's the way in this life. A big smile and the casual twist. Mark my words, I've studied the options."

Winston could hear Ed Worth grunt.

"Always this attitude. Aren't you taking your medicine?"

"Fuck medicine," said Ed. "Didn't I tell you this whole idea was bullshit."

"You did, Eddie, and maybe you were right, but it's too late to back out now. We aren't thinking along those lines, are we?"

Bill's question was a slowly enunciated threat. Winston couldn't hear Ed's answer but the man's tone was sullen. The two men were now standing on top of where Winston was hiding and he wasn't sure how much longer he could hold his breath.

"Where's the ladder?" asked Bill.

"In the hole."

"Well, that's a stupid place to leave it."

"Someone's been in these trunks," said Eddie, his voice suddenly loud in the close space.

"Damn, you're right," whispered Bill. "Who in the . . ."

Winston had heard it too. Incongruously, it sounded like someone calling his name.

"Get out of sight," whispered Bill.

Unexpectedly, Winston found himself crouching next to Ed Worth. The man stared at Winston in open disbelief.

"Hi, guy." Winston gave the surprised man a little wave.

"What the fuck?" Ed actually pointed at Winston.

"Shut up," Bill hissed from close by.

"It's the fucking history jerk. I'm hiding next to the fucking history jerk."

"I beg your pardon," said Winston.

All three men were standing, staring at each other, when Dr. Wetmore appeared at the top of the steps that led down into the cave. Squinting, she peered at the men standing in the shadows.

"Winston, are you there? I heard your voice."

"Turn around and run, Janice. Get the hell out of here!" shouted Winston.

"Get her, Eddie!"

Ed started off but Winston shoved him flying into a table. Such a dust cloud rose up it was difficult to see anyone. Two shots rang out, deafening and painful in the small space. Winston grabbed at his ears.

"Anyone moves and I'll shoot Mr. Wyc!" Bill shouted above the noise. The dust settled in sync with the echoing gunshot, revealing three people in various attitudes of flight. Dr. Wetmore was not present.

"I mean it!" shouted Bill, racing to the step end of the cave. "I'll shoot Mr. Wyc."

A moment passed and Dr. Wetmore's head appeared in the tunnel.

"Get down here, Doctor. It's in your best interest to obey."

"A gun, Bill? I'm impressed. Janice, what are you doing here?" Winston tried to ignore the gun in Bill's wavering hand.

"I'm not sure why I'm here at the moment, but I did come to tell you I'm sure now that there is a Mr. Berry."

"I think it could have waited," answered Winston, who watched to see if Bill had responded to Janice's disclosure. Instead of surprise, Bill's face showed fright.

"Another word and I'll start shooting again." Bill looked capable of doing anything. He waved his gun in the general direction of the tunnel end of the cave. "Eddie, do something with Mr. Wyc here. I'll see to the doctor."

"Like what?" asked Eddie.

"Use your damn head. I don't know. Tie him up. Throw him in the hole." Bill's voice was a harsh whisper. "Don't move, Doctor. We need to talk."

As Ed bound Winston in some torn raiment of old cloth, Bill talked in a low voice to Dr. Wetmore at the far end. Winston wondered who Janice thought was Mr. Berry. Winston had put together a whole scenario starring Bill Joyce, but he obviously wasn't the one Janice was talking about.

Winston was testing the strength of Ed's bindings when he was struck from behind. His last sensation was that of falling through the eye socket of a skull into a long, dark tunnel that ended in a hard crash of fiery red.

Chapter 32

Dr. Wetmore asked Bill if he wouldn't push so hard, for she couldn't see all that well in the dark, which was bunk of course; she could see as well as a healthy cat. She needed time to think. Winston was in trouble and she wasn't sure *she* would see the sun rise again on Wistfield. Little old ladies seemed to be this man's specialty, and she had left her mace in her bag in the DeSoto. The journey up the tunnel went too quickly, and they were standing in the cottage living room before Dr. Wetmore could devise an escape. All at once she felt disoriented and too old for this misadventure. Her mind refused to come up with any solutions. Her body wanted only to sit down and rest, its flight mechanisms asleep for the night. Silently they stood waiting for Ed. Bill wouldn't look at her and busied himself with watching the tunnel entrance. The wardrobe reminded Dr. Wetmore of that C.S. Lewis tale, only this time the fantasy land offered neither hope nor adventure. At last Ed's gaunt face smirked at the closet opening. Closing the cabinet door behind him, he motioned to Bill that all was secured.

"What have you done to Mr. Wyc?" Dr. Wetmore

realized she sounded like some fretful old teacher. She took a deep breath.

"I wouldn't worry about Mr. Wyc, Doctor. If you'll excuse us." Bill motioned for Ed to follow him. They stepped just outside the front door to confer. Dr. Wetmore looked back at the hideous wardrobe, worrying about poor Winston. For all she knew the boy was dead. If she could get to a phone she could leave a message with Mrs. Cog to call Captain Andrews. The captain had been right of course—this was not "Mystery Theater"—but she wasn't defeated yet. Watching the door, she inched toward the study. Ed came back in from outside just as Dr. Wetmore reached for the knob.

"That's enough exploring for now, Doc. Have a seat. Mr. Joyce will be right back."

"Where has he gone?"

Ed Worth only stared at her, his face drawn tight with a half grin. He took out a cigarette, packing it on the back of his thumbnail. Dr. Wetmore made a few attempts at conversation but Ed wasn't interested. He stood facing out at the night, smoking and tapping his finger on the windowsill. Fifteen minutes later, Bill Joyce could be heard crunching on the gravel outside the cottage. Snow blew in with him as he entered.

"You've been invited to a party, Doctor. It's come as you were." Bill laughed at his little joke and ducked back out the door.

Encouraged by Ed Worth, Dr. Wetmore followed Bill Joyce outside and was surprised to find it snowing quite hard. The flakes were large and covered her clothing quickly. She thought of Skippy and wondered if he was still waiting at the back door.

Bill Joyce's lantern threw a dim and hallucinatory

246

light on the driveway before them. The falling snow seen through the soft illumination gave Dr. Wetmore the unsettling impression of having stepped into a fairy tale, the terrible kind in which too many children get eaten. Suddenly the scaffolding loomed out of the darkness, a steel carapace that caught and reflected the beam of Joyce's lamp, giving the house beneath a metallic and sinister aspect. A delicate light in the first-floor windows moved and flickered, suggesting the play of candles. A dark silhouette billowed and stirred against the glass.

Standing in the unlit entrance hall, Dr. Wetmore shook off the snow and waited in the silence for Bill Joyce, who had gone into another room. Nothing seemed real anymore. Shadow and light played on the mind, confusing the limits between reality and illusion. Numbly she allowed Ed Worth to hold her arm. Within minutes Joyce was back and guiding her into the dining room. She remembered the room from her meeting here with Winston, when it had been partially gutted and littered with the detritus of renovation. The space had undergone some strange alterations since then. The debris had been pushed to the walls, and dominating the center of the room was a large plank table supported by sawhorses. In contrast, six finely carved Queen Anne chairs had been brought in for seating. Brass candelabra at either end of the table provided the light, illuminating the flatware and cutlery that had been laid and leaving the corners of the room dark. No food was evident, but a small covered platter sat shimmering at the head of the table near the fireplace.

Dr. Wetmore drew in a sharp breath as she recognized the woman already seated. Erika Phillips sat gagged and motionless, her eyes wild and entreating, searching Dr. Wetmore's face for answers, but the doctor could only look on in horror.

"Why is that woman being treated that way?" Dr. Wetmore pulled her arm away from Joyce.

"Please be quiet, Doctor, or you too shall find yourself in the same predicament." Bill Joyce motioned for her to sit down.

"I will not. I would like some answers right here and now." Dr. Wetmore moved to the middle of the room. "What in the world is this nightmare?"

"Be seated, Dr. Wetmore, and I shall tell you about a nightmare."

Dr. Wetmore turned toward the voice coming out of the shadows. She recognized instantly the man Mr. Shaw had picked from the photo: Bill's chauffeur, James. In the photograph he had stood off to the side in his chauffeur's uniform, cap in hand, glaring at the ensemble. Now he was elegantly attired in a tuxedo, a bottle of champagne in hand, true lord of the manor, ready to dispense hospitality or horror. Whatever he found appropriate.

"I apologize for the shabby condition of the room. I had hoped the house would be completed before this little party was thrown, but certain events have moved things forward. If you would please be seated."

Dr. Wetmore let herself be positioned into a chair by Bill Joyce.

"William, we need one more glass," said James.

"Yes, sir," said Bill. Joyce disappeared into a back room.

"Ed, would you light the fire?"

"Yes, sir." Ed Worth hurried over to the fireplace. Taking matches from his pocket, he fumbled with lighting the kindling. Instantly the fire flared up, wrapping James in a halo of fiery color. Bill returned with another glass, which he set down before Dr. Wetmore. James handed the champagne to Bill.

"You pour."

Dr. Wetmore exchanged glances with Erika and was happy to see her shake her head as if to say she didn't know what was going on. At least Erika was still lucid. Watching Bill in this role reversal confused the situation even further. Dr. Wetmore tried to concentrate on her glass as Bill filled with a small amount of the bubbling wine, its fizz distinct above the silence of the room. The candlelight dappled the walls and faces of those present. An eye, an expression, a finger tip would appear and then blur. James took his seat at the head of the table.

"My family used to live in this house. They ate at this table. It was given to them by a lady who cared and kept her promises to them. I left this house when I was ten to go away to school, returning only occasionally so that my bitterness might be renewed and not forgotten. You talk about a nightmare, Doctor, I have lived my whole life with a nightmare. A tapestry of horror that began with a word and grew into a life dedicated to revenge. Tonight my nightmare will finally end and I can awake and go back into the world."

"But the hunt committee is all dead," said Dr. Wetmore. "This revenge you speak of has already been satisfied."

"That's not true, Janice. May I call you Janice?"

"There's nobody left." Dr. Wetmore raised her voice in exasperation.

"Julia Westcliff remains, Janice."

"How's that?"

"She sits opposite you at the table."

Dr. Wetmore followed James's face as he looked over at a suddenly very still Erika. His mouth spread slowly, parting in a false smile, but the eyes blazed with such loathing that the doctor had to look away. The man was completely mad, she realized. He mistook Erika for her mother.

"I see sitting across from me Erika Phillips."

James bowed to the suggestion. "As did I until I began to understand the subtlety of the deception. William assures me that I'm correct."

Dr. Wetmore glanced quickly at Bill Joyce, who stood silently in the dim light, his face hidden but his hands tense and rigid at his sides.

"I'm sorry, but you're wrong. That is Erika Phillips. I delivered her myself." James would not take his eyes off Erika. "You are going to kill an innocent person." Dr. Wetmore's voice seemed too loud, too harsh for the room, and she began again, softer and more intense. "Too many people *know* now. You can't get away with this, so why continue?"

"Only you and that Winston person. I made a mistake there. I had wanted the house finished correctly, precisely. The way it had been in the glory years. I thought a young historian, a student, really, would be easy to handle, to manipulate with the immensity of the job. But William had to introduce him around. Had to like him. The historian became too involved."

"You're insane."

James stood quickly, pushing back his chair. He towered over the table, his shadow darkening the faces before him. Unflinching, Dr. Wetmore held her ground, straightening with resolve as James leaned toward her. His voice was low and intimate.

"It doesn't matter, Dr. Wetmore. To the world the Berrys no longer exist, *never* existed as far as Wistfield was concerned. Someone who doesn't breathe or walk can't kill people. Tomorrow Mr. Joyce will fire me and James the chauffeur shall disappear. After an appropriate time I shall come back and enjoy this, my home. No one will recognize me. No one really sees the chauffeur or the gardener or the cook." Ed Worth replaced the chair and went to stand behind Erika. James slowly reseated himself. "You are right, Doctor. I am . . . not well. But the death of this woman will heal me."

Erika went to stand, but Ed Worth touched a knife to the side of her head, his other hand on her shoulder. Erika let out a soft moan and slackened.

"You will excuse me a little melodrama," said James, removing the lid from the platter before him. Resting on the silver plate was a lucky rabbit's foot. "But this is the last one."

Dr. Wetmore and Erika watched with horror as James squeezed the good luck charm between his fingers, rolling the soft fur across his chin.

"But first allow me to tell a story."

Chapter 33

The damp musk of the earth was strong and comforting in Winston's nostrils. Coming to consciousness, he focused on the earthen smell to take his mind off the headache and the cold. His hands and feet were bound with cloth that sliced into his skin. Pulling his knees up to his chest for warmth, Winston slowly opened his eyes and peered out into a darkness so complete he blinked twice to assure himself that his lids had actually parted. Points of colored light began to dance in the void before him, only to vanish, then reappear. He realized his mind was not accepting this complete absence of light and was manufacturing its own. Leaning back, Winston focused on the dots, clearing his mind of the anguish and the cold.

The events leading up to his present predicament seeped back into his sensibilities like poison. Twisting his body violently into a sitting position, Winston shouted out from the pain in his wrists and ankles. Falling sideways, he lay perfectly still, allowing the pounding to subside to a manageable level. If he was going to get out of this mess, he needed to proceed cautiously and with some hint of intelligence. Ed and Bill might come back at any moment to check on him. Or worse.

Winston went back over his last conscious hour again. There had been a cave and Bill knew about it. Why the big secret? Unless it wasn't Bill's place to make that decision . . . or unless this space was being saved for dubious purposes. What did Bill do for a living? Was the cave in some way connected to the murders? Had Bantram come across the cave? And what about Janice? Too many questions for the moment. Winston wriggled slightly to his left. He seemed to be lying on a bed of sticks or kindling; the roughness was causing him considerable discomfort. Moving again, the sticks produced a dry rattle, a soft, jangly sound like bones being scattered on rocks. Winston probed behind him with his hands into the pile. The sticks were smooth and brittle. Winston's hands rested on a round stone that was pocked with indentations and . . . Winston tried to scuttle away. This rock had teeth. This rock was a skull.

Winston scrambled backward over the bones, trying to rid himself of their touch. Digging his heels into the pile, he catapulted himself straight into a wall. He tried rolling in the opposite direction and then back to his right, but the space was completely layered with bones and skulls, their rounded knobs and sharp edges stabbing into him as he thrashed to avoid them. The pounding in his head and wrists finally overcame his desire to escape this skeletal carpet. Great gasps of air slowly calmed his shaking body. In the silence that settled back over him, Winston imagined he heard a soft moan. He strained to hear it again. Somewhere in this hellhole was another person or animal, and it was breathing in a low, muted, guttural rasp. Every hair on Winston's body extended, his skin crawled with fear. He listened, his body frozen in time. The rasping was lower now, expiring. His movement had disturbed something. Winston waited, listening until he could no longer hear anything. The need to escape became overpowering. Pains and aches would have to be ignored. And skeletons couldn't hurt you. If they were dead . . .

Pushing his hands down, Winston tried to sit back up but instead slipped on another skull, his weight closing the mouth of this skull around his wrist and inflicting more pain. Winston squirmed to his right but the teeth still caught to his hand. An idea came to him. A little farfetched, he reasoned, but under the circumstances anything was worth a try. Forcibly twisting his hands, he felt the lower jawbone break loose from the skull. Slowly Winston worked the bone up and against his lower back, where he pinned it between his belt and the binding wrapped around his wrists. Moving his hands up and down slowly, tightly, he hoped the teeth might act as a saw and cut through the cloth. Testing the binding, Winston could feel a distinct loosening. The only problem was that the teeth had all come loose and the jaw was now toothless.

Cautiously pushing himself over the mound, Winston found another skull. An eternity passed and two more skulls sacrificed their molars, but suddenly the cloth snapped free and Winston sat rubbing his bruised and bleeding wrists. Untying his feet, he stood deliberately, calming his excited brain and concentrating on his next move. Bill had mentioned a hole and Winston remembered seeing such a hole at the far end of the cave. It had been covered with a metal grate. This is where he must have been tossed. A ladder had also been mentioned, and hopefully Fast Eddie Worth had once again forgotten to remove it. Easing over to a wall, Winston followed it with his hands, groping to one corner and then to another. Was it possible the ladder was standing in the center of the space? Maybe there was no ladder . . .

Placing his hands out in front of him, Winston batted at the air, crunching his way toward what he imagined to be the center. Twice he met the far wall. On his third crossing Winston stumbled on something large and soft and animallike. The animal moaned and Winston threw himself to one side. On his hands and knees, ten inches deep in bones, Winston pinched his eyes shut as tight as he could, squeezing from his mind the fear and horror. His body began to shake. Time to be intelligent, he thought. Time to be brave and calm and intelligent. Do not go gentle, and all that. Rising to his knees, Winston shook out his arms and hands, trying to relax and concentrating on the problem before him. Other than a lost spelunker, a hibernating bear, or the bogeyman, who could possibly be sharing this miserable hellhole with him? Only one person came to mind.

"Simon, is that you? Hello?"

Winston's voice was hollow and tentative in the cavern space. He was answered with another moan, this one more human. Crawling forward, Winston found a body. Speaking in a low voice and rubbing the person's face with his hands, Winston tried rousing the unconscious form, but the man was unresponsive, the moans becoming weaker. From the size of the person and from what Winston knew, this had to be the missing Simon Tart. Mrs. Cog would be surprised to learn that she had been right. Realizing he could do nothing to help Simon other than untie him and make him as comfortable as possible, Winston covered the moaning man with his own coat and went looking for the ladder.

The ladder stood just beyond the prone body of Simon Tart. Inching slowly up the rungs, Winston kept his hands out in front of him, feeling for the grate. Fifteen feet above the floor the rusted metal bumped his hand. Pushing upward, he raised the grate and sent it crashing to one side, a cloud of dust blasting him in the face. Leaning off the ladder, Winston slid from the hole and onto the cave floor.

Orienting his body at the end of the cave, Winston tried to recall where he'd left his lantern. Fifteen feet straight ahead and ten feet to the left seemed close enough, although once there he couldn't feel anything. The total darkness and chilling cold was beginning to unnerve him. That Simon Tart could still be alive was a miracle. His body weight had probably been the saving factor. Maybe his God. How long had he lain there, waiting to die? Waiting for the cold to ease the last ounce of warmth from his body?

Winston edged forward, feeling with his foot. Four feet and he struck a trunk, the same one that held the old uniforms. He had placed the lantern just to the left and . . . it was still there! The light felt like the sun. Instantly the cave was warmer, less frightening. Winston sat on the floor hugging the lantern to his chest, letting its scant warmth ooze into his body. Remembering Simon, Winston jumped up and hurried over to the hole and on his knees shone the light into the dark. Simon Tart lay on his side next to the ladder, unmoving, uncaring about the sun or the many skeletons that lay under and around him. Winston went back to the trunk and took out an armload of uniforms, throwing them down the hole. Clambering down the ladder to sit beside Simon, Winston arranged the dusty clothing under Simon's head and around his body, removing the sharper bones from under him. Winston wasn't an expert on bones, but he was sure these had been here a long time. It might have been an Indian burial site of some kind. Or were these the bones of runaway slaves? How weird had Colonel Worthwell been? If these were the remains of slaves, then the man had been a monster, lulling those poor people into a false sense of freedom and then snatching away not only their hope but their existence. And to what gain? From the look of the pile around him, forty or fifty people had perished to satisfy this man's madness.

Winston promised the silent Simon he'd return and went back up the ladder. He was cold, and the uniform jacket he had taken out before looked warm. Putting it on, Winston reached in the trunk and took out a cap. He put that on too. A little small but certainly warmer. An officer's saber completed the outfit. A big knife might come in handy with the Bill and Ed act.

The exit back into the cottage had been closed but not locked. Cautiously, Winston reentered the dark living room. Where was everyone, and what had they done to Janice Wetmore? At first Winston had thought that the good doctor might have had the sense to call Captain Andrews for backup, but that didn't seem to be the case. No revolving police lights played against the windows. From the cottage window Winston could see other, stranger lights though coming from the main house—the moving flicker that a fireplace gives off, or a candle.

Winston was unaware of the snow until he opened the door to the outside. It blew in around him in a great white gust, covering him instantly. Ducking into the wind, he ventured into the storm, heading toward the dim lights of the house. Winston wondered how long he had been underground, for the snow was four inches deep already. Slogging his way up the hill, Winston looked like a risen Civil War hero come back from the dead to haunt the Northern winter, saber ready to revenge some heinous betrayal. Ducking under the scaffold, Winston huddled against the house, peeking in through the window of the dining room. His Civil War fantasy was nothing compared to the phantasmagoria being played out before him in the candlelit room.

Chapter 34

Dr. Wetmore had never felt so helpless. It was almost the same as losing a patient with a terminal disease except that in this instance she could have prevented the outcome. Had it been pride or stupidity or negligence that made her not call Captain Andrews? Maybe it was none of those excuses, maybe it was just a need to pursue the ending quickly and without pause, to keep chasing and not stop in order not to miss out on the resolution. This headlong, tenacious quality had been invaluable as a doctor, but it was not what was needed in this case. She had run straight into the arms of a madman. James sat at the head of the table telling them a story.

"My father had been left this house, and stupidly he thought that social position automatically went with it. My mother and I used to look on in horror as Father went about inviting people to the house, first for dinner and then for drinks and finally just to see his gardens. He was a gardener, you know. Of course, nobody came. Ever." James paused, taking a sip of champagne. "Actually, that's not true. A Mr. Hardwell came over once for a drink, but he hardly stayed. Father had Mother make plates of

261

silly little things for this one man who didn't even finish his drink.

"I was young. Under ten years old at the time, but I was painfully aware of the situation. I would stand next to my father in the village as he made small talk with some pastyfaced ass decked out in riding habit, his riding crop nervously swinging against his leg, his eyes darting here and there to make sure no one was watching. Father seemed completely unaware of the others' attitudes toward him. I hated him, of course. Hated his stupidity and the senseless posture he put me and my mother in. I began to realize that I wanted him dead. It was the only way the embarrassment would end. I plotted against my father."

Dr. Wetmore watched Erika while listening to James. She appeared asleep and uninterested in what he was saying. Her breathing was shallow and quick, her forehead glistened with a thin film of perspiration. Erika was experiencing the classic symptoms of extreme fear, of shock. If something wasn't done she would faint and topple over. James droned on with his story.

". . . to join the hunt. Beagling was open to anyone in the community. Anyone silly enough to chase over the countryside after small dogs and invisible rabbits. Father would bundle me up every Sunday afternoon and make me tag along behind him as he pursued this inanity. Would introduce me as his 'growing boy' over and over to the same people who either never remembered me or didn't care."

James was talking in a singsong at this point, as though he had recited this tale aloud to himself over and over again. His eyes were watching the whole story unfold, moving as the situations changed, peering up to stare at an adult. If not for Erika, Dr. Wetmore felt she could probably just stand up and walk away.

". . . wanted more than anything to win his green coat, a symbol, a gesture by the establishment of having accepted my father in some small way. Mr. Bantram had all but promised him that at the end of the beagling season, when such symbols were bestowed on the precious few, he would receive his coat."

James stopped and took a deep breath. Seeming to snap back into the reality of the situation, he peered quizzically at those about him. Turning to Erika, a slow, malevolent grin spread across his face. Dr. Wetmore thought it best to distract him.

"What happened?" she asked.

"What?" James looked confused for an instant.

"The green coat?" asked Dr. Wetmore.

"It was all a joke, of course. My father had been set up. He had brought my mother and me along to witness the great event. I remember my mother was wearing a blue coat, and underneath, an apron."

James turned to where Bill was hiding in the shadows.

"She wore her damn apron to the ceremony. Can you believe that?"

Bill said nothing.

"Well, they awarded a few coats, and then just before adjourning for the gala hunt feast Mr. Bantram rose to say that a Mr. Gardener had been considered for induction but that no one could figure out who that person was. My father . . . my father raised his hand and said . . . and said he *was* a gardener, not *Mr.* Gardener. I was gone before the laughter stopped but my father stayed. He actually stayed and smiled and drank their booze and ate their food. My mother walked home by herself."

"You didn't kill him, though," said Dr. Wetmore.

"Oh yes, I did. In this very room, Doctor. Shot him dead. After that Sunday he began his own war against the hunt, not allowing them access to the land, snubbing *them*. I thought that life might become right again but I was wrong. He entered a madness. He became more obsessed with being part of the community then ever before, and eventually he decided to give the estate to the town, making it a park or something. Berry Park, it'd be called. Our name forced on Wistfield forever."

James stood.

"I knew what had to be done. Before he left my mother out in the cold like that, I shot him. In this room. My mother and I buried him in the cave, the same cave where Miss Worthwell's father used to kill slaves. You've been there, I understand."

"And that's why you wanted to kill the committee? For humiliating your father." It was a statement not a question that Dr. Wetmore spoke.

"No, no, Doctor. I killed the committee because *they* killed my father. Later I realized it wasn't me who had pulled the trigger of that gun, it was the hunt committee. *They* killed him. They manipulated me into killing him, but it took me a while to figure that part out. Those people had murdered an innocent man, a sick man, and gotten away with it by blaming me. But I began to understand. Now I can come back unafraid. I can reclaim my house, my existence."

The room was silent. Dr. Wetmore wondered about the slaves, about Mr. Berry, about Winston, and all the committee. James was fingering the rabbit's foot again and staring at Erika. Moving around the table, he took the knife from Ed Worth. It was the kind with the sharp hump in the middle, a Bowie knife. Dr. Wetmore had always wondered what that hump was for. She sat staring at it now, knowing she had to do something, anything, to prevent this man from killing Erika. She turned to where Bill Joyce was standing in the shadows.

"Bill, you must do something. You can't let this madman kill another person. How can you just stand there?" Dr. Wetmore went to stand, but Bill moved behind her chair and held her down.

"Don't interfere, Janice," said James. "I have no quarrel with you. Of course, you will die too, because you have to now, but don't make me hate you." James rested his hand gently on Erika's shoulder. He stood staring into the fire as if gathering strength from the flames.

Erika had sagged forward, her chin almost resting on the table. Dr. Wetmore gripped the table edge, preparing to push the table into Erika and causing her to fall if James tried anything. As if anticipating her movement, Ed and Bill took her arms on either side and held her tight. Dr. Wetmore shrank from the gleam on their faces. They stood mesmerized, staring over at James, who was now smiling back at them, a terrifying, twisted smile that shone from the reflection of the fireplace. Dr. Wetmore couldn't move. She found herself as rapt as her two keepers.

James reached down and ran his hand through Erika's hair, tightened his grip and pulling her up into a sitting position. Touching her cheek he said the name *Julia* to no one in particular. Erika seemed to have fainted. She was dolllike in James's hands,

weaving slightly as he handled her, seemingly unaware of the knife he held against her throat. Now
James drew the blade tight against her throat, causing her blood to seep out around the knife blade,
sticky black in the firelight, like the juice of some
exotic plum.

Chapter 35

Peeking through the dining room window, Winston saw Dr. Wetmore sitting at the crude table Ed had made earlier that day. James the chauffeur was standing behind another woman, who was sitting with her back to him. Hovering on either side of the doctor were Bill and Ed. The room had been decorated in some way, or was it the furniture? Winston squinted against the dim and flickering light. James seemed to be in control, holding court about something, the jester being given his day, except James didn't appear all that amusing. In fact, he must have been frightening and strange in the role he was playing. Janice's face was a mask of terror. Winston gripped the sill. James held a knife in one hand and the woman's head in his other. As the woman's face was forced upward, he realized it was Erika, her mouth slack, her skin waxy and tight. James was about to kill Erika. Winston leaned back against the house and tried to clear his head. What was going on? James was the killer? The Berry kid? Winston didn't wait to sort it out. Drawing his arm back to smash the window, he hesitated, realizing he couldn't stop James if he broke the glass. He might even hasten the act. Quickly ducking around the corner of the house, he stumbled his way to the basement door and into the cellar. Taking the wooden stairs two at a time, he fell into the kitchen. Winston waited for those in the dining room to come investigate his noise, but no one had heard him. They were too engrossed in the drama unfolding before them. Leaning in the dark outside the dining room door, Winston watched James's glowing face and heard him utter the name *Julia*. He stood horrified as James drew the knife slowly across Erika's throat, a violin player drawing his bow.

Chapter 36

"James, my son . . ." said the hurried, booming voice. "Come join your father. Come follow me back into the darkness. I forgive you. I still love you."

James looked stunned, as if hit by a board. Every muscle in his body tightened and he stood frozen, the knife held in midair. Blood gleamed on Erika's throat. James began to moan, a deep, guttural lament from within his chest that rose out his mouth and filled the room with its force and terror. A shade stepped into the doorway, a ghost dressed in a military uniform, sword drawn and pointing at James.

"Drop the knife, my son."

James let the knife fall to the table. Straightening, he turned his head toward the voice, the moan still issuing from his throat, his eyes glued to the apparition before him.

"Fuck this," said Ed Worth, who dove across the room and straight into the figure standing in the door. Both fell crashing into the dark kitchen.

Dr. Wetmore awoke from her comatose state realizing that this ghost was very solid indeed and sounded very much like Winston Wyc. Seeing her chance, she rose from the table and made for the front door. Bill Joyce stepped in her way, grabbing her by the arm.

"Don't be foolish, Bill. Why do you align yourself with this madman? Let me go. I will say you saved my life."

Bill held fast, his tongue silent, his eyes blazing. He forced the doctor back into the room. From the kitchen, Ed was screaming that someone had damn well better give him a hand, that this was no ghost but a red-blooded bastard with a sword. James stood dazed at the table, staring into the dark void that was the kitchen, his eyes slowly focusing, his breathing returning to normal. Bill had let go of Dr. Wetmore's arm to take out his pistol. He stood undecided about what to do, hovering between her and the kitchen door. Erika had come to life, flinging herself from the table and onto the floor. She hugged the near shadows, looking wildly around the room, her neck and blouse streaked with blood. Her hands tore at the tape across her mouth. Ed gave out another scream and Bill took two steps in that direction. It was all Dr. Wetmore needed. She was out the door and into the entrance hall. Throwing open the front door, she stood back briefly, amazed at the falling snow and the sudden cold. Hearing a noise behind her, she slammed the door and flew into the night. Within seconds she was enveloped in darkness and heading down the driveway. Light from the opened front door fell just short of revealing her but she knew its glow showed her prints in the snow and the direction she had taken. Tucking her coat around her, Dr. Wetmore reached deep within herself and drew upon all those years of keeping in shape. She felt like a teenager again running down the Joyce driveway, the cold pumping into her lungs, the razor of the night air pushing against her face, her heart racing ahead of her into the dark, into the welcoming, sane dark.

Chapter 37

Winston acted on impulse. Up until he spoke he had had no idea what he was going to do. Now he was wrestling on the floor with a very strong Ed Worth. Although Winston was twice the man's size, the carpenter was starting to get the upper hand. Winston had to do something before the others broke from their shock and came to Ed's assistance. Grabbing Ed by the hair, Winston pulled the man's head violently toward his own forehead. Blood erupted all over Winston's face, and though momentarily stunned, he could feel Ed let go. Staggering to his knees, Winston pushed the man away from him. Immediately Ed started yelling for help. Someone stood in the doorway waving a gun, but he obviously couldn't see into the dark kitchen. Winston dove in the direction of the cellar door, crashing into the jamb and rolling down the wooden stairs to the earth floor below. Above him he could hear running footsteps. A door slammed. Winston listened to the noise and wondered if he could move. His body felt like one big bruise and his head had started pounding again. Giving in to the madness would be easier than resisting. Death would come quicker.

Lights went on upstairs. A beam of light from the kitchen fell across his legs and Winston involuntarily rolled out of its revealing glare. Lord, he thought, I'm going to die of pain. Above he could hear James screaming "Kill them!" over and over. Winston got to his knees, then to his feet. Supporting himself on the stone wall, he worked his way over to the outside cellar door. A pair of legs appeared at the top of the basement stairs. Bill Joyce bent his head down to peer into the gloom, a revolver in his hand. Winston's legs found renewed energy as a bullet ricocheted off the stones next to him. As another bullet hit the jamb, Winston bounded outside and into the snow. The cold hit him like a slap. Without hesitating, he took off down the hill to the right of the cottage and into the low shrubbery just before the woods. The low fence caught him at the thighs and catapulted him into the air. Lying stretched out in the snow, Winston prayed for the feeling to come back into his legs, and soon. Rolling over, he could see that an outside light had come on, its edge of illumination cutting just at the fence line. Standing at the corner of the house were James and Bill. Ed came out of the cellar door with two outsized flashlights and raked their beams across the yard, and then, finding Winston's footprints, followed them up to the fence and beyond. Winston ducked as the light played over him. The men moved in his direction.

Winston ignored the pain in his legs. Rocking up, he came to his feet and started to run, the flashlights dancing in the snow around him. Shots were fired and then Winston was in the woods, the white crusted branches of the spruce trees closing in behind. Winston bounced off one tree and tripped on another that had fallen. Reeling forward, he suddenly felt the ground disappear beneath him as he tumbled down a steep embankment. Lying there, feeling the damp of the snow soak his clothes and listening to the calls of the men above him, Winston experienced a disquieting awareness of what the hare must contemplate when she hears the high cry of the hounds. He wondered if his instinct for survival was as strong. Winston had never hurt so much. Every inch of his body glowed with pain.

Rising with a grunt, he picked his way down the gully into which he had fallen. The shouts of James and the others reverberated off the frozen land, making it difficult for him to know exactly where they were. Winston noticed his tracks were highly visible in the snow. He would have to find some way to camouflage them. Veering off to his left for twenty feet, Winston retraced his steps at a half run and then leaped into the air as he came back to the spot where he had originally halted. He landed in some low evergreens, rolled another few feet, and came to rest on the other side of the bush. He glanced back at his flight path. Only ten feet of untrampled snow, but it might be enough to confuse them for a few precious minutes. James's cries had become unnaturally high and tight, a crazed hound screaming at the cold.

Winston couldn't make out what he was saying but he could hear Bill warning the others of the embankment and shouting "Over this way!" In a low crouch, Winston took off, keeping the steep rise to his right, figuring that if he kept in this general direction he should eventually come out on the driveway or the main road. Picking his way among the shrouded trees, Winston hurried through the dark as best he could. The snow had drifted two feet in places and the trail was rough. After five minutes he stopped, his breath coming in short gasps, the wet cold numbing his entire body. The wind made owllike sounds in the evergreens, and as hard as he strained, Winston could hear nothing but the wind and his thudding heart. Was it possible his pursuers had gone back? Winston stood and listened. Knowing all three men had followed him outside gave him hope that the women might have escaped. Maybe they could find help.

Winston had read somewhere that people freezing to death just wanted to lie down and go to sleep, but his body was beginning to shake violently; his fists stuffed between his legs could have held an imaginary jackhammer. Rest was the last thing on Winston's mind. Hearing sounds off to his left, he began running.

Halting at the edge of a clearing, Winston looked around him to see if he could skirt the open area and avoid leaving such an obvious trail, or . . . A thought came to him. Listening intently for any hint of his pursuers and hearing only the wind, he ran out into the center of the clearing and then off into the woods on his right. Going only ten feet into the trees, he retraced his steps to the center of the meadow, listened again, and then repeated the process until eight trails led off in all directions. Congratulating himself on his deception, Winston noted movement at the other side of the open circle, a figure coming to a stop among the shadows. Winston dared not move. Warily, Ed Worth entered the clearing, and from his attitude, Winston realized the man must not have seen him. Ed stood puzzling out the many directions the trails took into the woods. In one hand he held a flashlight, which he had switched off. Ed peered hard into the surrounding woods. The men stood only fifty feet apart, but Winston could see that Ed's nose had been flattened, the dried blood on his face looking like a crude black mask. Ed's eyes rested on Winston but then moved off to the left. Winston prayed that Ed would pick a trail that gave him the edge he needed to get away.

Ed picked the path next to Winston. It was the one that scribed a straight line across the opening and was therefore the shortest way back into the woods. Clenching his teeth together, Winston pressed his arms to his sides to try and keep them from shaking. Ed passed within fifteen feet of where he stood and disappeared into the shadows. Winston listened for the man but could hear nothing. The minutes passed. Was Ed making a wider, outside circle of his own, hoping to pick up the path Winston had taken? Of course there was no right path at the moment. He'd gone nowhere. Would Ed figure this out?

Winston almost missed noticing that Ed had reentered the clearing. He had been peering into the woods, trying to avoid being surprised by Ed, when he heard a muffled "shit" and, turning, saw the man heading for the opposite end of the meadow. The second Ed entered the trees, Winston was gone.

The close encounter with Ed Worth infused Winston with the extra resolve he needed to find the main road. The woods had thinned and he was able to cover more ground. At one point the trees opened enough so that Winston could see the house above him and off to his right, its dark silhouette providing no clue to the whereabouts of its owner and his friends.

The thinning trees became no trees at all, and Winston suddenly found himself in the middle of an immense meadow. He heard shouts off to his right. Two shapes appeared at the dim borders of his vision, shapes moving in his direction. A shot was fired. Someone yelled. A third figure came out of the dark on Winston's left, loping across the expanse, its tall, gangly shadow vaguely familiar. Our nine lives have finally been used up, Winston thought. Somewhere it was written that Winston Wyc must die at the hands of a madman, his tennis shoes frozen to his feet, his body clad in a Civil War uniform. Where was the sanity of New York when he needed it?

Mr. Cog went past Winston still at a run, his hand up at his mouth, trying to keep his teeth from falling out.

"Follow me, Mr. Winston. And hurry."

Winston stared after the man, shook off his bewilderment, and started chasing him across the field. The others were shouting louder, a few more shots were fired. Someone yelled his name, but Winston didn't stop to see who it might be. Mr. Cog waited for Winston at the edge of the field. He held his side.

"Haven't run like this in many a year. Mother *said* you might need some help. Come, I know of a place we might be able to hide."

"I don't think I've ever been happier to see anyone in all my life," said Winston.

"This is just like when I was a kid and Mr. Berry would chase me and Harry Boynton away from the Worthwell place. I can remember once . . ."

"I think we'd better save it for later," said Winston, looking over his shoulder.

"Good idea," reasoned Mr. Cog, glancing past Winston.

Winston followed Mr. Cog back into the woods. Almost immediately they came upon a stream bed, the banks of which were lined with ice. Mr. Cog stepped over the ice and into the flowing creek. Winston looked down at his snow-caked tennis shoes, shrugged, and plunged in. Strangely, the water felt warm against his frozen feet.

"Go up that way and stop at the culvert. I'll be right there."

Winston watched Mr. Cog take off up the opposite creek bank and into the trees. Hearing voices approaching, Winston moved swiftly up the stream, heading around a bend and straight for fifty feet before coming to an immense culvert. The shouts behind him seemed confused and angry, but they didn't sound like they were following him. Winston stepped up on a rock shelf just inside the mouth of the tunnel. The minute he did his feet began to scream with pain. Winston was banging them against the culvert wall when Mr. Cog came swinging down on his right.

"The men chasing you won't jump into the water and get their feet wet," Mr. Cog chuckled. "They think we went across to the other side. Now follow me, Mr. Winston."

"I don't know if I can make it. My body temperature must be around ten degrees and my liver has frostbite. And my feet . . ."

"You must keep moving them. You know I almost didn't recognize you in that funny coat. It reminds me of . . . that's it! Make believe we're on the frozen

279

tundra of Russia, Mr. Winston, and the Cossacks are after us. We have no food or proper clothing and to be caught is certain death."

Winston stared at the man in amazement. Mr. Cog's whole life has been an imaginary adventure, he thought, and now that the real thing is upon him, he wants to make it even more fantastic. "My name is Wyc, Mr. Cog."

"Wyc Winston, call me Herb. Let's go."

Mr. Cog pulled a flashlight out of his jacket pocket and started down the water pipe, his voice echoing back to Winston.

"This was all built one hundred and fifty years ago to bring water to all parts of the original farm. Wind pumps brought water up to several cisterns, which fed the big barns. One of these tunnels down here goes to a main cistern located on the hill overlooking the house. Quite unique in its day. It's not used anymore. Pity."

Winston nodded, afraid to open his mouth for fear his teeth would shake out. The cold was becoming critical. His hands and feet were experiencing a new ache, the pain of a thousand dull needles being forced under his skin. Unless he got warm soon, Winston was freezer meat. The water tunnel was much warmer than outside, and the pipe was relatively dry, but Winston's clothes were soaked through. Some parts were solid ice at this point. He concentrated on Erika to take his mind off the cold. Hopefully, she and Janice were warm and safe. Winston wondered if Erika would marry a man with no toes.

After what seemed hours, Winston drew up to Mr. Cog, who had stopped. Above them was open sky, the dark snow clouds visible as they scudded across the round opening.

"These metal rungs will take us up and into the main cistern. At the far end is another set of rungs that will take us out and in back of the barn about two hundred yards behind the house. We can hide in there and get warm."

Winston stammered his gratitude and went up after Mr. Cog. At one time the cistern had been covered with a roof, but most of it had rotted away and fallen into the concrete reservoir, causing Winston to stumble and fall as he crossed over to the opposite side. Maybe I actually died in that cave with the bones, thought Winston, and these last hours have been my introduction to hell.

Suddenly the cistern was flooded with lights that were attached to the back of the barn. Winston and Mr. Cog stopped just short of the metal ladder, blinking up at the lights and the men looking down on them: James, Bill Joyce, and Ed Worth. James's voice was calm now.

"I had a feeling you'd pop up in this hole, Mr. Wyc. I wondered who had come to the rescue. Mr. Cog there isn't the only one familiar with this land.

"I'm sorry, Wyc." Mr. Cog bowed his head in Winston's direction. A small boy caught in his neighbor's apple tree.

"And such a merry chase. The rabbit and the hounds, eh?" James was holding a hunting rifle.

"They call it a hare, Mr. Berry. But you wouldn't know that. You have no class." Winston tried unsuccessfully to keep his voice from shivering.

James's throat tightened, the words barely forming in his mouth. "You're not my father, I killed my father a long time ago. He's still in the cave."

"Shoot him, for christsake!" yelled Ed Worth.

Winston could see Bill Joyce moving off to the left and away from the cistern. Mr. Cog stood frozen by the metal ladder. The sky shone white above Winston's head, a sterile, phosphorescent white that glowed and shimmered in the cold.

James looked like a little boy whose every wish had come true, an evil boy with his finger on the wrong button. Lifting the rifle to his shoulder, James aimed the barrel down into the cistern. Winston closed his eyes and found himself wondering what to buy his mother for Christmas. He felt a part of the shimmering white cold, felt suddenly invincible, as if the cold protected him with a wall of iciness.

Someone yelled and Winston heard shots. He felt the bullet tear into him, hours it seemed before he heard the report. Going over backward, his eyes opened and he could see James falling in slow motion toward him, the man's eyes wide, the mouth in a toothy grimace. Winston looked up as he lay in the snow, James lying across him, and far away above him on the cistern wall he could see Captain Andrews in a low crouch, a gun in his hand, shouting at someone on the opposite wall. Winston smiled. Captain Andrews had gone to hell also. They could keep each other company. Winston was last aware of a flash of light and then brilliant warmth and then darkness—far-away, you've-never-been-born darkness.

Chapter 38

Winston had been awake for hours, but he feigned sleep every time someone entered the room. His body ached. A dull pain nagged his entire body and made it difficult for him to focus on what caused that ache. Eventually the past had sorted itself out, and Winston marveled at the fact that he was still alive. If indeed he was. Heaven wouldn't allow such pain, he reasoned, so he must still be in the land of the living. And the others? Every time he closed his eyes he had a vision of himself sitting at that table, James sliding his knife . . . It was this image that finally compelled him to face the real world. Hearing someone enter the room, Winston forced his eyes wide, using the light to shock himself awake. A nurse in a tricornered hat was opening the blinds. From behind, and with her arm raised, she looked to Winston like the Statue of Liberty. Was he back in New York, safe among friends and places he loved? Had the lady that takes care of the downtrodden and weary taken a special interest in Winston's trials? He raised his own arm and gazed at the tube coming from his hand. Another tube could be seen snaking out from under the blanket. The stiff rustle of the nurse's uniform was heard crossing the room.

"Mr. Wyc?" The voice authoritative but caressing at the same time. Hospitalspeak. "Mr. Wyc. How are we feeling?" The hospital *we*.

"Okay, I guess." Winston's voice sounded like it was being controlled by a ventriloquist. Pulling himself up slightly, he felt a sharp pain in his right side. "Ohhh."

"No moving about, please. You must remain still for a few more days."

"I'm alive."

"Of course you're alive, Mr. Wyc, although you did everything in your power not to be. Frostbite, hypothermia, and a gunshot wound to the right side. This is not the way to pursue a long life."

"Frostbite? Am I all here?" Winston peeked under the sheet.

"Everything's accounted for, I believe."

"Sure doesn't feel like it. How long have I been here?"

"Two days."

"I'm in a public hospital for physically sick people, I take it?"

"That's correct, Mr. Wyc. Where else would you be?"

Winston could imagine any number of private sanatoriums for the bewildered. Touching his side, he found it swathed in bandages. James had shot him in the side. It would account for the dull ache.

"Do I still carry the bullet?"

"Went clean through, Mr. Wyc. Nothing to worry about."

"Easy for you to say. What time is it?"

"One o'clock. In the afternoon." She busied herself straightening the sheet. "I think you have a visitor, if you feel up to it."

284

"Is the visitor a lady?" asked Winston.

"She is."

Winston could remember dreaming about Erika, but it seemed so long ago.

"I'd love some company. How do I look?"

"Terrible."

"Thanks. Show the lady in." Winston ran his hand through his hair and restraightened his bedsheet.

"Hi! How's my detective partner?" Dr. Wetmore placed a large apple pie on the bed stand. "Here's a little something from your landlady. Said it would make you feel better." Dr. Wetmore removed her hat, causing her hair to cascade down her face and shoulders. Winston's face fell with it.

"Well, I'm glad to see you, too," said Dr. Wetmore.

"Sorry. I've just now returned from the arms of Morpheus."

"You were expecting Erika."

"Actually . . . Is, eh . . . ?"

"Erika okay? She's fine. I expect her along any minute. No one's supposed to see you for a few more days, but being an ex-doctor has its privileges."

"Erika's all right." Winston relaxed back against the pillows. "What happened?"

"Lots of things. We can go over the details when you feel better. Briefly, I can say that your odd heroics at the last minute allowed me to escape down the drive, where I ran straight into Captain Andrews and a patrol car coming up to the house."

"Hurray for the police. How did he happen to come by?"

"He had found out that the clue Simon left me

285

was from the Epistle of James. The captain then took a chance and ran a check on our James. James was using the last name Fielding around here, but his chauffeur license had been issued to a John Berry. Fielding turns out to be Mrs. Berry's maiden name, but that's another story."

"On the strength of that he came up to the Joyce place?"

"Well, that and some things you'd told him and the fact that Mrs. Cog called the station shouting that her crazy husband was going to get himself killed up at the Joyce place. Needless to say, she convinced him to hurry on over there."

"And we're glad he did. And Erika? You say she's okay?"

"I accidentally slammed the door in her face when I made my getaway. In the darkened foyer, she managed to slip up the stairs and hide until she saw the police arrive."

Winston suddenly sat up in the bed. "Ohhhh, God! Simon's down in that cave."

"Simon's down the hall. I was just visiting him before I decided to look in on you. He's not doing so well, but he'll be okay. Bill Joyce told them where he was. Bill claims he was the victim of James's demented mind. The verdict's still out on that, if you ask me."

"I can't believe I've been knocked out for two days," said Winston.

"The doctors kept you sedated because your body was exhausted. Erika and I have been checking on you after lunch every day, hoping you'd wake up. I thought it might hurry along the healing process if you knew the world out there was doing okay."

"Thanks. I appreciate that."

Erika's long form leaned into the room.

"Do I hear voices?"

"Come in," said Dr. Wetmore. "Our hero has finally awakened."

Erika stood at the end of the bed. Winston held her eyes for a full minute. He'd sift through the tumble of emotions some other time. Right now, he decided, he was very happy to see her.

"You look like the hare that didn't get away," said Erika, smiling.

"Thanks. You look pretty good yourself. I like the choker."

Erika's throat was wrapped in gauze. "Merely a flesh wound. Isn't that what they say in the movies? I feel I've been in one." Sitting on the edge of the bed, Erika took Winston's hand. "The nurse says you need to be kept quiet, with no more excitement."

"What excitement? I'm from the Big Apple, remember? Gunshot wounds are part of everyday experience. Without massive doses of pandemonium each day, New Yorkers tend to shrivel up and waste away."

"Then we'll have to guard against that."

"Ahem. If you two don't mind, I must hurry along. Skippy's all alone in the car." Realizing they hadn't heard her, Dr. Wetmore smiled and slipped out the door.

Winston still held Erika's hand. "I had the worst nightmare. I dreamt that you were married to Jack Glenn and you kept giving birth to beagles."

Erika laughed.

"Jack called and apologized for acting like a fool. I think he finally got the picture."

Erika moved in closer.

"You know, there were some moments two nights ago when I thought I'd never see you again. I started missing you."

"You did?"

"You like dogs, Mr. Wyc?"

"The little mutts are called hounds, don't ya know nothin'?" said Winston.

"You pretending to be a hilltopper, Mr. Wyc?"

"As a matter of fact, I don't know what I am anymore. A week ago I lived a normal life with normal fears and normal worries—like how to find a job, how to pay the rent, how to stay alive on the city streets, worries that will seem fine from now on. I looked forward to a little scotch in the evenings and maybe wondering about the future with a few friends and . . . and then I came to the peaceful countryside for a few months of rural bliss. You know, something different and friendly."

"I can be different and friendly. The country isn't just nonstop excitement, Mr. Wyc, there *is* a quieter side."

"The name's Winston, and that's not what I've been told. They say that even from the beds one can hear the thunder of cannons."

"I've heard that too." Erika leaned over. "Winston?"

"Boom," said Winston.

"Boom," said Erika.